I0662457

The Wastelands of OZ

The Wastelands of OZ

The Return to Oz *series*

Kasey Hill

Azoth Khem Publishing
Huntsville, AL
April 2025

AZOTH KHEM

ISBN: 978-1-945987-10-6
First Edition 2016
Second Edition 2018
Third Edition 2025

Azoth Khem Publishing
29931 Copperpenny Drive NW
Harvest, AL 35749
www.azothkhem.com

Ordering Information:
Quantity sales and exclusive discounts are available on quantity
purchases by corporations, associations, and others. For details,
contact the publisher at the address above. For orders by U.S. trade
bookstores and wholesalers, please contact
Azoth Khem Publishing: Tel: (256) 221-5498 or visit
www.azothkhem.com

Printed in the United States of America

Dedication and Thanks:

A very special little girl's love for all magical movies inspired me to write this spin-off of The Wizard of Oz. Modernizing it with more knowledge of magic and merriment was my initial intent. Filling it with the coming of age and love that every teenager goes through just flowed from my pen. The Wizard of Oz was always my favorite as a child. Now, my child is the same age I was and enjoys it one and the same. I hope the multitudes of readers enjoy the recapturing of the essence of the Wizard of Oz through this reclaiming of magic story. Always believe in magic, Maryjane Hill. Mommy loves you!

To my friends and family who stood by me while I wrote and published it, thank you!

L Frank Baum (1856-1919): Thank you for instilling in me a love of your work. Without you, I would have never had something to go from, and all success goes to your original storyline.

Check out these other series by Kasey Hill

The Guardians of Light Series
Firefly of Immortality
The Shining Ones
Firefly: The Half-Blood Angel
The Valley of the Shadow of Death: Nephilim Rising

Dark Woods Series
Devil's Claw

The Whispering Spirits Series
The Haunting at Foxwood Village
Dark Coven

Coming Soon to The Guardians of Light Series
Firefly of Immortality II
Black Wings of Death
Firefly of Immortality: Anniel Unveiled
Alpha and Omega
Firefly of the Apocalypse

Coming Soon to The Guardians of Light Series Universe

The Guardians of Light: Darkness Falls Series
Bloodlines: Into the Shadows

The Wastelands of Oz

PROLOGUE

THE WORLD HAS GROWN and changed since the beginning of man upon the land. Groups of nomadic travelers settled down and formed villages. The villages soon turned into towns, then into cities, into nations, and then into countries. As time passed, many technological advances found their way into the world. However, no matter how advanced the human race could become, there was always magic that existed within the world. This magic circumvented anything a scientist could boil in the laboratory. Along with this magic, existed lands never before seen by humans. Their enchantments were so powerful that even sorcerers and witches in the human world could not see past their cloaks.

There existed a land where magic flourished, and within its grasp, every magical creature imaginable was present. Birds chirped, and animals danced around gaily in the bright, warm sun that shone across the green valleys and forests. All the inhabitants grew together in balance and harmony. It was simple and peaceful here in this enchanted land. Blessed by the fairies, this land named Oz had once been a powerful and thriving kingdom led by a young, fairy Princess who looked no older than your average teenager. Dark times had befallen the kingdom, which caused the Princess to step down from the throne, leaving it open for the rightful heir deemed fit to earn it. The Princess gathered a group of her closest friends and allies, creating a council to mentor and oversee the new powers to take the throne. This council was known as the Elders.

"We must take action before this land is lost to Evil," the former Princess persuaded.

"What do you propose we do?" The council sat awaiting an answer as she walked over to her magic mirror.

"Show me, Dorothy," she said, waving her hand over the mirror.

"You can't be serious! Dorothy left us years ago!"

"No matter how long ago she left, she will always remain a princess here!" she retorted. Dorothy popped up in the mirror entering a hospital. "I have been watching over her for years. I propose an action to be taken on her behalf for what she has done for us." She turned and faced the Council. "The answer lies not with her, but the child she carries within."

"What are you suggesting? Making a mortal child the Queen of Oz? Preposterous!" The council murmured amongst themselves over the proposal that was ludicrous.

"No, but the rightful heir to the throne does need a companion." The Princess stood her ground.

"You know the rules! Mortals and Ozmites will not marry!"

"That's why I have called you all here..."

Chapter One

TALL WHEAT GRASS blew in the soft wind rolling across the fields of dreams. In the distance, you could hear the soft tones of melodic singing as the workers went about their day. It was a peaceful and gay portion of the world that evil left untainted. The foliage that spread from one end of the land to the other was lustrous and unequivocal to that of the rainforests that existed in the Amazon. Fairies fluttered about tending the gardens of flowers while the gnomes worked hard harvesting the jewels from the mountains on the outskirts of the land. Everyone worked in harmony to bring about their day's work for celebrations later on in the evening. Not one job was harder than the next, so all lived civilly without jealousy or discontentment.

Just outside of a quaint little town that lay toward the east of the land, there was a barren spot in the field where a nest sat with bones and decaying animals lying around it. A young, teenage girl who wasn't indifferent to the marvelous land frolicked through the fields free of worry or fright. Maryjane had been making daily visits to this peculiar place for quite some time now, and the inhabitants had fallen in love with the child. She had stolen their hearts upon her arrival and was treated with the utmost care. She roamed the valleys always exploring and looking for a new adventure to embark on.

As Maryjane made her way over to the massive grave

of animals, she couldn't help but cover her mouth as her eyes watered. She tried not to choke on the pungent stench. She had been warned not to venture to close to this new addition to the land, but curiosity had gotten the best of her. She now wished she had listened as she was unable to force down the bile that had risen to the back of her throat. She covered her nose and mouth with her shirt in an attempt to block the reeking, decaying bodies, but the putrid smell had sunk into the stitching of her clothes. Once she laid eyes on the rotting corpses of animals and the maggots squirming around inside, she lost all control of her stomach and heaved with huge spasms, putting her to her knees as she tried to force herself away.

Her ears caught an indescribable sound that sent chills and fear throughout her body. She carefully stood from her doubled-over position and turned around to find the source of the sound. Her body went rigid with dread. Careening toward her was a winged creature with no feathers. It had the body of a human, with feet and hands as talons. Its head was large, with the disposition of a reptile. Its mouth was a fanged beak, and it squalled a spine-tingling shriek of death. She had never seen or heard about this creature, even in a warning, but prayed with all her heart that she would get away unscathed. As it closed in on her, with every ounce of whit she tried to move, but her entire body stood frozen like a statue.

"Ch-ch-Charlie!!" she managed to scream before the beast closed in for the attack.

The sounds of laughter mixed with screaming filled her ears, and she opened her eyes. Her vision was blurry as she tried to focus, and her head felt tremendously heavy. Through her hazy vision, she was able to make out trees; green foliage had replaced the wheat grass she had been in, as well as a blurred blob of faceless people. When she was finally able to focus, she realized she had been having one of her nightmares, and to her dismay, her outburst was in public. The screaming she had heard was her own. The laughter coursed through her body as her peers joked about her public display of "crazy."

She sat at the base of a tree while her notebook spilled open with her sketches and writings. She scrambled to pack everything up in the notebook before the group of bystanders could see them. She kept her eyes to the ground as she hurriedly placed all the papers back in the notebook. She heard the whispers from the kids who stood around her, watching her every move.

"Her mom's crazy. She was in an insane asylum," one of them barked.

"She's not far behind her," another one chided.

Her face grew hot from embarrassment, and she could feel the tears welling, but she brushed them aside. She reached for her last sketch when a foot stepped down on it. She closed her eyes, took a deep breath, and looked up to the perpetrator.

"Do you mind picking your foot up? You're stepping on my sketch," she mumbled.

A boy her age bent down, picked up her sketch, and looked at it.

"This sketch?" he mocked as he tore it in front of her.

The pieces fell to the ground, and it took every ounce in her to hold back the urge to burst into tears. He then picked up her notebook and began tearing sheets of paper from it. She jumped up, trying to grab it from him.

"Please, don't," she pleaded while everyone gawked and laughed at her.

The earth beneath her began to spin as she grew lightheaded and disoriented from the anxiety.

"Listen to this," the boy began, "Today, Glinda showed me how to use my powers and told me I'm a powerful witch," the boy stopped reading and looked at her, "You're a witch! This is a magic book!" he exclaimed holding it up to everyone.

The crowd exploded in laughter. The faces whirled around her in mockery, and she was to the point of passing out.

"Stop!" she bellowed, and the crowd came to a silent halt. Everyone looked at her in astonishment. She had never fought back or said anything as they taunted her before today. "Give me my book," she demanded, stretching her hand to meet his.

"Or what?" the boy enticed, tearing another sheet from the book.

The skies began to grey, and clouds began to roll in as the kids all stopped and stared at the sudden weather change. They looked from the sky and back at Maryjane as her expression hardened.

"Do you really want to know what?" Maryjane glared as lightning struck a tree several hundred feet from the crowd.

Everyone jumped and screamed, terrified of the warning bolt.

"You really are a freak," the boy stammered, tossing the book to the ground.

The crowd dissipated in haste before the rain came pouring down on them. Maryjane bent down and picked up the torn pages that surrounded her feet. She stopped at the one sketch torn from the book, but not ripped in two.

"Charlie," she whispered. The weather changed from the impending torrential storm back into the sunny day it had been with a light drizzle as her tears fell. She rubbed her fingers across the face of the sketch and sighed. An emotional dam broke loose from within and tears streamed down her face. She packed away all the torn pages, slipped the notebook into her bag, and started on her walk home. In the distance, she could hear her mom calling her name from the front porch of the farmhouse.

"Maryjane! Maryjane! Where are you, Maryjane!?" Dorothy looked out toward the long road leading up to the house, but could see nothing in the distance aside from the thunderclouds that had moved in. Her eyesight had started to fail along with the rest of her body from old age.

Maryjane was a couple of tenths of a mile from the house. She lollygagged down the road, brooding over the events of the afternoon. She looked into the distance at her mom standing on the front porch, and she remembered her mother's stories of her Uncle Henry and Auntie Em. They had long since passed before Maryjane was even thought of.

"Maryjane! Child! Where are you!?" Dorothy yelled with a tired voice.

Maryjane was always late coming home from school, and knew what to expect when she got home. Her mom was always sick to her stomach, so she would fix dinner, and then would lie down after fixing dinner.

"Maryjane!" Dorothy yelled more exasperated.

Maryjane groaned and put a little hitch in her step. "Coming, Mama!" Maryjane rounded the corner and opened the gate.

Dorothy frowned at her when the absence of the cat that disappeared five years ago wasn't on her heels. When the kitten had been given to her, she was barely learning to talk and couldn't yell kitty-kitty, only Kiki. So, the name stuck with the cat, and the two had been inseparable until it disappeared. Dorothy told Maryjane stories of frolicking along through the field with Toto. That dog had gotten her mother through all of her life's hardships. Dorothy explained how it was a total heartbreak when he took his last breath in her lap.

She was pregnant with Maryjane and had endured so much during the pregnancy. Maryjane's father had been killed in an accident on the farm while tending to the animals. She was left to raise Maryjane alone while also tending to the care and upkeep of the farm. Now, fifteen years later, Maryjane was nearly full-grown, and the farm was flourishing. Dorothy had offered room and board to whoever would work on the farm in return. It took a couple of months, but finally, there was a family that stopped in to take her offer.

"Come in, child. It's dinner time, and I feel a storm a brewing." Dorothy turned around to walk inside as Maryjane neared the steps.

Maryjane stopped on the top step and looked around the farm. Every day, the same routine ensued between her Mother and her. She was never questioned as to what took her so long to respond, or what she had been doing that took her so long to get home. She couldn't gather the courage to tell her how she was treated by the other kids. She didn't dare speak of her notebook, which was full of magical spells, potions, and herbal information. She thought surely her mother would pitch a fit and would have her committed to an insane asylum if she knew the secret she kept within.

Since she could remember her early childhood, she had dreamt every night of a faraway place called Oz. It was a beautiful and spectacular place with evergreen forests, rolling fields of flowers, and farms as far as the eye could see. Each visit, she was always greeted by the friendly people of Munchkin Land and her mentor, Glinda, the beautiful witch of the South. She had no friends outside of Oz. She had always been a social outcast, with most of the children's parents putting an end to whatever friendship could have blossomed. Her mother was noted as an insane and ludicrous addition to their small town in Kansas. She would cry herself to sleep each night from heartache and loneliness - the anxiety the town had placed on her small shoulders.

After finding Oz, the people there had become the

only friends she ever had and ever truly cared about. She missed each and every one of them, especially her best friend Charlie. Charlie had gotten her through some of the most challenging moments she had faced in Oz. Outsiders were few and far between, so not many people smiled at their presence. Charlie didn't care, though. They were the same age, and he took to her as if he were an outsider himself. The people of Oz slowly came around to her presence, and within months, she was seen as a person of Oz herself. It was the only place where she truly had people who loved her dearly instead of treating her like dirt.

Each visit she had in her land of love and magic, she learned spell work from Glinda. For the past five years, however, she hadn't been able to slip back into the remnants of Oz. She felt lost without her nightly trips, and her depression sank deeper into her heart and mind. It was her sanctuary from the real world. So, as a means of escape from the harsh treatment the townspeople expressed to her, she would slip off into the field and practice what Glinda had taught her. She had taught her herb usage for various healings. She could make tonics, tinctures, sachets, nearly anything herb-wise. Along with the herbal knowledge came the gift of spells. Her mom thought it was the family that moved in that helped make the farm flourish. However, she had cast a fortune spell in favor of her mom so that she wouldn't worry so much. The stress and worry had put so much strain on her body; she had grown weak and sick. This sickness was not curable with her herbs, though, and she had exhausted her resources by trying to heal her mom.

Every night, she shut her eyes, hoping she would make it to Oz to speak to Glinda about a cure. To her dismay, each night she was met with the same wall. The wall went for miles, blocking any possible entrance there could possibly be. She had walked for what seemed like forever in each direction, only to be disappointed and weary from her plight. Glinda had warned her the last time she left that she may not be able to return. There had been a strange feeling in the air during her last visit, along with a vague memory of a woman dressed all in red. She had pondered quite often if this woman was the reason for her inability to return to her land of freedom and happiness.

Her memories of Oz had become hazy, but she clung to the memory of something dark that had been nesting there for a while, which Glinda had spoken of. Every time she urged her memories to return, a haze went through her mind, blocking what was essential to remember. She could only remember the faces and names of those close to her there, and the memory of her last conversation with Glinda before her final visit ended.

"Oz used to have a balance of power. There were my twin sisters who had reign over the East and the West, along with my sister to the North. My twin sisters had become power-driven and soon found themselves drowning in wickedness and morphing their part of Oz into desolation and evil." Glinda sat down and patted the fountain beside her. Maryjane complied and rested beside Glinda as she wrapped an arm around her. "It was quite disheartening to watch them turn from the loving people they had once been into evil tyrants."

"What happened to them?" Maryjane peered up at Glinda with an eager face, hoping her eyes would force the story from Glinda's lips.

Glinda giggled. "You mean you haven't heard the story, little one?"

"No," Curiosity overtook Maryjane. There was something odd about the way Glinda asked the question that left Maryjane's mind roaming wildly.

"Well then, that is a story for a later time. However, with their destruction, the balance of power diminished. I am the last of the four, and I am afraid my power alone isn't enough to battle the power that is brewing from Emerald City." Glinda stood and motioned for Maryjane to follow as she walked to the edge of Munchkin Land.

The beautiful, golden road that originated in the center of the city had begun to crumble and gray on the outskirts. Maryjane followed Glinda's gaze past the road and saw the enchanted fields dying, dwindling away to wastelands. Emerald City, which was once too far away to see through the enchanted forests, was now visible as if the land was shrinking, and a pillar of black smoke rose from the center. It was no longer emerald in color but was darkening from the center. What parts of the castle that were still emerald were slowly losing their luster. Maryjane didn't know how much longer the beautiful city would have until the darkness completely enveloped the once sparkling ray of hope it had been.

"This is why it is so important for you not to wander off as you did today. If it weren't for Charlie being there with you, I don't know what would have happened to you." Glinda frowned, picturing Maryjane's future.

"What's there now, Glinda? Or should I say who? Why is there smoke where beauty used to be? Why would this person wish me harm?" Maryjane turned around from the sight of the city with her heart beating rapidly in her chest. She had never known anyone in Oz who wished her harm.

"Child, do not fret. In good time, it too will be fixed. I have one last lesson for you to learn before you're off back to your home," Glinda assured, placing her hands on Maryjane's shoulders.

"What lesson is this one?" Maryjane asked.

"You have within you a tremendous power brewing just under the surface. I have taught you the basics of power. I want you to take this last lesson to heart. After your run-in today with a special kind of evil, you need to learn whatever I can teach you." Glinda walked her back to the fountain.

Maryjane nodded in acknowledgement.

"Okay, my dear, close your eyes."

Maryjane obeyed, closed her eyes, and adjusted all her senses to her surroundings. She inhaled and exhaled, slowing each breath.

11

She could hear birds in a nearby tree feeding their babies with insects from the morning hunt. There was a soft rapping in the distance from where the workers cut down trees and busted the wood up to season for firewood so that they could keep warm during the nights. The wind started to blow slightly past her, and she could smell the fragrant flowers in bloom just outside of the little town. Apple pie flitted by her nose as one of the Munchkin bakers placed one in a nearby window to cool. The sun beamed down on her, heating her skin to where sweat trickled down her forehead. She didn't flinch and stood unmoving as all of her surroundings grew louder and stronger in sense. Just as fast as her senses reached out to everything, she withdrew them, concentrating on her immediate surroundings. Her ears trained in on Glinda's inaudible breathing and heartbeat, calm and collected without a hint of worry to cause a jump or flutter of tachycardia.

"Now, imagine a bright, white light starting in your center and filling your body. Let this light surround you. Once surrounded, take your hands and place them an inch apart. I want you to feel the energy radiating between them. Expand your hands until you have a nice ball formed. Gently press together and feel the push like magnets against one another."

Maryjane listened as Glinda spoke. With her eyes still closed, she envisioned a startling white light growing within her center, her Ki point. She let the light grow from her belly button, and without her, surrounding her entire body in white light. Once she felt the energy radiating from her body, she took her hands and held them slightly apart. She funneled all of the white light into her hands and felt them vibrating with power. She concentrated all of her efforts on maintaining the energy within the spaces between her hands and fingers. She then pushed her hands together and felt the immediate push back, just as Glinda described. The energy resistance sent tingling up her arms and into her spine. She felt the power of this manifested energy as it coursed and spun in her hands.

"Open your eyes and concentrate on this ball."

When she opened her eyes, she saw a beautiful, bright purple sphere in her hands. She had tapped into the violet flame of power.

The energy was astounding, and the purple ball looked like fire did in a fireplace. She turned the grenade of energy over in her hands, expecting it to disappear. The sphere grew brighter and stronger as she played with it, and the flames flickered in her hands without searing her.

"Do you see the color?" Glinda asked.

Still concentrating, worried that answering would diminish the unfathomable globe of purple fire in her hands, she squeaked, "Yes, it's purple."

"Excellent, little one. Now, concentrate on the orb. Imagine it growing hot like fire."

Maryjane did so, and the tumescence of energy began to change into a fire orb. It turned from the violet flame into a molten ball of lava. Fire tendrils whipped from the orb, and she could feel the heat growing in intensity as she let it sit between her hands. She began to sweat from the heat wave radiating around her body. The power held within her hands started a fire up her arms. Panic shot through her body until she realized the fire did not burn her skin.

"Marvelous! Imagine it cold like ice."

Once more, Maryjane changed her concentration, and the orb shifted into a ball of ice. The rondure felt solid, but she could still see straight through it as if it were translucent. It was a numbing and freezing feeling that crept throughout her body. Ice began to grow up her arms and down her legs as the power sat growing in intensity within her hands. A frigid wind emanated from her hands, and the ground below her feet began to freeze over.

"Stupendous!"

Maryjane followed her gut instinct, tossed the ball in the air, and it began to snow. She stared in awe as tiny snowflakes drifted down from the sky onto her and the surrounding area. It didn't melt, and clumps of snow began to form around them. The fountain that had water coursing from its top froze into shards of solid ice as the last bits of water dripped from the spout. The entire fountain turned to ice.

As fast as it had begun to snow and ice, it stopped, and the remnants of what her powers had caused melted away in the heat of *the Oz sun. Maryjane stood in utter awe of everything she had just witnessed with her own hands. She looked down at them, turning them over, peering, and speculating over the power that she had witnessed them create.*

"I…I can change the weather?" Maryjane was still in awe over the ball of power she had held within her hands. The power still coursed through her fingers, waiting for another one to be let loose.

"You can do far more than that, my dear. You can manifest energy balls to heal as well as to harm. You are very powerful." Glinda smiled at Maryjane. She rested her hands on Maryjane's shoulders, looked her directly in the eyes. "You are destined for something far greater than your imagination can think of. When you're older, you will understand, but right now isn't the time to elaborate on that." She looked to the sky and back to Maryjane. "Right now, it's time for you to return home."

"Okay," Maryjane replied, dropping her head. Whenever she would run off and come close to danger, Glinda would always send her home. It wasn't a punishment, but rather a fear of Maryjane being hurt while in Oz.

"Glinda?" Maryjane asked.

Glinda turned around and faced her with a smile. "Yes, little one."

"Don't be mad at Charlie." Maryjane scratched the back of her head anxiously. "And…tell him I said goodbye."

Glinda smiled as she always did. "It is never goodbye. Remember, even if you can't return one day, never give up or stop trying." Glinda said as she floated away.

Maryjane walked to the center of Munchkin Land, tapped her heels three times, and said, "Take me home." She took three steps through the whirling winds of Oz and awoke in her bed as daylight approached the horizon.

Maryjane sighed. She was about to open the door and walk in when she heard the familiar sound of Scarlet Gulhimer approaching on her bike. She had been trying to steal their farm from beneath them for years.

"Mama," Maryjane called out. "Miss Gulhimer is

coming."

Dorothy opened the door and walked onto the front porch as Scarlet dismounted her bike at the picket fence gate.

"Good evening, Dorothy. I heard you aren't feeling well in town and thought I'd drop this basket off with you. It's not much, but it's the thought that counts," Scarlet said as she walked up the sidewalk.

She was dressed in a red, polka-dotted dress with a deep red lipstick that was nearly scarlet in color to match.

"Thank you," Dorothy said flatly with no emotion behind it.

"I'd hate to see anything happen to you," Scarlet said smugly.

"Scarlet, I know what you're thinking, and I'm in no mood to battle over my farm. You're just as snide as your mother was, and frankly, I didn't care much for her. However, unlike the rest of the county, I will not bow to your pigheadedness. You do not own me or what is mine, and never will. So please, kindly leave," Dorothy said, handing the basket back to Scarlet.

Scarlet snorted, her hands tightening around the handle of the basket.

"One day this farm will be mine just like everything you have ever dreamed of, as yours is." She smiled an evil smile, turned, and walked back to her bike at the fence. She mounted it, glared at the two on the porch, muttered something under her breath, and pushed off down the road.

Maryjane watched her mother shiver. She had heard the stories of how menacing Miss Gulhimer's mother was and how much she was like her. She had disappeared when Scarlet was a child without a trace. Dorothy walked inside with Maryjane trailing. Dorothy was silent as everyone ate, but she sat and ate nothing. Once the workers cleared out, it was Maryjane and Dorothy who were left at the table. It was Maryjane who spoke first.

"Mama?" she asked, looking up from her plate of fried chicken and mashed potatoes.

"Yes, Maryjane," Dorothy replied, looking at her through weary eyes.

Maryjane started, "Is this sickness going to kill you? I've worked on countless remedies and none…"

"Oh, hocus pocus," Dorothy said, cutting her off. "You can't cure cancer, child!" Dorothy exclaimed.

Maryjane protested, leaning forward over the table to emphasize her point, "If I could just get back to Oz, I could cure you, I-"

"What did you say!?" Dorothy enquired, not giving her a chance to finish the sentence.

"I said I could cure you…" Maryjane said meekly, sitting back in her seat and looking down at her plate.

"No, before that. You said…Oz," Dorothy said, squinting her eyes at her in suspicion.

Maryjane sat quietly, wishing she had kept her mouth shut. She replied, "Yes."

"Who told you about Oz?" Dorothy demanded with her face flushing.

"No one…I…I used to go there in my dreams," Maryjane said regretfully, wishing she hadn't.

Dorothy was silent. "Whoever told you to play this joke is cruel, and you…you're just as cruel to go along with it," she hissed as she stood up, knocking her drink over.

"Mama, it's not a joke, honest!" Maryjane cried, standing up, running to her mother.

"Enough! No more talk of Oz. Clean this kitchen up and then off to bed!" Dorothy yelled and walked from the room.

Maryjane sat back down in tears. Her mother was clearly upset with her tale of the kind of dreams she had. This is one reason she never told her, or anyone else, for that matter. People already thought she was weird and strange. She stood up and started clearing the dishes off the table. She carried them to the sink and looked out the window.

"Glinda," she whispered, "please help me return to Oz. I need to so desperately." She turned to walk from the room when she saw her mom in the doorway.

"Oz...what...what does it look like now?" Dorothy asked with wide eyes like a child staring at candy.

"I don't know. I haven't been able to return in nearly five years. There's a wall up now blocking me," Maryjane replied, sitting back at the table.

"I heard...you say Glinda..." Dorothy said, following her to the table.

"Yes, she's the good witch of the South, well, the only witch left now. Her twin sisters, who had turned wicked, were destroyed years ago, and her sister of the North not too long ago. There's an imbalance of power that made way for a new power to emerge. This new power is what has me blocked from re-entry," Maryjane said.

Dorothy was silent. Thoughts whizzed through her head. *Could it be true? Has my daughter been taking the trips I wished for?* She thought quietly to herself.

"People used to call me crazy. Uncle Henry and Auntie Em finally told me to stop telling my tales to people. The townspeople held a meeting and forced Uncle Henry and Auntie Em to commit me to an asylum for three years. When I was finally released, I ran away," Dorothy said, pausing in reminiscence. "I was barely a teenager when I went to Oz," Dorothy began as she started to tell her daughter of her trip to Oz and all the friends and foes she had made. When she was finished, Maryjane sat there looking at her.

Finally, she spoke, "So, it was you who destroyed the wicked witches of the east and west."

"Yes, well, of course, they were both accidents. I

never intended to harm either one of them," Dorothy said. "You have no clue how wonderful it feels to share the story and not be treated as a mad woman. I finally convinced Uncle Henry and Auntie Em that Oz existed, well, Princess Ozma did. We lived there until they died. I asked Ozma to return me home, and she complied, sending jewels and gold for me to buy back the farm. I met your father, and you know where it goes from there." She smiled in relief as she shared her story for the first time in years.

"Mama, we must go back! Glinda can heal you! I know it!" Maryjane said excitedly. She grinned at her mother. Her smile faded when her mother did not return the same enthusiasm. "What's wrong?" she asked.

"I haven't been able to return to Oz since I came home, child," Dorothy replied with a grief-stricken look. "Ozma told me once I left, I would never be able to return."

"I can help you, Mama! If you really want to go back, I can get you there!" Maryjane exclaimed, running to the sink. She pulled some herbs out of her basket and began to brew them.

"What are you doing, child?" Dorothy asked, exhausted from the conversation.

"I'm making you a tea to drink to help you sleep and dream. The herbal blend will take you on a journey of the heart. I'll meet you at the wall," Maryjane said as she handed her a cup of tea.

Dorothy looked at her daughter. She saw a glimmer in her, something she had never noticed before. She drank the tea, and Maryjane walked her to her room to lie down.

She looked at her daughter, smiled, and said, "You have always been my glimmer of hope to keep pushing forward."

Maryjane smiled, and as she shut her mother's door, said, "I love you, Mama." She walked to her room, shut the door, and crawled into bed. "Glinda, we're coming home!" She closed her eyes and drifted off to sleep. She felt her body getting lighter and lighter. Soon she was asleep and ready to begin her journey back to Oz.

Chapter Two

MARYJANE WALKED through the haze that separated the two worlds. So often she had made this journey, and she was no longer frightened like she had been many years ago. A child barely five years old walking through the mists of a strange land is hard to fathom. However, even as the fear mounted, she trudged on until the glow of the village washed away the mist, and she had landed in Oz. It was a strange adventure for her. She had met people she hadn't known could even exist.

She kept her head up high as she trudged the same path, hoping and praying to reach Oz once more. As the haze disappeared, the wall became visible to her. Her mother stood there with a solemn look upon her face.

"This is Oz, but it's blocked off." Dorothy walked toward the wall surrounding Oz and placed her hand on the cold stone.

"I know. This wall has been up for five years. I was hoping traveling with you would bring it down," Maryjane replied, walking up beside her mother as she eyed the wall for a hidden passage.

Her heart sank in her chest, and immediately, she felt the urge to cry. The wall had been up for years. It was silly of her to think that it might have disappeared just because her mother came along with her. She turned around and leaned her back up against the wall. She was out of ideas and options for returning to Glinda. Her mother wouldn't be healed, she would die; then Maryjane would be left alone, devoid of compassion from a cruel world she didn't belong in and never had.

She glanced around at what was left of Oz outside the wall. The land was barren and dying even before the desert could be seen. The trees had long since withered away into pieces that couldn't even be used for firewood. The rivers had dried up and turned into cracked trenches of death. It appeared as if it were the wee hours of twilight. However, Maryjane knew that it was always daytime when she would arrive in Oz. To her dismay, hanging in the sky were black, dark clouds of death and decay. As far as the eye could see, there wasn't a shred of light. There was only darkness and the ever-so-often bleeding red of the sky. You could feel the heat of the sun through the clouds, but not a ray of light peeked through them. It was ominous and a bit frightening to witness.

"How long has Oz looked like this?" Dorothy gazed around her surroundings and stood alongside her daughter. Her brow was furrowed, and tears glistened in her eyes as she looked in horror at what her beautiful world had become.

"It was becoming a wasteland, my last lesson here. The sky wasn't as dark as it is now, but it was starting to get gray over. Plants had begun to starve from the lack of light. Even though there were clouds for miles to see, there was no rain that poured from them, so the rivers dried up. This is what is left after wicked takes over a place full of happiness and life." Maryjane ignored her mother's emotional crisis as she crouched down at the wall and pulled her knees into her chest.

"Lesson?" Dorothy's confused, yet curious face, peered down at Maryjane.

"Yes," Maryjane began, "Glinda was helping me develop my uh…my powers."

"Powers!" Dorothy exclaimed. "You're a witch?"

"Yes, Mama, a powerful one according to Glinda."

Maryjane looked over at her mother, who stood there staring at Maryjane with her mouth agape.

"How do you have powers? You are my daughter. You were born in the mortal world. I don't understand..." Dorothy trailed off in thought.

"I don't know, Mama. Glinda never told me why I have powers. She just taught me how to use them." Maryjane didn't know if her mother was afraid of her or afraid of what she could do as she stood with space in between them.

Trailing in the wind was a familiar soft voice. It sounded far off, but close at the same time. "Don't forget your lessons."

Dorothy looked at Maryjane uneasily. "That's Glinda's voice. I remember it as if it were yesterday, her speaking to me." She paused for a moment with a serene look on her face. "Well, what was your last lesson?"

"She taught me how to use energy and manipulate the elements." Maryjane didn't dare to look her mother in the eyes. She sat in her crouched position, turning her lesson over and over in her head, when a thought occurred to her. "Maybe...no, that's ridiculous," she said, shrugging it off.

"What?" Dorothy asked.

"Well, I thought I might be able to use the power against the wall. Silly, huh?" Maryjane said, shaking her head at the sound of it.

Dorothy was silent. "Well, the elements include fire, water, air and earth. Stone is earth."

Maryjane looked at her mother, and her eyes brightened. "Of Course!"

She stood up, faced the wall, placed her hands on the cobblestone formation, and closed her eyes. She repeated the process Glinda had taught her in her lesson. The ground began to shake, and it frightened her. She removed her hand from the wall and looked at it with cautious eyes.

"Do it again," Dorothy urged.

Maryjane placed her trembling hands back on the wall and closed her eyes once again. The ground began to shake, and this time the wall started to tremble. She didn't stop her concentration and pressed her urgency for the wall to fall harder into her hands filled with magic. The wall began to break and crumble. She pushed one last time with her mind, and the entire wall fell to the ground like a domino effect.

"You did it, child!" Dorothy exclaimed, running through the remnants of the wall and taking her first step back into Oz since she was a teenager.

Maryjane opened her eyes and saw the wall falling to rubble as far as her eyes could see. She walked over the rubble and into the midst of a ghost town of what was once Munchkin Land. There was no color inside, just as there was none outside of the wall. The grey loneliness blanketed the streets just as the lack of movement in the town.

Dorothy stood, not moving, as she gazed around at the remnants of Oz. "I can't believe this is what's left," she uttered, moving her feet over the rubble. "Where is the light? Where are the beautiful colors? These hills used to sing. Now, it's…it's…barren! Where is my beautiful, dream land?" she asked, walking around the fountain that sat in the middle of Munchkin Land.

"It's been this way for years. I remember when I was very, very young, it was so beautiful. Each time I came back, it seemed to have gotten darker and grayer. This is a complete change from the last time I was here. It's…empty," Maryjane mumbled, walking carefully through the center of the town.

A wave of panic washed over Maryjane. She ran to each of the houses that the Munchkins lived in, banging on the doors, "Munchkins!? Munchkins?! Where are you?

It's me, Maryjane!"

There was no answer from any of the houses. A slight breeze blew her hair, and she looked behind her as fear crept up her spine. She looked off toward the sky and saw the floating mists descending to the remnants of Munchkin Land. Within the floating mists, there was a beautiful woman dressed in a glorious gown that shone brighter than the sun itself.

"Glinda," Dorothy murmured, watching her descend in a spectacular fashion.

"I see you finally found a way to get back into Oz." Glinda smiled at Maryjane and bowed with respect for her feat.

"Why didn't you just tell me?" Maryjane asked, looking at Glinda.

"You had to figure it out on your own." Dorothy looked as if she were in a serene dream, gazing at Glinda.

Glinda turned to her, and a warm glow washed over her face. "Welcome back, old friend. I see the years have been kind to you." Glinda tried to look sincere and forced a smile as her eyes looked over Dorothy's frail body.

Dorothy gave a half-hearted smile in return to the strained words. "Not too kind." Dorothy touched her hand to her stomach, reminded of the cancer that was eating away at her insides.

"Glinda, you have to help me heal her. She's sick, and nothing I've done has helped her," Maryjane pleaded, tears glistening in her eyes.

Glinda touched Dorothy's stomach, and with a pained look, turned toward Maryjane. "Darling, there are some things that even my magic cannot heal."

"Then, it was a wasted effort." Maryjane flopped down on the side of the fountain behind them.

"No, my child, it was not." Dorothy sat down beside her on the fountain. "You returned me to my real home, my place of happiness. This was the best gift you could give my dying soul."

"I have no one but you, Mama." Maryjane teared up as she thought of her mother slipping into a sleep she wouldn't wake from. She leaned over and wrapped her arms around Dorothy's waist. Dorothy gave her squeeze back and pulled back from the embrace.

"This is a discussion for later, my dear, right now there are more important matters at hand." Dorothy wiped the tear from Maryjane's cheek and kissed her forehead. "Glinda, what power has seized Oz? Is Ozma ok?" Dorothy's face filled with concern as she brushed aside the heavy emotions lying on her heart.

"Do not fret. Ozma is safe. This power is wretched. She goes by the name the Red Sorceress, but I have had my run-ins with her and know her by her true name, Scarlet. She would have given those wicked witches a run for their money. She is what you call pure evil."

"Where are the Munchkins?" Maryjane asked once again, giving a look around for them.

"She has taken most everyone prisoner in the Land of Oz. She keeps them locked away in the remnants of the Emerald City. Even my power is no match against hers. She has taken every magical being and turned them against any good left in Oz. She has turned our beautiful land into a wasteland. All of those freed by you, Dorothy, have been enslaved once more. And this time, by a power far greater and more sinister than my sisters."

"What of Lion, Scarecrow, and the Tin Woodsman, Nick? What has become of them?" Alarm spread over Dorothy's face as she was delivered the news of Oz's enslavement. Glinda placed her hand on her shoulder and sent her calming vibes to alleviate the anxiety.

"They went into hiding. They knew they would be her first targets. Everyone in Oz has always spoken of your triumphs in helping the land. They knew she would find out about you and how they had helped you when you were here. Nick was especially fraught since he was the emperor over the Winkies." Glinda looked out into the field of Oz and peered in the direction of the Emerald City. Her eyes were glum and meek as she turned back to them and offered a smile of encouragement.

"How do we find them?" Dorothy hastily walked up to her and watched her for an answer. Glinda was aware of everything at all times, just as the wicked witch was. It was a sacred power they held through the looking glass.

"You will have to find out about the three of them on your own. Right now, I must teach Maryjane as much as I can to develop her powers further and ensure a safe passage for you two as you journey through this changed land," Glinda said.

A bright pink light enveloped everyone, and they found themselves standing in an enchanted castle and no longer in Munchkin Land. The floors of the castle glistened as if they were crystals. Maryjane looked around and noticed that every facet of the castle was inlaid with precious gems and silver.

"Your lovely castle. Oh, how I have dreamt of coming back here again to admire its beauty. This was much faster, if I do say so, than the traditional cross-country crossing." Dorothy chuckled, Glinda shook her head, and she snickered as well.

"My friend, you never forgot anything, did you?" The two chuckled together and began walking down the corridors of the castle. Every cathedral ceiling that they walked under had a chandelier different from the one before, but each was unique and spectacular in sight. Each room was filled to its capacity with elements of the craft.

Maryjane walked past an alchemy room while the other two continued to chatter and walk ahead. It was a laboratory filled with beakers of potions, herbs to distill, a distillation column, a condenser, and a mortar and pestle for grinding the herbs. All of the potions were on one wall with plaques beneath them stating what they were. On the back wall, you had all of the herbs in glass containers with labels of the genus and species on the plaques. The wall adjacent to the herbs was full of old books labeled with different numbers and letters signifying their order in the alchemical texts.

The next room she walked past was an incredibly large library. When she peeked inside the room, the walls looked as if they had outgrown the castle itself. Even those who knew nothing about magic could conclude it was magically enchanted. She glanced at the closest title and read, "The Secrets of Conjuring and Banishing." It was evident how powerful and knowledgeable Glinda was just by the anthology of books that graced the walls. Maryjane never assumed how powerful or how disempowered she was. She felt a surge of admiration for Glinda. She was thankful that it was she who taught her the basics of her powers.

The last room the group entered was where Glinda held her ceremonial rites. There before the small group stood an altar lavishly decorated, with all of Glinda's tools she used for magic laid out on it. Maryjane gazed upon Glinda's exquisite athame, which had a pentagram etched into the blade and strange characters engraved into the handle. Her besom was on a stand mounted over the table. To the sides of the table, there were two statues adjacent to each. One was of a man draped in a cloak and bearing a wreath upon his head. The other was of a woman who was also draped in a cloak, but had a pregnant belly, and held a star with both hands above her head. In the middle of the table, there was an inexplicably large, leather-bound book. The pages of the book looked ancient and worn.

"Normally, I would teach you in Munchkin Land, but there are ears everywhere. Word travels quickly through the grapevines to the Red Sorceress. Here, nothing can get in to harm us or hear us. It is guarded by a multitude of crystals and layers of magic that evil cannot touch." Glinda motioned to the castle's window for them to see for themselves.

Maryjane walked to the castle windows and peered out at the surrounding area. All around the castle were walls of crystals that encased the entire castle in a rainbow glow. Within the fields were rows and rows of gorgeous roses blooming. She immediately thought of Charlie. Her head was flooded with all the memories of their time together during her trips to Oz. Her fondest memory was of when he took a seed and held it in his hand. He closed his eyes, and within his hand, she could see a glowing light. When he opened it, a single rose lay in his hand, which he tucked behind her ear. She smiled to herself, but the smile was painful and heartbreaking. She lowered her head and walked back to Glinda.

"What about Charlie? Where is he?" Maryjane's heart begged for an answer. Had he been towed off along with the rest of them as a prisoner?

Glinda passed over the question without even a glimmer of hope for Maryjane to have. She feared the worst for Charlie, and it seemed like Glinda didn't have the time to speak of him to her. So, she turned her full attention to Glinda, pushed Charlie from her mind, and listened intently as Glinda began to speak.

"Maryjane, you have powers you could not possibly dream of within yourself. You tasted what you could do with the wall. I'm going to help you open the flood gate, so you can put a stop to the tyranny that has overtaken Oz. Walk to the center of the room, please. It's a consecrated, sacred space. Even if anyone were to get around my enchantments, you are safe within that circle of power."

Maryjane listened and walked to the center, where

there was a large pentagram glowing on the floor. She had never seen such a sight and immediately thought of how powerful this space was. She stepped into it, and a bright, white light descended around her.

"The Elders provide us with a multitude of weapons to defend against other types of magic. Here you will choose your first weapon, which will be a wand. A wand helps you direct your power to a central source instead of affecting the entire surroundings. Once you choose your wand, the rest of your tools will descend automatically to you," Glinda said, motioning to the light.

Five wands descended in front of Maryjane. They were all so intricately designed, and she marveled at their beauty. However, her eyes rested on one in particular. It was intricately twisted like a unicorn's horn.At the top of it was a star that had a triquetra at the bottom of it and two crescent moons; one to the left and one to the right of the star, all wrapped in a circle just as the pentagram to her feet looked. She picked it up, and it began to glow a purple flame around it.

"You have chosen your wand wisely, young one. The symbol etched upon your wand is a symbol pertinent to your soul. It is your personal sigil of power. The star represents the five elements within nature working together: Earth, Air, Fire, Water, and Spirit. The two crescent moons, to the left and right of the star, indicate the stages the Goddess goes through: waxing, full moon as the circle around the star, and waning. This is her as a maiden, mother, and crone, which symbolizes her mounting, peaking, and waning periods of power."

The next object to descend to her was a deep purple robe. It had the same symbol at the top of her wand embroidered upon it. The touch of the fabric felt like caterpillar silk. She wrapped the robe around her body and tied it where the hood was. Her body vibrated with energy. She looked at her hands as she felt the surge course through her fingers, up her arms, and down her spine.

"Your robe is one of the most powerful additions to your wardrobe. Most do not know the power that it wields. It will protect you against all types of elemental magic. Fireballs will not harm you, nor will any type of magic that would resonate from the elements of nature or conjured from nature."

She looked to the light as a ring and necklace descended to her. Once again, the emblem that had been on every single item she had received was adorned in her jewelry. She grasped the ring out of midair. She placed the ring on the pointer finger of her power hand. Electrical sparks began to arc from her fingers. The necklace draped around her neck as it completed its descent and began to glow a bright red along with her aura. The power mounted in her Ki point, and soon she found herself engulfed in an emerald and purple blaze of fire.

"These are your talismans. You must wear them always. Not only do they emit magic to raise your powers, they also work as a natural defense against the magic of the black arts. Those who wish you harm will have to go to extra lengths to cast any type of mind-altering spell on you."

Again, from the light, another item began to descend. She looked up as a leather-bound book floated softly down toward her outstretched hands. She watched as her sigil was etched on the cover of it as it descended from the light. When it touched her hands, it opened, and each page flipped over as blank pages that were immediately filled with spells, incantations, recipes, and herbal magic. Everything that she had written in her notebook at home, which had been torn and shredded, was within the pages, along with new information.

"This book is your Book of Shadows. I know you started a small notebook at home, which contained everything you had learned over the years. This one has everything you have learned and everything you will begin to learn on your journey to becoming a young sorceress. You will begin to progress and grow in your magic. Each time you pass a level of learning, your book will grow larger. Keep it safe, for in the wrong hands, it can lead to your destruction. To mortal eyes, it is blank, but to those trained in magic, it is not."

The last few items to descend were an athame, a sword, and a pair of beautiful silver slippers.

Dorothy gasped, "Are...are those the—" She trailed off.

"No. These are slippers that are designed for her favor. The slippers you speak of are right where you left them." Glinda motioned down to Dorothy's feet.

Dorothy glanced down, and upon her feet were the silver slippers that took her home. "How? They disappeared."

"Magic can work in mysterious ways." Glinda winked at Dorothy as she bent down to touch and inspect her shoes.

Maryjane slipped hers on and felt the power contained in them. Glinda swirled her finger, and the slippers were cloaked as black, ankle-high, leather boots to prevent the knowledge of the power she wore on her feet.

"Your slippers will remain cloaked as long as they remain on your feet. As for your athame and sword, they each hold unique qualities, as each is a different extension of your powers. The athame enhances your courage and the creative spark within your heart. Like the wand, it can centralize your power and turn it into a deadly stream of energy. The sword enhances your thoughts and intellectual nature. When used in up-close combat, it enhances your reflexes and helps to calculate your moves with better dexterity as opposed to your enemy."

Maryjane slid the sword into its sheath and donned it around her waist. She placed the athame in her boot. She looked ready for battle, and Glinda gave her a half-hearted smile.

"One more thing, we need to do something about your attire. We can't have the future queen of Oz walking around looking like a farmer, now, can we?" Glinda snickered as Maryjane blushed.

Glinda gave her finger another twirl. The outfit Maryjane had been wearing faded and was replaced with a pale white, Victorian-era styled gown. The gown laced up in the back-corset style. The front of the gown was embroidered with white lace and layered in quartz crystal in the shape of her sigil. Maryjane assumed the quartz was for power amplification. The gown didn't hang loose but clung tightly around her waist and chest. Atop of her head was a small tiara. It had her sigil fabricated from silver.

"Now, listen well, my child. Your final lesson, and the only help I can truly give you with your powers, is this: Be careful what you say, for your words manifest from power. Herbs will enhance your spells. Crystals can protect, heal, remove toxins, and much more. A lighted candle holds power that can either protect or cause harm to those it is used against. Those whom you meet along your way may or may not know who you are or your status within the Arc Coventry. Those who do know and accept you will help you pass along with ease. Those who do not know you will cause great interference and delay. You must touch them in order for their mind to be unscrambled. All the people of Oz know who you are and have awaited your return. Those who see your tiara should automatically know who you are, although the Red Sorceress has brainwashed most citizens of Oz, so be wary of who you trust."

"So, if my words manifest power, if I say I wish to

return to Munchkin Land, we will?" Maryjane asked, looking down at all of her weapons and gifts from the Elders.

"Look around, my dear. We're already here." Glinda motioned away from her body to her surroundings. Maryjane looked around, and to her astonishment, they were in the center of Munchkin Land.

"Did…did I do that?" She was still stunned from the power that coursed through her veins. It felt nothing like it did five years ago. She could feel that it was much stronger and more powerful than the taste of what she received on her last day in Oz.

"Yes, dear, you did," Glinda smiled, and her eyes twinkled with approval.

Maryjane thought to herself for a moment. "So, if whatever I say manifests…Can I use my powers to bring the Munchkins back?" She looked at Glinda's face for a sign of relief. She remembered the storm that had appeared from nowhere when she had gotten angry at her tormenters in the park.

"Try and see for yourself," Glinda wasn't giving her any more tips on her power.

"Alright." Maryjane gathered herself, raised her hands toward the sky, and declared, "The Munchkins are to return to their home, Munchkin Land, and no one shall ever harm them or take them again." She waited a few seconds. "It didn't work," she said, glancing around for at least one munchkin to come skipping along. She didn't understand how the storm came out of nowhere, but the munchkins didn't appear.

"Be patient," Glinda said.

Maryjane stood there, and was about to turn around to admit defeat, when she heard a giggle, followed by another and another, then soon there was a parade of giggles, and she whirled around. "Munchkins!"

The ground began to tremble as crystal walls

sprouted from the ground around Munchkin Land. There was quartz, obsidian, blue kyanite, and other protective crystals that all assembled a very powerful barrier between Munchkin Land and the ruins. The crystals sparkled and shone as if the sun's light had reached them through the dark clouds that hung in the sky.

"Well done, young one." Glinda bowed to her in approval.

"You are amazing, child," Dorothy said in astonishment as all the munchkins swarmed around them.

Thunder and lightning began to clash all around them. The munchkins ran and hid in their houses while Dorothy, Glinda, and Maryjane stood their ground awaiting the arrival of their foe. Within seconds, a figure emerged at the edge of the crystal gate. She was fiery in nature, everything scarlet red from her head to her toes.

"Who dares to defy me with magic? Who has snatched my Munchkin slaves?" the Red Sorceress demanded.

Maryjane stepped forward. "I have."

"Do you have any idea who I am and the power I wield?" the Red Sorceress boomed.

"Why, of course, I know who you are. Apparently, your memory has failed you in your old age, but we have met once before." Maryjane smirked snidely as the Red Sorceress scowled.

"I do not have to acknowledge your existence nor answer your questions. However, I do know of your friend who stands by your side in her old age. Dorothy isn't it?" Dorothy gasped as a smile spread across the lips of the Red Sorceress.

"How do you know my name or who I am, for that matter?" Dorothy demanded.

"All in good time, my dear. First, I have to settle this tiny arrogance of power. Munchkins, return at once to the Emerald City." Silence followed. "Now!!!" she yelled.

Once again, silence followed, and the Munchkins stayed safely tucked away in their homes.

"Your powers are useless against the declared magic within this crystal circle," Glinda stated, smiling ear to ear as if she had won a game.

She glared at Glinda, "Whatever magic you have learned to wield will not compare to mine."

Lightning rained down all around them. Maryjane ran over to her mother, and a bolt dropped down right in front of her, preventing her from offering safety to her mother. Her fear soon turned to anger, and she turned around to face the sorceress. Her purple shield radiated like flames and engulfed her as she levitated from the ground. The Red Sorceress was astonished by the look of anger on her face, and without words, she sent a bolt of lightning careening directly at Maryjane. Maryjane raised her hands in front of her, pushed with her energy, and the bolt returned, landing directly next to the Red Sorceress. She then lifted her hands and head to the sky and gathered all of the lightning together into a twisting vortex of electricity.

"You have but one choice, and I say this with meaning: leave now, and never return to bother these innocent people. If you do not, this vortex of lightning will end your reign. What do you say, live to fight another day or meet an early death?" Maryjane taunted, holding the electricity steady. She had no clue as to whether the vortex would really end the sorceress, but it was worth a try for arbitration. She knew she could not take on the sorceress right now. She was new to her powers and knew she would be defeated.

The Red Sorceress sneered, "We will meet once again, and you will not have Glinda at your side to help defend you." She glared at Maryjane.

"Oh, I plan on meeting once again, Scarlet," Maryjane sneered back.

"I see Glinda has taught you almost everything you need to know to survive here," the Red Sorceress said uneasily. Maryjane could sense that no one called her by her name, Scarlet. The Red Sorceress glanced over to Glinda, who stood by herself, watching Maryjane use her magic.

"No, some things you learn on your own. Now, be gone," Maryjane demanded without flinching in fear or apprehension.

"Oh, Glinda, next time, dearie, we fight to the death," the Red Sorceress sneered, and as fast as she appeared, she disappeared, taking her storm with her.

Maryjane walked to the edge of the crystal fortress and stared off at the Emerald City. She turned and faced Glinda. I know what I must do now," she said, glancing behind her at the black and red clouds that swirled above the darkened Emerald City.

"You are our only saving grace. Heal this land and eradicate the evil that dominates it. I must go now. If you need me, you can always summon me," Glinda said, bowing to them both.

"Wait, what about Charlie?" asked Maryjane. "Where is he?" Glinda had floated away before she could finish asking about him.

Maryjane stood there and turned to face her mother. "We must find your friends, but I'm afraid I do not know where to start or what to do."

Dorothy smiled, "Well, that's easy. There's only one way to the City of Emeralds..."

Chapter Three

THE TWO OF THEM started to walk the path of what used to be a beautiful, golden road. Like everything else in Oz, the road had long since blackened from evil and crumbled nearly into dust in some parts, but with each step Maryjane took, the road returned to its lustrous, golden hue. Even with no sun out to shine upon the road, it lit up the valley as daylight would, breaking through clouds. Maryjane watched in awe and horror as the road behind her changed from death to life. It was what she wanted, to heal the land, but she didn't want it at this cost. The Red Sorceress would know precisely where she was by the path they were leaving, with it turning to the yellow brick it had once been. To her relief, but discouragement as well, the road that had sprung back to life once again turned back into the color of death. They walked along the path in silence as Maryjane cautiously looked around the surroundings on alert. Dorothy, remembering her own journey along the path to the Emerald City, slipped a giggle. Maryjane glanced at her.

"What are you laughing about?" she asked.

"Oh, nothing.I was just remembering my own journey down this same road. It is very different, however. Everything here has changed. It was once so beautiful here, and now it's just a dark, black hole from the deep-seated evil rooting itself into Oz," Dorothy said solemnly.

They continued along in silence, both eyeing the devastation the sorceress had placed upon the land. It was barren and dying like the surroundings on the outskirts of Munchkin Land. The sight fell on their hearts heavily, as they knew the rest of Oz had the same overbearing lack of love. They were hopeful to think that some light would appear somewhere along the walk, but to no avail, it remained dark, black, and a rotting atmosphere, just as the love the Red Sorceress held within her had long since wilted. What should have been fields of corn were rotted pieces of stalks, where no farmer was present to harvest them. There wasn't a person for miles on end during their hike. Everyone in Oz was under the rule of the Red Sorceress. The fields that were once alive with abundance were just scant pieces of dried-up earth.

The Red Sorceress' plan had worked perfectly when she put the wall up around Oz. Maryjane had been the only person to keep Oz alive and the land from dry rotting with her pure love of the magical land. Once she was barred access back to Oz, the land had no more love to latch onto. The only thing left to feed from was the evil and hatred in the Red Sorceress' heart. The land now reflected what her heart looked like: death, darkness, decay, and lifelessness. Maryjane's eyes searched the fields on either side of the road to see if there was any life whatsoever left to the fields, but, to her dismay, everything was dead.

They came to a broken fence lying on the ground. Behind the fence was a post where a farmer had once hung a scarecrow, but it had long since been taken down. "This was where I first met Scarecrow. Oh, how I miss him," Dorothy cried.

Maryjane looked at her mother. If only she cared that much for her...She had never had an established relationship with her mother. She loved her mother unconditionally, but her mother was never there for her when she really needed it. Like most mothers and daughters, their relationship revolved around small talk over dinner. There were times she wished she could have talked to her mother about things that happened with the kids at school, and the horrible things they would say to her. She trudged through life being labeled as the daughter of an insane woman. Her mother never spoke of her asylum years, for obvious reasons, but it still left Maryjane in the dark about everything. If she had told her years ago about Oz, this trip may have come a lot sooner.

Up ahead, there was another field of decaying corn. Amidst the field was a post with what appeared to be a mangled body of an old scarecrow. It was falling apart with its clothing ripped and torn. You could see the hay stuffing poking out in bunches, ready to fall out of the man-made carcass. Its arms barely clung to the body with just snippets of thread. Dorothy walked closer to it, peering at it, and straining to see if there was a resemblance to her old friend. If she could find the farmer and the farm where he had been created, she might be able to find him. When she was within reaching distance, her hand outstretched to touch the mangled body, red eyes ripped open on its face, burning into her eyes. It lunged from the pole and grabbed Dorothy by the arm. Dorothy screamed in fear and panic as the hideous creature dragged her from the field and onto the road.

It smelled awful, like a mixture of mildew and raw sewage. Dorothy tried not to breathe in the pungent stench of the creature as he jostled her around like a rag doll. It bellowed, malevolence dripping like water from its voice, "Who dares to trespass in my fields!?" It yanked Dorothy closer, and she let out a more deafening scream, trying to squirm out of the creature's grip and get away.

Maryjane, outraged, stomped her foot hard on the ground and yelled, "You will not harm her! Let her go!"

The ground roared with tremors, and a hole opened

beneath the creature. As it fell, it tightened its grip on Dorothy and hauled her down to the open hole with it.

"Let me go! Let me go!" Dorothy shrieked.

"Witches!!" the creature hissed. "At least one of you will go with me!"

Maryjane ran to Dorothy, dangling for dear life from the ledge of the hole. Not knowing what else to do, she grabbed the creature's arm to pry his grip loose from her mother's arm. The arm started changing from a deep, blackish, grey color to a colorful, yellow and blue fabric arm. Soon, the entire creature changed from the mangled, menacing creature into a scarecrow.

"Scarecrow!" Dorothy yelped. Maryjane pulled her mother out of the hole. They both leaned back over the hole and pulled Scarecrow from the hole. The hole immediately closed behind him once he was out.

"How do you know my name, witch?" he demanded, backing away. He looked at his hands, feet, arms, legs, and then at the two women standing before him. "Who are you!?"

"Scarecrow, it's me! It's Dorothy!" Dorothy cried as she walked closer to him.

"Lies! Dorothy was no witch and wouldn't consort with witches either!" He glared at Maryjane.

"It's me! Honest!" Dorothy pleaded with him.

"Prove it!" he snapped.

"I helped you to get to the Wizard so that he could give you a brain," she said, scrambling to think of things.

"Everyone knows that!" he hissed.

"You were the first friend, and best friend, I made while here. When I helped you slip off the post, it was down the road that way." Dorothy pointed to the broken fence and empty post.

Scarecrow looked at her. He was taking it all in. It had been such a long time since he had seen Dorothy. The woman who stood before him was aged and frail, and then his eyes stopped on her slippers.

"The slippers! Why, it is you!" He ran to her, threw his arms around her, and hugged her tightly. "I can't believe it's you. I knew one day you would return. I told the others you would come back. We waited forever, but you never did."

"I know it's been a while since you two have chatted, but before everyone starts to get reacquainted, we need to get off this road and now!" Maryjane barked off the order as she looked off into the blowing wind. "She's coming!"

They all glanced at a whirlwind bounding down the road. The three of them took off into the field when they realized the whirlwind was following a carriage up the road. Maryjane fished her spell book from her bag and flipped through the pages as swiftly as she could.

"What are you looking for?" Dorothy watched her thumb through the book and skimmed the pages.

"An invisibility spell." Maryjane landed on a page and read through the words with her finger trailing below the lines. "I found it!"She exclaimed, tapping the book page. "Encase us in a globe of light, which is blind to see in others' sight. Turn us invisible to the eye unseen, so as I will it, so mote it be!"

Sparkles ascended from the ground and surrounded the three in a swirling ball. The energy encased them in a globe, and it was just in time as the Red Sorceress rode up in the carriage to the spot they had found Scarecrow and halted. She stepped out of the carriage, wielding her staff, and looked around.

"They could *not* have gotten very far!! Find them!" she thundered as two of her henchmen climbed from inside.

Maryjane stayed still as the Red Sorceress eyed where they had knelt down. She put her finger to her lips to make sure her mother and Scarecrow didn't make a peep.

"Ma' Lady, we will track her. You return to the city." It was a handsome young man who couldn't have been older than Maryjane. His voice sounded gruff, and Maryjane watched him as he knelt in front of the Red Sorceress. There was something strangely familiar about his persona, but she brushed it aside. Beside him stood a young woman who looked around the same age as well. She could have passed as Maryjane's sister. She had the same shade of red hair and the same body build. She was almost an exact copy, if only Maryjane could see her face...

"Why should you two be the ones to track her?" hissed a second man who jumped from the carriage. Maryjane watched the second man saunter up to the first one. The distaste between the two was evident as they sneered at each other.

"We both know that I'm faster and better at tracking, hunting, and killing than you are. Emma can control people with her mind. What better two to track and go after her?" The handsome man grabbed the other's shirt and pulled him in closer to prove his point. "If you like, we can show you how we could handle them now," he cautioned through gritted teeth.

The Red Sorceress broke her gaze from their spot. "Enough, you two. Ashe, you come with me back to the city." The one she called Ashe muttered something under his breath and climbed back into the carriage. She looked to the other one, "You both had better find her and the older woman she is with!" She glowered, returned to her carriage that sprang back to life, and left for the city.

The young man stood watching the carriage until it was no longer visible, and glanced in the direction they were all kneeling in. He motioned with his hand for the girl to follow him, turned around, and they both started treading through the corn field on the other side of the road. When they were no longer in seeing or hearing distance, Maryjane motioned for them all to stand, and she let the bubble of invisibility down.

"We have got to keep moving. If you talk, please do it quietly. I don't know how far away those trackers went in the other direction, and we mustn't get caught," Maryjane spoke softly. She began to walk back to the road.

"I cannot believe you are consorting with a witch, Dorothy," Scarecrow huffed as he trailed behind her.

Maryjane spun around, annoyed and proclaimed, "I'm not just a witch to her. I'm her daughter!"

Scarecrow looked at Dorothy. She had not flinched while Maryjane had spoken. She didn't look or seem baffled by Maryjane's declaration.

"It's true. If it were not for her, I would not be here right now. She helped me return to Oz to find all of you. Do you know where Nick and Lion are?" Dorothy asked, staring off into the field to see if the tracker was lurking around.

"No, after the Red Sorceress invaded, we went our separate ways so that we could survive. I have not seen or spoken to them since our departure from one another," Scarecrow replied, looking around for the tracker as well. He eyed Maryjane. "Have we met before?" he asked.

Maryjane paused and looked as if she were about to answer. She shook her head to the trivial question and brushed it off. "Enough talk. Let's get moving. We only have a few hours of what can be considered daylight left, and I don't know about you two, but I would like to find somewhere to hide for the night," Maryjane replied. "Which way do we go to get to the Emerald City?" she asked.

Scarecrow pointed to the left path. They continued their journey on foot once more. They walked in strained silence and eyed their surroundings with each step. Every step they made seemed like it echoed throughout the valley. Maryjane stayed a few feet ahead, keeping a cautious eye out for trouble as she looked at the surroundings. As they walked past an area of termite-infested trees, Maryjane remembered the orchard that used to be in the spot. The trees were barren when they used to hold fruit and nuts. What had once been a vivacious orchard was now a toothpick factory. There wasn't a single living plant in view, nor were there any animals to be seen. Oz was as empty and hopeless as the plains of Kansas. She had escaped her home to come here for the freedom and pure beauty of the land. Now, her place of solace was in shambles, and her heart began to break from the sight of the ghastly devastation.

Memories flooded her mind. Charlie had taught her all the tricks of tracking. What to look for, what to listen for, what to expect when animals would leap from the woods. He was able to sense all of these things and keep them out of harm's way. Why had Glinda not spoken of him? It was all rushing back to her, and it began to weigh in on her mind. Were the trackers following them? Did they know which way their traveling party had gone? Had they heard her mother and Scarecrow talking any? She wished she knew where Charlie was or what he even looked like now. He could take the two trackers out with ease and precision.

They walked for what seemed like miles with Maryjane in her thoughts, Scarecrow and Dorothy chatting away, when they came upon a slightly dense area of trees. The trees had long since died and were being demolished by the hunger-driven termites. Up ahead, to the right of the road, was a small cabin. They walked up to the front of the cabin, walked to the back, and inspected around it. Maryjane peered through the windows, but they were so dusty and webbed from spiders that she couldn't see inside. She turned to Dorothy and Scarecrow.

"I can't see inside, but it would be the best place to rest. We have maybe an hour of daylight left," she said. Dorothy and Scarecrow exchanged glances. "What?"

Maryjane asked, confused at their silent stares.

"This is where Nick used to live," Dorothy replied, looking around the familiar area.

Maryjane turned around and looked at the cabin again. She listened inside for any sign of movement. No one is in there. There isn't a door in the back, so if we want to go inside, we will have to go through the front of the cabin," she said.

The three of them walked to the front of the cabin, and just as Maryjane was about to open the door, something caught her attention in the reflection of the window. She whirled around in fright to look at what she had seen with her wand drawn and ready to do damage. In the middle of the road, sunk into the ground, was a deeply rusted figure. What seemed like what had once been silver in color was now black and rusted through in places. It was missing an arm that had fallen off and lay at the base of the rusted heap of metal. It made neither movement nor sound.

"Stay right here," she told the two as she carefully walked closer to the menacing remnants of junk.

The closer she got, the more fear tore through her. It was a ghastly sight to look at, but she knew she had to inspect it for any evidence that the Red Sorceress was spying. She reached out and was about to touch it when two red eyes surged open, and a terrifying wail escaped its lips. Maryjane tripped and fell backward.

The figure pulled its sunken feet from the road and started treading toward her. She felt like kicking herself. She had not noticed the axe it held in its one arm. She was crawling backward on the ground, trying to get distance between her and the creature so she could get her footing. It swung the axe as she rolled away, barely missing her, and that was all she needed. She was on her feet, but no sooner had she stood up than the thing was swinging the axe. She ducked out of the way and ran behind the creature.

She had no time to think, no time to read off a spell. *What can I use for a weapon?* She thought to herself. She remembered the sword given to her in the castle. She pulled it from its sheath and met the axe with her blade. The creature was powerful with each blow from the axe. The swings had become faster and more erratic. It swung the axe, and she jumped back with the blade barely missing her throat. She stumbled back and nearly lost her footing as the axe came down at her again. She threw her sword up, catching the impact once more. She gave the creature a hard kick, and it awkwardly stumbled back. Having had enough of the dancing back and forth with blades, she picked her sword up, looked at the creature, and thrust it as hard as she could into the ground.

The thrust erupted electrical sparks throughout the ground that surrounded the creature. The heat from the electrical shock instantly melted and cooled the metallic body of the creature in its place. The only thing left free to move was its mouth.

"Away witch!!" it bellowed in anger and fear.

Maryjane motioned for Scarecrow and Dorothy to walk over. When they were within a few feet of the creature, Maryjane looked at her mother and said, "This is Nick."

"How do you know my name, witch?" Nick growled with his eyes dancing back and forth between the two women.

"I know a lot about you, but more importantly, I'm here to set you free from the damnation cast over Oz." Maryjane lifted her hand to touch him.

"Don't touch me!" he screamed at her. He tried to wiggle from her reach, but his body was a solid chunk of melted metal. Scarecrow stepped forward to talk him down from his madness.

"Old friend, I'm sure you remember me. It's

Scarecrow. She will not harm you," Scarecrow said, stepping closer with his hands out in front of him as a sort of surrender.

"She has brainwashed you!" Nick cried out.

"I know you think your friend has been made a slave to a new evil, an evil worse than the one who had caused Oz to rot away, but he hasn't," Maryjane offered.

Nick sneered at her, "Thou shalt not suffer a witch to live!" he hissed.

"No, it is true!" Dorothy cried, walking forward to Nick. "We're not here to hurt you."

"And who are you? Another witch!" Each of his words was menacing, and the disdain melted from his lips. His eyes flicked from Dorothy to Scarecrow.

"No, it's me, Nick. It's Dorothy," she stated as she walked closer to him.

"Lies!!" he cried. "Dorothy left years ago, and not one word have we heard from her. Now you are here claiming to be her and look nothing like her. If she had wanted to return to us, don't you think it would have been sooner?"

"No, I have returned!" Dorothy said with pleading eyes.

"Lies! Dorothy would never consort with a witch! Leave me at peace with my memories of her! Don't drag her name through this mockery," he cried out, dropping his head.

"Good friend, it is Dorothy, just look at her feet. She still has the slippers," Scarecrow said, pointing to Dorothy's feet.

Nick looked to the ground where Dorothy stood. The slippers gleamed in the setting sun. He looked up at Dorothy. Without a warning, Maryjane touched his arm. The black rusted mess he was began to melt away and was replaced with a platinum sheen of tin. The arm that had fallen off was regenerated, and the melted metal lubricated so that he could move freely. He glanced over at Maryjane.

"How do I know I can trust you?" he asked Maryjane, eyeing her suspiciously.

"Because I'm the only hope you have left to defeat this evil that has turned your home into shambles. Neither you nor the others are my mission. I am simply helping my mother find her friends."

"Your...mother?" Nick asked breathlessly. He looked at Dorothy, and he realized the age that the years had truly put on her face.

"Yes, friend. She is my daughter," Dorothy replied, smiling and looking over at Maryjane.

"How can she be your daughter and a witch?" Nick asked, slightly confused.

"That I do not know," Dorothy replied, looking at Maryjane. Maryjane returned the look but spoke no more of herself.

"How often do patrols come through this area?" Maryjane eyed her surroundings and looked up and down the road for a sign of the cavalry.

"About twice a day. Why?" Nick asked.

"Do they ever check the cabin?" she asked, glancing over at the wooden structure.

"Yes, each time they come through, they do," Nick replied.

"Great!! We barely have any light left to light the way, and we need a hiding spot," Maryjane said, sitting down.

She was trying to think while the group talked to one another. The same questions were being asked as before. She didn't know what to do. She was running short on time and options, and not to mention, she was growing sluggish. Her energy was nearly depleted. She needed to rest.

I wish Charlie was here, she thought. *He would know what to do.*

Chapter Four

A CLAMMY EERINESS settled in the atmosphere, and Maryjane became uneasy. She quickly glanced around the woods and road as her senses urged that there was danger. She saw nothing to corroborate her feeling. She shrugged it off and set thinking more on what to do with thoughts of Charlie invading her mind more. The air began to grow humid and thick. Maryjane found it a bit difficult to breathe. The eerie feeling that had settled over her earlier was now past panic mode and into full alert mode. Maryjane looked to the sky while the others continued to talk, and she shushed them.

"Shhh.....listen," she said, looking off into the sky. In the distance, she heard a faint, buzzing sound. She arched her head back and stared off into the sky, scanning the dismal darkness for any signs of the faint noise she was hearing. "Is that...bees I hear?"

"Oh no!" Nick yelled, breaking Maryjane's concentration. "Another patrol is coming through!"

Maryjane jumped to her feet. "Everyone inside the cabin!" Everyone stood motionless and in fear. "Now!" she barked and broke their concentration. They moved nimbly as she ushered everyone to the cabin. She looked at Nick and said, "If anything happens to me, make sure my mother is protected."

Nick nodded, closed the door behind him, and locked it. Maryjane made her way back to the road. The buzzing was closer than ever. She looked to the skies to see what her next enemy looked like. She gasped in horror. Flying overhead was a swarm of oversized bees. They were at least as big as a foal or a calf would appear in size. They spotted her and swarmed down toward her. She threw up her protective shield and drew her wand. They hit the shield as if it were glass. It was impenetrable. They covered her entirely in one large, bee ball.

Aside from the buzzing that was deafening to Maryjane in her silent cone of power, everything remained quiet on the outside as well. Then, from the cabin, a noise broke the barrier of silence. "Ah-Choo," escaped Dorothy's mouth as she let out a loud sneeze from all the dust. The bees were no longer interested in Maryjane. Instead, they began to swarm the cabin. She could hear the gnawing of the wood as the bees chewed it, trying to get inside. This put everyone on the inside in more danger than she was on the outside.

She panicked. She didn't know what her next move should be. *What to do, what to do? They have nearly gnawed the structure in half...* She dropped her shield and yelled to get the attention of the swarm of bees, "Hey! I'm who you really want. Come and get me, if you can!" She took a step back and prepared for the bees to swarm.

One by one, they left the cabin and hovered in the air above her. She lifted her arms to the sky. Thunder and lightning moved in fast over the area. The lightning turned into an electrical storm and zapped a few of the bees from the sky. The wind picked up, the air cooled, and water poured down over the bees. They slowly dropped one by one as their wings were ripped and torn by the gale wind; a rain storm that blew around them, but even being grounded did not stop them from advancing as they crawled toward her.

From beyond the trees, you could hear the sound of rushing water. A tidal wave of water came bounding through the woods. It swooped in and took all the bees with it. It careened out of control toward the cabin. Maryjane threw a hand up as if she had placed a wall around the cabin. She threw her other hand up in front of herself. The water came crashing through. It cut a V around her, and through the waves, she could see that the cabin was untouched by the water as well.

As soon as all of the bees had been carried away with the water, it quit raining, and the water flowed away in an instant. She dropped her hands, and the weather changed back into the typical day it had been, with the rain and lightning being halted. She fell to her knees, exhausted. She couldn't fight anymore and had no clue what she would do if anything else decided to pop up on her. Everyone began to emerge from the cabin. She just sat on the ground, trying to get a grip on her dwindling energy. The ground was spinning beneath her as she felt the mounting panic and fear turn her faint and dizzy.

Dorothy stepped out on the porch, admiring her daughter. Nick and Scarecrow had already stepped down from the porch. Dorothy was following when she saw a figure in the brush, maybe twenty feet from where Maryjane sat.

"Maryjane, behind you!" Dorothy yelled a moment too late. An arrow whizzed through the air, catching Maryjane in the arm, and another followed, piercing her leg. She wailed in pain as the arrows hit her body. "No!!" Dorothy screamed as she ran to her daughter. Nick and Scarecrow grabbed her and held her back.

"No, it's too dangerous!" Nick cried, remembering the oath he had sworn to the child. "We promised her we'd keep you safe!"

"Let me go! She needs me! It's my daughter!" Dorothy cried out, struggling to get loose from their grip. Neither one loosened their grip on her arm.

Maryjane rolled over in agonizing pain. She ripped the

arrow from her arm and leg and howled in pain as she did so. She climbed to her feet and whirled around to face her challenger. A muscular man stepped from the brush. He had a cape over his head, so she could not see his face.

"Who are you?" she demanded, still frightened and shaken up from everything that had happened in the past few moments.

"I might ask you the same thing!" he hissed back. He drew another arrow and pointed it at her. "Now, who are you?" he demanded.

He stared at her even though no one could see his face. Maryjane was up against a wall. She had no choice but to tell this stranger about her journey.

"I am sent by the Elders and Glinda, the witch of the South, to Emerald City to destroy the Red Sorceress and reclaim the Land of Oz. The land has become a barren wasteland compared to its grace and beauty before her wickedness came to this land. She has damned the land and everyone who inhabits it that cannot protect themselves by magic. Her power does no good to anyone, and it needs to be stopped."

"I don't believe you. I have known Glinda for years and have never heard her mention you or seen you in person. The Red Sorceress is too far out of your league anyway. Glinda would never send someone like you after her. Now, tell me again who you are, or you will meet your death by an arrow," he said, tightening the draw on the arrow.

"It is true. I have known Glinda since I was a child. She trained me with my powers. She taught me what I needed to know to get by, and the rest came naturally," Maryjane said.

"So, you're a witch? Witches cannot be trusted around here. Especially unknown witches. I have never seen you around before now. No good can come of witches just dropping from the sky," he said, his arrow steadfast in its point at her.

"I'm a good witch. My powers grow in leaps and bounds each time I use them. I am *not* an ordinary person or an ordinary witch. I shouldn't have to explain my mission or defend myself to you. You are no judge or jury," Maryjane said, struggling to her feet. "And you never answered my question as to who you are!"

"I am one of Glinda's subjects. I have been hot on the trail of the Red Sorceress to destroy her, and I don't need you meddling around in my affairs and ruining my chances of defeating her," he said, his voice tight with hatred.

"Well, it seems as if we have the same mission. We should hunt her together," Maryjane offered on a whim.

"I work with no one," he hissed.

She lifted her hand from her wound on her arm. It was bleeding pretty heavily along with the wound on her leg. She winced from pain as she cupped it with her hand again.

"My name is Maryjane. What is yours?" she asked.

"My name is of no importance to you. You are not an Elder, you are not Glinda, so you have no role in my hierarchy, so I need not share it with you," he said, lowering his bow. He watched her as she limped to the edge of the road and gathered some herbs. "What are you doing?" he asked.

"I'm making a salve to speed up the healing of the punctures your arrows left," she said as she smashed them between her hands.

She placed the sticky herbs on her wounds and ripped some of her dress to make bandages. Once she was finished bandaging herself up, she looked at him.

"How do I know you aren't lying about being one of Glinda's subjects? She made no mention of you when she sent us from Munchkin Land," she said, eyeing him suspiciously.

"How do I know you're not?" he retaliated.

"I have no reason to lie. You are the one who hides behind the shadow of a cape," she said, glaring at him. "Prove it."

"Prove it, how?" he asked, glaring back.

"Summon her."

"No one has the power to summon her," he challenged.

"I do. She told me whenever I needed her, she could be summoned on the spot," Maryjane said, slowly taking a step back.

"You are not powerful enough to summon her!" he yelled.

Maryjane stood in place watching the man in the cape. It was odd he didn't know how to summon her, and even more strange that he felt no fear toward her. A wind began to swirl around her. She stared him down.

"Glinda, good witch of the South, I summon thee to this space," she said. Lightning flashed, and the hooded man jumped back. In an instant, Glinda appeared.

"What is it, child?" Glinda asked Maryjane, her voice full of alarm.

"Ma' Lady," the caped man said while taking a knee.

"Who are you?" Glinda asked him.

"You mean you do not recognize me?" he asked through gritted teeth, malice trailing in his words. You could feel the hatred behind his simple question.

"No, I do not," Glinda replied. "You have your face hidden. Show yourself," she commanded. The young man stood up and removed his cape from his head. Maryjane's eyes grew wide. She was filled with dread and fear as she moved toward Glinda.

"You lied to me! You are not a subject of hers. You are in league with the Red Sorceress," she yelled, jumping in front of Glinda. He snickered.

"What are you talking about, Maryjane. Do you not recognize him?" Glinda said, stepping from behind her.

"Yes, Glinda, I do. He was with the Red Sorceress today. He is her tracker. I saw him follow her out from the carriage while she was hunting us after we left Munchkin Land," Maryjane said tensely.

"Yes, it's true," Scarecrow chimed in, glaring at the tracker. "We hid with an invisibility spell, and sure enough, he was the tracker who took out on foot for us."

"I've been following you ever since the field. I have been waiting for the right moment to strike," he said, circling them like a wild animal to prey.

Glinda looked stricken. "Charlie! What are you talking about? How long have you been working with that evil harlot?"

"Charlie!?" Maryjane gasped, nearly toppling over. She looked at him long and hard. He had grown so much. He was chiseled in his features and no longer the thirteen-year-old boy she loved so dearly. Now, in his place stood a young man with death in his eyes. Where there was once love and happiness, there was now hatred and emptiness. The boy she loved so much, who protected her from anything that could or would possibly harm her, was now standing here with an arrow pointed at her. She didn't know what to say. She didn't know how to react. She didn't know what to do. *Can I really hurt him?* She thought to herself.

"You abandoned me! It was nearly two years with barely a word from you. My own mother! You hid in your castle from fear while I was left to protect Oz on my own!" he snarled at her.

"Charlie, she's filled your head with lies and false memories," Glinda said slowly, inching her way closer to him.

"No, no, she hasn't. She has given me so much more than you ever could have given me. She gave me a home, she gave me powers, and she gave me a renewed sense of life. She loves me like her own son!" he yelled.

"No, Charlie, everything is a lie. She is just using you," Glinda said as calmly as she could while inching closer to him.

"No, you don't know her like I do. She was there for me when no one else was. When I was completely left alone in this god forsaken world, she was there to help me. She was there to offer me a friend. Now I honor her by completing my first task," he said, drawing his bow and arrow.

Maryjane realized what she had done when she summoned Glinda here on his whim. Glinda was his target as well. His bow and arrow were quick to release, but not as fast as Maryjane's hand.

She threw her hand up and yelled, "Dust!"

The arrow disintegrated right in front of Glinda's heart. Glinda breathed out a breath of relief. Charlie drew another arrow and was about to shoot when Maryjane stepped in front of Glinda.

"Your arrows will not pierce her skin.I will make damned sure of that," she said raising her hand.

He sneered. His sneer turned into a wicked grin that made Maryjane's skin crawl. The girl who had stepped out of the carriage with him, whom he called Emma, emerged from the brush. She, too, had an eerie grin spread across her face. Maryjane reached for her wand.

"She...looks just like you..." Glinda stammered.

"Yes, but I can guarantee she can do far more damage than the one who stands in front of you protecting you," Charlie remarked as Emma stepped closer to him. Maryjane's wand followed her every move. She was standing directly beside Charlie.

"Please, do not hurt him," Glinda begged. "He doesn't know what he's doing."

"I'm more worried about the girl than him," Maryjane

replied, pointing her wand at the girl.

"Oh, I know exactly what I'm doing," he said, tensing the bow string tighter. "First, I will take care of this little mishap that was allowed into Oz, then I will take care of you, Mother," he said, aiming his bow at Maryjane.

The love of her life was standing in front of her, swearing to put an end to her life. She didn't know how to react. "Charlie, why? Why do you not remember me? Why have you gone so far off course from your destiny? Our destiny?" Maryjane cried.

"I do not remember you because I don't know you! I have never known a…Maryjane. The only person I have grown up with has been my future bride, Emma. She is my destiny," he hissed as Emma wrapped her arms around his waist and sneered at Maryjane. "Hit her with your mind control," he said to Emma.

"It would be my pleasure, love," Emma said, stepping away from Charlie, grinning, and staring Maryjane down.

"Oh, you will never have power over my mind. You hold no power over me. You may look like me, and sound like me, but you will *never* have power over me," Maryjane uttered to the girl. Emma's eyes flashed a golden color as she grinned. Maryjane stood still, holding her wand ready to strike. The girl faltered with her expression and looked at Charlie, baffled.

"I…I don't understand. I can't control her," Emma whispered to Charlie. "This has never happened before with anyone."

"It must be because she is a witch as well. I will take care of her, don't worry," Charlie said, aiming his bow directly at Maryjane's heart.

"Charlie, you know me!" Maryjane yelled, stepping forward. "Please, do not make me battle you," she said, pleading with him while tears were burning in her eyes.

"Oh, there won't be a battle, I can assure you of that!" he sneered, waiting for the right moment to release his arrow in surprise.

She didn't know what else to say to him so that he would remember her.She took a step closer to him and closed her eyes. "The one thing I fear is leaving, and never having your presence delight my heart," she said.

He faltered with his bow and arrow for a split second. Emma looked from Maryjane to Charlie and shot him a dirty look. He closed his eyes and then composed himself. He glared at Maryjane and released the bow and arrow. Maryjane pushed her energy with her hand as if she were hitting the arrow, and it flew upward in the sky. Their attention was drawn to the arrow long enough for her to take and push their bodies away the same way as the arrow with her other hand. He went flying through the air and landed in a patch of sticker briars.

"We'll be back!" he yelled as they climbed from the thicket and disappeared into the trees.

"That's a promise," Emma yelled.

Maryjane collapsed to the ground, sobbing. She was so weary. She was heartbroken, injured, and drained of all energy. She felt like giving up. How could she defeat the Red Sorceress when she had already won the love and heart of the only person she cared about in this world? Charlie was now on the other team. She didn't know how to sway him back to the good side. Glinda ran to her side.

"You need to rest," she said while turning to the others. "Find a spot in the woods to camp. There are plenty of caves around that you can hide in. She needs to rest and regain her strength. In the meantime, I will speak with the Elders and see if they know anything about this Emma girl." She turned back to Maryjane and kneeled to hug her. "We will get him back. I promise," she said, standing back up.

She was engulfed by her mists and floated away, leaving everyone standing in the middle of the road that at one point used to have meaning and importance behind its name.

Chapter Five

THE FOUR TRAVELERS gathered what supplies they could from Nick's cabin and started on their way into the forest. Nick helped Maryjane as she limped through the trails. Her arm had nearly healed; however, her leg was still badly wounded from the arrow.

"Is it infected?" Dorothy asked as they stopped for a moment for Maryjane to rest.

"No, I don't think so. It's just painful to walk on," she said, grimacing as she touched the wound. "It pierced the bone. I didn't think I would have the nerve to pull it out."

She didn't want to think of everything that had just happened. Her heart had already been broken years ago. Thinking of everything and about Charlie would only make things worse for her in her mind and heart. The two had been through so much together, and this was a knife in the cake.Her heart was already cracked. She never told Charlie goodbye personally when she left the last time. If he believed Glinda had abandoned him, she knew that he must have felt the same way toward her. If he ever remembered her, that is. She didn't need her heart shattered thinking about the past, especially not in a time like this.

She strained every muscle she had but rose to her feet. "We need to keep moving."

They began walking again, this time, deeper into the forest. It had already fallen to what would be considered night outside, and in the thicket of the forest, it was even darker than the blackest night. None of them could see one foot in front of them. They all stumbled around blindly, tripping over roots of trees, and swatting away the cobwebs they ran into. The sounds of the forest made them more uneasy as they looked around in the dark, straining their eyes to find the source of the noise. The noises of the dark were creepy and disturbing to hear. Every creepy crawly that existed seemed to be awake as they trudged through the trees. Scarecrow let out a howl as something slithered across his foot. No one laughed, for they all felt the edge of the darkness creeping into their minds. Even Maryjane wasn't her normal, fearless self.

"I can't do this stumbling blindly through the dark any longer," she said as she stopped and picked up a stick. "Scarecrow, stand either behind me or ahead of the other two." Scarecrow did as he was told and stood ahead of Dorothy and Nick. Maryjane ripped another piece of her dress and wrapped it around the stick. Her hand began to glow red as she concentrated. A fire began to surround her entire hand. She cupped her hand; it grew in intensity and became a ball of fire. She placed the stick in the fire and created a torch to carry. She handed the stick to Nick and closed her hand. The fire snuffed itself out.

"Do you know where about we are?" Dorothy asked Nick.

Nick looked around at the trees that surrounded them and inspected them. "We are close to where Lion used to nest. He had many caves he would hide out in throughout the forest. This is one of his areas, but I don't see where there has been any activity in this one, so he must have chosen a different spot to hide," Nick said, checking trees for markings.

"But, he has a cave nearby, though, right?" Scarecrow asked, looking around. He looked spooked from all of the night sounds. "I mean, I don't want to run into any trouble in the middle of the forest. You know, like animals that eat…straw," he said, gulping the last word.

"Don't be silly, Scarecrow," Dorothy said, chuckling.

The mood of the group was starting to lighten a little. Maryjane remained silent through all the chatter. If she didn't find somewhere to rest soon, her leg would give out on her, and Nick would be carrying her. "I hope the cave pops up soon," Maryjane said faintly.

They came to a small clearing. The group stopped on the edge and listened. It was completely silent. Everyone looked around to see if there was any apparent shelter. It was Maryjane who saw the hidden cave. The cave's entrance had been overgrown with tree roots, hiding it from plain sight.

She pointed in the cave's direction, "There." Everyone looked and started for the cave. "Wait, put the fire out. We don't want to be seen." Nick stomped the fire out on the end of the stick and wrapped his arm back underneath Maryjane's to help her walk. Everyone proceeded toward the cave. When they got to the entrance, none of them could fit through the gaps of the roots.

"Now what?" Scarecrow asked.

"I could chop them away," Nick offered.

"No, that would be too loud," Maryjane replied.

She lifted her arm from around his neck. The full weight of her body on her leg sent streaking pain throughout her entire body. She winced and sucked her breath in. Nick reached for the arm she had lifted from his neck and said, "Do you need me to…"

"No, just give me a second," she said, gathering her strength.

She lifted her hands together and pushed them apart. As her hands slid apart, so did the roots of the trees so that everyone could slip through. She hobbled through the entrance of the cave, and once through the roots, collapsed to the ground, and the roots sprang back into place as if they were never touched.

Dorothy helped her to a corner of the cave where she sat down and removed the bandage from her leg. The wound was far deeper than the one on her arm. She took some more herbs out of her pouch, and instead of just sticking them to the outside of the wound, she sucked in a breath, and filled the wound with the herbs. The pain was excruciating and dizzying. Dorothy finished her dressing by putting a clean bandage around it and tying it.

She looked at her sternly and said, "You need to eat something."

Maryjane looked at her mother, surprised by her worry. "So, do you. You know the doctor said you need to eat three square meals a day to keep your strength," Maryjane said, taking the worry and placing it on her mother instead.

"I'm not important right now. You are the one who needs the attention. I have never in my life feared for your safety the way I did this evening." Dorothy stroked Maryjane's hair and put it back in place.

Maryjane stared at her mother. "You have never been worried about my well-being. Why are you now?"

"I have always worried about you, child. It was your strength and courage that have always reassured me that you will be just fine." Dorothy smiled at Maryjane. Maryjane stared back and had no clue as to what to think about her mother anymore. She never showed a shred of interest in her life, and now, since she knows she has powers, she was acting as if they had been the closest of friends during her teenage years.

Nick pulled out some apples and other fruit and began cutting them up. It was fairly dark in the cave. Maryjane picked up a stick to the left of her and blew on it. The end began to glow as if it were lit by fire. She handed it to Scarecrow. He was apprehensive about taking it and tried to scramble away from her.

"It's ok. It's not real fire. I would never do that," Maryjane said reassuringly.

Scarecrow looked like a critter taking food from a human's hands. He took the stick and placed it in the center of the cave. Maryjane wiggled her fingers, and the light grew brighter.

"I don't know if I'm alone on this question, but can anyone see the light from the outside?" Scarecrow scratched nervously at the straw poking through his hat.

"No. The roots are too dense in the cave," Nick replied.

Maryjane nibbled on some of the fruit but was too tired and nauseated to eat. She lay down on her side, which wasn't injured. Scarecrow removed some of his straw from his middle section and offered it to her as a pillow. She thanked him and laid her head on it.

She was so exhausted. She knew she had lost a pretty good bit of blood. Her body was still buzzing from the adrenaline that had taken over her earlier. Even though she didn't want to, her mind trailed off to Charlie. Her heart felt like it was literally being torn from her chest. She was utterly crushed. He couldn't even remember her. Tears began to betray her will and slid down her cheek. One after another until it was a silent sob.

"You two were in love, weren't you?" Dorothy asked as she sat down beside her. The other two remained closer to the entrance, talking and catching up with one another.

"I loved him, but I wasn't too sure of his feelings for me. We were best friends, but I guess I got my answer because five years later, he doesn't remember me and replaced me," Maryjane said, choking back the sobs that wished to escape her breath. "The last time we talked, we fought. I left without saying goodbye and was unable to return because of the wall. Now…he's lost to that monster, the only friend I have ever had," she cried.

"If he loved you, he *will* remember you soon enough," Dorothy said. "Love conquers all."

"You're wrong, Mama. I'm destined to be alone," Maryjane sobbed. "No man stays in my life, Mama. I'm cursed."

"What do you mean?" Dorothy asked, confused.

"Daddy died before I was born, and Charlie is consorting with the enemy. If I cannot sway him back to our side…I will have to destroy him along with the Red Sorceress," Maryjane said.

Dorothy was without words. She had never really spoken of Maryjane's father to her. "You're not the reason your father died, sweetie; it was a careless accident. I wish you could've met him. You two are so much alike. Both of you were courageous and strong, taking the world head-on without a care. He would have loved you to death. You are the most wonderful gift of a child that could have been given. I would ask for no other child to replace you. You have been the best daughter. You are so full of life, and you care for everyone selflessly. Look at what you have done for Scarecrow and Nick. If not for you, they would still be the menacing monsters they had been turned into by that tyrant who calls herself a sorceress," Dorothy said, stroking Maryjane's hair.

"I just want him back. The way he used to be. He used to be so protective and courageous. He would have never hurt me before. He was so afraid of me being hurt," Maryjane cried. "I never fit in at home with the other kids. I was their personal joke. This place, Charlie, they were my escape, and now, half of my world is gone."

"In due time, things will be set right. Now, you must get some rest. You have done so much and fought so hard today. Close your eyes and sleep; daylight will be fast approaching, and you need your strength," Dorothy said as Maryjane finally closed her eyes and let the day melt away from her thoughts.

When she was sure she was fast asleep, Dorothy slipped back over to the other two and sat down with them. Her mind was heavy and filled with not only her troubles, but her daughter's as well. Maryjane had never told her that she had problems with making friends in town or that they made fun of her. She looked up at Nick and Scarecrow, who were eyeing her. She gave a halfhearted smile.

"What took you so long in returning, Dorothy?" asked Scarecrow. "We really have missed you."

"I have tried for years to return and had no luck. No one would believe this place existed since Uncle Henry and Auntie Em weren't around to testify to it, and after being accused of insanity and locked away for three years in an asylum, I believed it myself," she said. She looked over at Maryjane, "If it hadn't been for that child's love for everything good, I would not be here right now," she said. She placed her hand over her stomach as a pain spread throughout her torso.

"Are you okay?" Nick asked.

She smiled another faint smile. "The doctors call it cancer. I call it endless hope," Dorothy replied. "They do not know how much longer I have to live. I haven't even told her it's that bad yet. She still believes I can be healed."

"You're dying?" asked Scarecrow with concern-filled eyes.

"Yes, but don't say it too loudly. I still have to tell her…I'm all she has left. Her father's family abandoned us after he passed, and I have no brothers or sisters of my own. So, there is no one to be there to comfort her when I do pass. She brought me back here one last time, so that I could see all of you again. I couldn't go without telling everyone one final goodbye," Dorothy said, tears glistening in her eyes.

"Well, why don't you stay here?" asked Scarecrow.

"Because I'm sick here as well as I am at home. There is no cure for it nor a magical cure," Dorothy said, dropping her eyes to the ground.

"You mean Glinda can't heal you?" asked Nick.

"No, the main reason the child brought me here was to see Glinda for a cure. She was so heartbroken when Glinda said she couldn't help me. It's really unfair to her. She has so much hope and an outlook to save the world. The entire occasion completely crushes her. I just wish I could offer her some peace," Dorothy said, looking at her sleeping daughter. "I haven't even had the time to make any arrangements for when I do pass. I have no money saved up, and there is a snake breathing down my neck to steal the farm from us. I'm so worried that child will end up in a dark place she can't escape from."

Nick and Scarecrow bowed their heads in silence. "I wish there was something we could do," Nick said, sniffling.

"Now don't go crying. You will rust yourself, and we don't have your oil can," Dorothy said, and a giggle slipped out. They all caught on to the inside joke and laughed along with her.

Once again, the cave grew quiet. Dorothy sat nibbling on the fruit they had brought from the cabin. So much had happened that day that none of them dared speak of the events. They all shared the same thought, though. Maryjane was a spectacular girl. She would make a good ruler of Oz. It had been a long time since a good ruler had ruled over the land. Ever since the wizard left, Oz had turned into shambles. Even though he left Nick, Scarecrow, and Lion as his successors, they had no power over the Red Sorceress when she rode through bringing her devastation.

Dorothy was the first to break the silence. "Why is it

the Red Sorceress came after you three first over everyone else? Glinda mentioned that you three had to separate because she had come after all of you."

Nick and Scarecrow exchanged glances. Scarecrow was the one who replied, "Our one and only run in with her, she spoke of you. She disliked you. She said she would ruin what you loved so much, and to teach you a lesson, she had planned on destroying everything you loved."

"Why? I do not know this sorceress, and she is not a sister to the wicked witches, so she has no grudge to hold against me," Dorothy said, thinking hard.

"We do not know why. We just knew what she was here for. We all went our separate ways, so we could survive here without her knowing where we were. Together, we were easy targets. Separate, however, she didn't know who we were. But alas, when she turned the land into wastelands, her magic not only turned the land into devastation, but whoever had defied her allegiance were changed into hideous monsters. So, we changed when the land changed. We could feel her hatred as we turned, and it bled over into our emotions. It's all we could feel, all we could see was red," Nick said, still shaking off the feeling.

"Hmm," Dorothy said.

"What is it, Dorothy?" asked Scarecrow.

"Oh, it's nothing. She just reminds me of someone from back home," she said, still thinking back to a day ago. She quickly brushed it off. "Well, I'm tuckered out. I'm not the teenager I was when I lived here. I need to get some sleep. Not to mention, I'm still having some pains. We will chat more tomorrow," Dorothy said, standing and moving over to another corner.

"I may not go to sleep, but you're more than welcome to lay your head on my lap for a pillow," Scarecrow offered her, walking over to her.

"That would be lovely," she said, smiling.

She let out a yawn as he sat down beside her. She rested her head in his lap and began to doze.

"I'll keep watch in case anyone tries to chop through them roots," Nick said, scooting closer to the entrance.

Dorothy smiled. "So brave, you two. It's why I loved you two so much."

She drifted off into sleep while Scarecrow and Nick sat quietly waiting for dawn to approach. Neither of them could hear anything from beyond the cave. They did not know that Maryjane had cast a protective barrier around it so that no one could get in right before she fell asleep. She didn't stir once while dreaming away.

Chapter Six

"Maryjane! Don't go over there!" Charlie yelled.

"It's ok. I won't get hurt," Maryjane replied as she galloped through the field. Charlie came running up behind her and grabbed her arm to pull her back.

"It's too dangerous! You don't know WHAT it is!" Charlie exclaimed.

They were both looking at some sort of creature's nesting area. What bothered Charlie the most was all the skeletal remains that surrounded it. There was an odd and vague remembrance of the place, as if they had been there before, but he brushed it off. Lately, the more he tried to hone his powers in, the more forgetful he became.

"Please, Maryjane, come on. Let's go tell Momma what we found," he begged.

"No!" She had never yelled at him before. She stood there staring at him, daring him to make her.

"Why not!" he retorted, trying to grab her arm and tow her back to Munchkin Land.

She ripped free from his arm before he could get a grip on it. "Because I don't want to go home!" she cried.

His throat nearly swelled shut, holding back the tears. He hated seeing her cry. It tore through him like a sword. He walked over to her and gave her a hug. He felt her tears hit the bare skin of his neck, and he choked back his own.

He cleared his throat to speak and brushed aside the tears that had yet to fall so she wouldn't see them. "If keeping you safe meant sending you home, then it's the best choice…this isn't **your** world. You visit here and there, and that's it! But…if you die here…you don't wake up at home," he said solemnly.

"I belong here! I've never felt so happy or free. I would stay here forever if your mother would allow me to! It may not be my world, but I feel like it's supposed to be! Why was I chosen to come here all of these years?I'm supposed to be part of this world, part of your mother's world…part of **your** world," she said, grabbing his hand.

He closed his eyes and shook her hand loose of his. He could see the pain behind her eyes as he did this. "I care about you, Maryjane, I do. But you're an outsider. I can't be with you, now or even when we're older, the Elders will not allow it. I am the sole heir to the magic and witchcraft left in this land. I will not let my mother down by disobeying the rules. We are the last witches left. I have to keep that alive!" he said.

He looked at her in what one would construe as pity, but it was utter heartbreak. He knew she was about to cry. He knew he had crushed her. The truth is, he did more than just care about her. Even at the age of thirteen, he understood the feelings that swirled around inside. His heart dropped to his feet when she was near danger, he got butterflies at the sight of her, and her touching his hand sent electrical sparks throughout his body. He was in love with her and had no clue how to fall out of love with her.

She was not plain looking in the least. She was gorgeous and one of the most beautiful girls he had ever laid eyes on in Oz. She had startling green eyes and the deepest shade of red hair. Every day she left, he was afraid she would never return, and her sight would never delight his eyes again. With the growing power in Emerald City, that time would be soon. He could feel their time together shortening. Just as long as she was safe, however, he didn't care if she was ever to return or not. It would break his heart, but she would be out of harm's way. He could then destroy whatever was causing Oz to regress to such a putrid state of being.

As she stared back at him, her heart slowly began to break. He was the one reason she kept returning. His piercing, crystal blue eyes made her melt away into a puddle of lust. All the time they spent together, she thought they had grown so close. She fought back the tears and turned away so that he wouldn't see them. He went to reach for her, to draw her close to him, when suddenly, a loud crash of thunder interrupted the two of them. Thunder and lightning swirled the fields as an electrical storm popped out of nowhere. It startled them both.

Standing in the field was a woman dressed in a Victorian scarlet red gown. In the back of the dress, there was a black collar wrapped around the back of her head. It cascaded down her body, gripping the body parts necessary and billowing out at the bottom. She had a crown dazzled in rubies attached to a headdress that resembled horns. She had fierce blue eyes, fiery red hair, and a shade of lipstick to match. She held a staff in her one hand, which was glowing an eerie red, and was adorned with a large crystal ball. Her fingers wrapped around it with nails like an eagle's talons that had just killed its prey in its claws. He pulled Maryjane behind him to protect her as the sorceress snickered.

"Who are you?" he demanded.

"Why you have struck me deep, young Charlie, all of Oz knows me. I am Scarlet." She indulged him with an insidious grin.

He didn't budge from the spot in front of Maryjane. He remained there in the same protective manner he always did when he placed himself between her and harm. Even for his age, he was strong-willed and didn't let his faltering fear interfere with his immediate need to protect Maryjane.

"What do you want?" he hissed.

"Why, I just want a friend for a young girl who has been staying with me," she babbled as she walked to one side, eyeing him. Her gaze slipped from him to the girl standing behind him. "And who is this radiant young girl?" she asked. Her mouth parted in a wide grin where her white teeth shone brightly.

Both Maryjane and Charlie were uneasy as they exchanged glances. He slightly shook his head no, trying to warn her not to share her name. The people of Oz who needed to know her name already did. However, still wounded from their previous conversation, she didn't listen and defiantly answered the Red

Sorceress.

"My name is Maryjane," she said, stepping forward to greet the mysterious woman.

"Maryjane. That is a beautiful name," she said, still smiling.

"Thank you," Maryjane replied.

Scarlet looked from Maryjane back to Charlie again. "Come on, Maryjane, let's go back; it's getting late," he said, pulling her arm and trying to lead her away.

"Going so soon? Why, we've just met," Scarlet said as her eyes lit up as if fire was engulfing them. "How about we chat a little bit, get to know one another?"

"No, we need to leave. She has to return home," Charlie said. Scarlet snickered at him again. "Come on, Maryjane," he said, tugging her again. She stood frozen.

"Come closer, child. Let me get a good look at you," Scarlet beckoned.

Maryjane started to step closer, and Charlie's grip tightened on her arm. She tried to shake him loose, but he had a good grip on her arm. He turned her to face him and saw why she fought him. Her eyes were burning the same way as Scarlet's were. She was mesmerized by magic.

"Drop your magic against her, and let her go!" he growled.

"I don't know what you mean," Scarlet laughed.

"Drop the hypnotism!" Charlie demanded.

He didn't know what to do. He couldn't leave her to get his mother, but he couldn't fend off the magic. His mother hadn't spent much time with him to develop his powers, and he knew he couldn't take on magic that was at this level of expertise. The sorceress let out another cackle.

"Ah, decisions, decisions. Are you afraid to leave her here with me to get your mother? Oh, drat, what's her name again?" she asked, tapping a finger to her cheek. "Oh, that's right. Glinda."

He sucked in his breath. How did she know who he was, or for that matter, who his mother was? His fear was beginning to take over him. He faltered with his words. "W-what do you want?" His fear was evident as he stammered through his words. Her smile grew *in size as he watched her toy with him and Maryjane.*

"Oh, I don't want much. I just want a friend for the young girl I mentioned earlier. You see, I live all alone in my fortress of solitude with her. There are no other children for her to play with, and it saddens me so." *She pretended to pace and pout.* "She has no one to talk to but me, no one to share her feelings with but me. I just…" *she stammered, starting to fake sniffle and cry,* "I just want her to find a friend," *she wailed and turned away from him. He couldn't see if she was crying real tears or not. Charlie didn't know what to say or do. He knew where it was leading, and he would fight to the death to keep Maryjane from her grasp.* "And this young girl will be a perfect friend for her. I mean, she's a good friend for you, isn't she?" *Scarlet asked with pitiful eyes.*

Charlie looked at Maryjane, and his face began to flush with anger. He balled his fists up and gritted his teeth. Her face was blank, but her mind was screaming. She was trying to mind tap him, but it wouldn't work. She knew it was a trick to get him to go with her. Charlie gazed at her, and she knew what he was already thinking.

"How about I be her friend instead?" *he said.*

No! She was screaming in her head. If she had only listened to him and gone back when he said to, they wouldn't be in this situation right now. She always managed to get them into some sort of mishap. She was helpless and couldn't even protest his words.

The sorceress took in a short gasp and placed her hand on her chest, acting out her plan perfectly. "You would do that for me?"

He looked at Maryjane, then at Scarlet, "Yes, if you let your enchantment on her down."

"Very well," *she said, and her eyes went to their standard blue color. He looked at Maryjane, and her eyes returned to their normal green color. He sighed with relief.*

As soon as she regained normal functioning, she yelled out to Charlie, "Run!" *She grabbed Charlie's arm and turned to look at him.*

He did not move even though his eyes were normal. "No, you go," *he said.*

74

"Charlie, I'm not leaving you," she said.

"Maryjane, go home! I don't want you here anymore. I have a new...love to spend time with," he said solemnly.

"I'm not leaving without you, Charlie. The one thing I fear the most is leaving, and never having your presence again to delight my heart." Maryjane breathed, fighting back the tears. She turned to Scarlet, "You will not have him! Leave us alone!!"

Scarlet was stunned and slightly confused from her outburst. She couldn't empower the young child any longer, and when she tried her powers on the boy, they wouldn't work either. She felt a spark around her like an invisible force field. Apparently, she wasn't the only one who felt power radiating in the area. Glinda appeared instantly.

"Scarlet, what a nice surprise. Please, next time, do call ahead." Glinda smiled, holding her wand with both hands in a defensive stance.

She walked behind the children and placed her hands on their shoulders, still holding her wand in one hand. Scarlet looked at Maryjane, then at Glinda, and smiled a smile that would belittle an evil witch.

"You have taught her well, Glinda," Scarlet said, eyeing the young girl.

"I have taught her nothing, but from this day forward, I will. Be gone," Glinda said, shooing her away with her wand.

"I'll be back. Not a threat, not a warning, but a promise!" Scarlet sneered.

The thunder cracked, and lightning swarmed around her, and as fast as she had appeared, she was gone.

Glinda turned to the two of them with anger dripping from her face and said, "What have I told you?"

"This is my fault, Glinda. Charlie was just trying to get me to go back. I didn't listen," Maryjane said, looking at her feet.

Glinda softened her eyes and expression. "Come on. It's late. You have to go home."

They walked in silence. Maryjane was still bruised from Charlie's words. They reached the edge of the clearing, and he

75

stopped and grabbed her hand. She didn't look up at him.

"Maryjane… I'm sorry I said those things. I didn't mean them. I was just trying to keep you safe, and the only way was to have you leave," he said softly.

"Yes…yes, you did. I understand, though. You wouldn't want to disappoint your mom by being with me," she said as she faced him. Tears had already run down her face. "Don't worry, though, when I come back, I won't bother you. I will stay in Munchkin Land and with your mom. You won't have to get in trouble by running off for me. You don't have to worry about the Elders, just worry about yourself," she sobbed and ran off, leaving him standing there.

His heart felt exactly what her heart did. Empty. Breaking. Dying. He felt stupid.

By the time he had reached Munchkin Land, she was gone. No goodbye. No hug. Just gone. Glinda stood there looking at him.

"What were you thinking, Charlie!" she yelled, shaking him by the shoulders.

"I tried to get her to come back, honest! She wouldn't listen," he said, pushing away from her grip on his shirt.

"I'm not talking about that! Why didn't you call for me? Run for me!" she bellowed.

"And leave her there alone? I couldn't, Momma. She was defenseless against her gaze. She had already put her in a trance. She would have taken her," he cried.

"You do not understand, Charlie. Maryjane… she can take care of herself," Glinda said, straightening up back into a formal stance.

"No, she can't! She's just a human girl and not part of this world!" he cried, glaring at his mother.

"How can you be so bright, but blind to see her for who she truly is?" Glinda said with pleading eyes. "Come sit beside me," she said, motioning for him as she sat down. He walked over and sat at the fountain with her.

She turned to him, "You are my only son, the only rightful heir to this land. There is a reason why the Elders let her into this land, unlike her mother, who was an accident in the beginning. You must listen to me when I tell you this, because in the end, it will save you and all of us from the damnation of Oz."

"What are you talking about?" Charlie asked.

"She is special, Charlie. How do you think I knew you were in trouble? Why do you think the sorceress had no powers once she yelled a command to her?" Glinda asked with impatient eyes.

"I don't know, you showed up right afterwards. You were shielding us," he said, shrugging her question off.

"No, my son. Maryjane has a higher purpose in this world," she said, cupping his chin in her hand. She started, "She will save us from…"

"No, she won't! She is just a girl, Momma! I heard the stories of your sister. I refuse to become a target of the Elders!" he yelled, cutting her off.

"That is where you are wrong. She is a witch, Charlie. A witch! She has powers!" Glinda yelled, standing up in anger.

"Stop with that nonsense. She has no powers. She is not a witch. I wish with all of my might she were because I love her!" he yelled and then realized what he had said. Panic rose throughout his body. Glinda stood unfazed by his declaration. "I cannot be with her. The rules of Oz forbid it, and I hate it!" he cried.

"Charlie, one day I will be gone, and you two will rule Oz: you the King and she the Queen," Glinda softly said.

"Don't fill my head with wishful thinking, Momma!" he muttered as he looked to the ground in defeat.

*"It is **not** wishful thinking. You two are destined to be together. If she wasn't who I said she was, I would have never let you two get close. She may not have been born in this world, but this is her world. The Elders smile upon her. They have blessed her because of what her mother did for us, and she **was** just a human girl. You have done no wrong in falling for her. Just never go near Scarlet, or Maryjane will never be a part of your heart or mind again. The bond you two share is powerful. If she finds a way to break it, to erase the love you two share, she wins!" Glinda declared. "You are the last witch of Oz and heir to the throne. Do you*

honestly think they would make you rule alone? Think of that," she uttered in a soft tone.

Charlie watched as his mother floated away in her mists to her castle. He could never stop loving her. They can erase his memories, but his heart is too full of love for her ever to stop caring or to forget who she is. When she returned tomorrow, he planned to tell her how he truly felt and how no one would take it away from them. His mother finally gave him her blessing so that the two of them could be together. He looked off toward Emerald City, and all he saw were eyes in the sky staring back.

Chapter Seven

"THE GIRL you sent us after…I know her, don't I?" Charlie asked as he sat facing the Red Sorceress. His eyes flicked from hers to Emma's and to Ashe's eyes, the other tracker. Charlie couldn't stand the sight of him. He was a true monster. Nothing Charlie had ever done could amount to what he had done in his past. Pillaging villages, raping and murdering women, he was a sadistic, evil, little man with no self-worth.

"Why are you asking me? If you knew her, you'd remember her," Scarlet replied, brushing off the question.

Ashe sat forward as if he enjoyed the questioning in the cat-and-mouse game. His amusement annoyed Charlie even more than Scarlet's answer. Emma played with her knife, trying to ignore Charlie's question.

"Well, you see, that's the thing. Every time a memory starts, it is tapped out, and replaced with something else, as if someone is spying on my thoughts," Charlie said, his eyes not moving from her. "When I feel the name Maryjane, it means something to me, but the only person in my head is Emma. I feel like a game is being played in my head, and I'm the joker." Emma cracked her knuckles from annoyance as Charlie glanced uneasily between her and Scarlet.

"Oh, that's rubbish. Do you honestly think I'm replacing your memories?" Scarlet scoffed.

His gaze didn't falter on her. "I don't know, you tell

me," he said.

The dream he had had with the girl younger in age was too absolute not to be a memory. When their gazes locked, and she uttered the exact words to him that were in this dream, memory, whatever you wanted to call it, he had felt a pang in his heart. It was a jumble of heartache and longing, and it sent chills down his spine. At that moment, even before he had the dream, he absolutely *knew* there was something familiar about her. It also left the question of Emma out on the table. How did she look so much like this girl? Why is it the memories he tried to recall, when they were replaced, they were replaced with Emma's face? They could pass as sisters, but Maryjane's features were unique, a uniqueness he couldn't see duplicated perfectly.

"Charlie, don't be foolish. Now tell me, how close you were to destroying Glinda?" she asked, eyes flashing colors.

Emma sneered at the mention of the battle. "Please, don't be foolish, Siress. He wasn't close to anything." Emma jumped onto a sofa chair and propped one leg up in the air as she tossed a ball of energy back and forth in between her hands.

"I could have gotten her if it weren't for that Maryjane girl, well, witch," he said, watching Scarlet for a reaction.

"She's a witch!" Scarlet exclaimed, her eyes dancing back and forth in thought.

"Yes, and a very powerful one too," he said, eyeing her suspiciously. He knew she had already had a run-in with the girl earlier that day. It is why he was released to hunt her.

"Yeah, so powerful I couldn't even use my mind against her," Emma said, sitting up on the side of the chair.

"I had no idea the little brat had powers! I thought

Glinda had started studying black magic this whole time!" she hissed. She sat on her throne. She toyed with the fur throw that lay draped across it. He watched her, wondering what her next move was going to be. Ashe walked up to her with a tray that held a goblet and a glass, a corked bottle of the liquid she drank.

"This changes everything." She was calm and collected, pouring her drink into the goblet.

"How so?" he said uneasily, reaching for his cup of water. He took a swallow and set it back down, still watching the sorceress. Emma was watching the two amused, waiting for bickering to begin.

"Because your target is no longer Glinda. It's…what did you call her…oh, Maryjane," she said, smiling.

Every muscle in his body tensed at hearing his assignment. Scarlet could not read minds, but he knew she sensed a difference in his tone over the girl. What should have been obedience was replaced with malice and rage. He cracked his fingers on his hands and sat there in silence. His face had begun to flush with anger.

"Is there something wrong with my orders?" Scarlet's eyes turned black as she stared at him. She glared at him, urging him to defy her. Charlie looked over at Emma, whose eyes were on fire. He knew she was angry and ready to explode. He couldn't help the situation any more than she could have. Ashe looked at him with amusement.He hesitated with his answer. He did not want the assignment but had no choice but to accept it.

"I'll take the assignment," Ashe said cheerfully, taking a bite from an apple.

Charlie scowled at him. He kneeled before her and replied, "No, Ma' Lady, I accept the assignment, but I go alone." He bowed his head so that he couldn't see Emma's face, and to where no one else could see the distasteful look on his face.

"Good! Now, start it immediately," she said as she

stood and left the room.

He remained in the same spot as she danced through the hall and up toward the tower. His reply was just a whisper in the wind, "Yes, your highness."

He stood to his feet, and Emma was right there behind him. "Alone? Since when have you done things 'alone'? Ever since you saw that girl, you have acted weird in general and even weirder to me. Don't forget who owns your heart and soul, Charlie. I saved you from Scarlet's pit. You would still be trapped in there if it weren't for me. Remember that!" Emma barked as she pushed Charlie out of her way, leaving the room.

Charlie didn't know what to do or say. He was stuck in the middle with a decision to make. The outcome was unknown, and no one else could make this decision for him.

Ashe looked at him and laughed, "You're going to screw this up, and I will be the one that has to fix it. Well, Emma and I will have to fix it," he said chewing on the apple and taking another bite from it.

Charlie glared at him, fished a dagger from his boot, and threw it at him. It struck the apple in the center while Ashe was taking a bite. Ashe took the apple from his mouth, removed the knife, and took another bite from it, smiling in triumph. He tossed the dagger back to Charlie. Charlie threw it at a bookcase, left the room, and made way for the gates. Even though he took the assignment, everything within him willed him not to; however, it was better for him to take the assignment and not Ashe because he would take the girl out without even batting an eye. When he thought of how Ashe would've completed the task, his heart dropped to his knees.

What is wrong with me? He thought to himself. *This should be an easy task. There shouldn't be any reason for me to risk my life for this girl to survive. I would be giving up everything, including Emma. We have been through so much together.*

He then replayed the dream in his mind, again. His heart already knew what his mind did not want to acknowledge was wrong. He was in love with Maryjane. He was in love with the enemy, and he didn't know what to do about it. He felt trapped. He couldn't disobey orders, but he couldn't betray his heart either. Scarlet was a monster and would find a way to make him complete the task. He was ruthless and ready to kill his own mother on orders from her. He couldn't even remember the real reason he was so angry with her. His mind has been clouded and vague for a while now. No original thoughts are sacred. He couldn't do as he wished or as he pleased. He was stuck in the middle of a bog, slowly sinking, and he couldn't reach the shore. He couldn't bear the thought of harming Maryjane. Even as a simple mark, before he knew who she was, it took every ounce of energy he had to release those arrows at her, and he didn't understand why. Emma had no power over her, and there was something oddly familiar with that scenario, and he couldn't wrap his fingers around it at the time. Now it was all perfectly clear to him.

He emerged from the lights of Emerald City and into the darkness beyond the gates. He began walking the path back into the barren lands of Oz. He remembered how it once looked when he was a child. He thought of the dream once more. She was even more beautiful now than she was in the dream as a child. He felt more alive than he had ever felt in the past years when he thought of her. Looking into her eyes made him melt into a puddle. The sound of her voice echoed in his mind and mesmerized his heart. The touch of her skin sent electricity through his body.

This is nuts! he thought. *She is my assignment, my mission. I must destroy her.*

Still, to no avail, the thought of him harming her or causing her demise put him to his knees. He stumbled and came to a stop. He doubled over, trying to collect his thoughts. He had never been this torn over a simple task before. He wanted to make his Siress happy, but he felt and knew that if he did that, he would never again be happy himself. In his heart, he knew Maryjane was his joy, his passion, and his reason for still existing to this very day. He knew the inevitable was true.

He didn't know what to do, though. On one hand, he had his Siress counting on him, along with Emma. He didn't even truly know if he cared for Emma or not. He thought he did, until he saw Maryjane. She looks just like her, almost as if she were copied to make him forget about his true love. Maybe it was all set up by Scarlet. Maybe Emma isn't truly a real person...but he's touched and felt her hand before...you can't fake that kind of stuff. So, how did Scarlet make Emma look so much like Maryjane? A thought occurred to him that had been rolling around in his head. She made her look like Maryjane, so it would be easy to fabricate his memories. He would find out the truth about everything. The important thing was that he knew what he felt was real. He knew...

It must be true...now what do I do?

He already knew what he had to do. He heard someone talking up ahead. He hadn't realized that what had started as walking had advanced through to a sprint, then to a run. He glanced around but saw no one. The voices seemed close, but off the path. He quietly stepped into the brush and tracked the voices. He came to a small clearing. The voices were more distinct. He could make out through the hushed talk the voices of the group Maryjane had been with. His stomach did flip-flops as he listened to them speak. And then, instead of voices, he heard sobs. His heart sank as he listened to her speak to one of the group members while sobbing.

"You two were in love, weren't you?" Dorothy

asked.

"I loved him, but I wasn't too sure about his feelings for me. We were best friends, but I guess I got my answer because five years later, he doesn't remember me and replaced me," Maryjane said, choking back the sobs that wished to escape her breath. "The last time we talked, we fought. I left without saying goodbye and was unable to return because of the wall. Now...he's lost to that monster, the only friend I have ever had," she cried.

"If he loved you, he will remember you soon enough," Dorothy said. "Love conquers all."

"You're wrong, Mama. I'm destined to be alone," Maryjane sobbed. "No man stays in my life, Mama. I'm cursed."

"What do you mean?" Dorothy asked, confused.

"Daddy died before I was born, and Charlie is consorting with the enemy. If I cannot sway him back to our side...I will have to destroy him along with the Red Sorceress," Maryjane said.

"You're not the reason your father died, sweetie, it was a careless accident. I wish you could've met him because he would have loved you to death. You are the most wonderful gift of a child that could have been given. I would ask for no other child to replace you. You have been the best daughter. You are so full of life, and you care for everyone selflessly. Look at what you have done for Scarecrow and Nick. If not for you, they would still be the menacing monsters they had been turned into by that tyrant who calls herself a sorceress," Dorothy said.

"I just want him back. The way he used to be. He used to be so protective and courageous. He would have never hurt me before. He was so afraid of me being hurt," Maryjane cried. "I never fit in at home with the other kids. I was their personal joke.

This place, Charlie, they were my escape, and now half of my world is gone."

She remembered him as he remembered her. *How did she keep her memories?* he wondered. *How did she not forget about him the way he had her?* His heart thudded in his chest as he listened to her speak. *Stupid,* he thought, *it doesn't matter if you love her, or she loves you. You have a mission.*

He waited outside the clearing until daylight. Once the sun had begun to rise, and the birds began to chirp, he saw the roots of the tree drawn back. He took his bow from his back and placed an arrow in the drawstring. He pulled the string tightly back and held it there. The first to emerge was Nick, followed by Dorothy and Scarecrow. The last to emerge was Maryjane. She was still limping from the arrow yesterday. His eyes stayed steady on her, and he pulled the string tighter and tighter. He stared at her as they talked about where they would walk next. He watched her expressions as she spoke to the group and made their plans.

"What if we run back into the guy with arrows?" Nick asked, glancing around, looking for him.

He waited for her to answer. It was silent for a few moments. Her face had gone expressionless as if she were thinking deeply about something.

"Maryjane?" Scarecrow asked, breaking her concentration.

"Hmm," she replied.

"What if we run into the guy with arrows again?" Scarecrow asked this time.

"Oh, umm, just leave that to me," she said, glancing around.

"Are you in good enough shape to handle him?" Scarecrow asked with concern.

She didn't answer right away. She was in deep thought once more. She finally replied, "Don't worry about me. Everyone just concentrate on keeping yourselves out of danger and out of harm's way."

"Ok, well, we need to get a move on," Nick said.

"Which way to Lion's next nesting area?" Dorothy asked. "Should we stick to the forest or head back to the road?"

"We stick to the forest," Maryjane replied. "We're less likely to run into trouble." She stepped off the log down onto the ground and nearly collapsed. She winced in pain.

"How are you going to get around? You can barely walk!" Dorothy exclaimed.

"I'm fine." Maryjane took another step and nearly hit the ground again.

Dorothy rebutted, "No, you're not. We can't go…"

"We can't stay here! It's too dangerous. Whether I can walk or not is not important right now. What's important is getting to Lion and then completing what I set out to do in the first place." Everyone could feel the anxiety and stress behind her words.

Nick walked over to her and helped her to her feet. He threw her arm around his neck and helped her walk through the thicket. Charlie eased the bow down. He couldn't bear shooting another arrow her way. He wanted to run to her. He wanted to hold her, kiss her wounds, the wounds that he had caused. He hated himself for shooting her.

He shook off the feelings that overtook him for a moment, redrew the bow and arrow, and aimed directly at her back where her heart would be. The bow was unsteady as he shook with fear and panic. He nearly released the arrow but stopped. He couldn't kill her. To kill her was to kill a part of himself, and he couldn't do it. Even if it meant that he would betray the Red Sorceress, he didn't care. All he cared about right now was that Maryjane never saw harm again.

His power-driven mind began to fade, and love completely took over his thoughts and actions. *What do I* *do?*He mind-tapped Scarlet to deliver a message, something he used to do with Maryjane when they were kids. *I will protect her and destroy anyone who tries to harm her,* he thought. *And I will never hurt her again or break her into pieces again. I will no longer serve you, Scarlet.*

The ground began to tremble as Scarlet began speaking to his mind. *"You WILL serve me, or you will die!"* she hissed.

"I would rather die than do what you want me to do. Nothing in this world can break the bond we share. You tried to erase her from my memories. It didn't work, for my heart will always remember. If you try to harm her, I will stand in your way. If you send anyone else, I will destroy them. I'm the most powerful tracker and hunter you possess. Without me by your side, you are helpless in her destruction. I no longer care about you or Emma, even if it was falsified adoration. Your foolish love spells will not work on me anymore. I am no longer a minion of destruction for you. You tried to make me destroy myself by destroying everyone I care for. You had me brainwashed to slay my own mother! It will happen no more. It ends today."

She laughed and laughed maniacally. *"I own you. Remember, I created what you have become, and I can take it away. You, foolish boy. You are my toy, and I control you through your own blood, or have you forgotten about the blood pact? Or should I say the blood pact tying you to Emma? I may have just influenced your actions before, but I can control you completely if I wish to. Remember, my darling, little Emma can lead with her mind the way the piper did with his pipe. So, you can either complete the task I gave you willingly, or watch yourself do it, and do it the way I want it done. It's your choice,"* she sneered. *"Be careful of your choice because it's not just me you would make angry; you will be waking a sleeping beast!"*

Her voice disappeared, and the ground stopped trembling. He sank to the ground with his hands to his head. He was out of ideas and roads to turn. *So, I either have to kill her out of love, or by mind control when I wish to do neither,* he thought.

Only one person could help him, and he didn't even know how to reach her. *Why would she come help me anyways?* He thought to himself. He had destroyed any bridge between people he had. Even his own mother. He stood up, walked back to the road, and sat back down. He was out of options and nearly out of time. If he didn't have her head on a platter for the Scarlet within the day's end, then she would use Emma's mind control on him, and do it the way she saw fit.

"Oh, Momma, what have I gotten myself into?" He slumped backward on a tree stump as he spoke aloud. He shook his head and bowed it in shame. "I have to save her, and I don't know how. I'm up against a wall. I've really messed up." He felt like a child again as he pulled his knees up and buried his face in his legs.

"Charlie?" a voice asked hesitantly.

He looked up. "Momma! Oh God, I know I've messed up. I'm so sorry I didn't listen to you before. I don't know what to do now. I can't stop her. Scarlet has control over my actions through Emma. She has changed her mind about what to do to Maryjane, and if I do not complete the task myself, she will kill her through me. I cannot let this happen. My heart cannot bear the thought of…" he trailed off.

"I see you are starting to remember her again. How much do you remember?" Glinda asked, staring at him nervously.

"Nearly everything. It's slowly returning. However, I do more than remember her, I…I love her," he breathed. The last time he said that to his mother was when he didn't believe Maryjane had powers. How foolish he felt for it.

"And what do you need from me?" Glinda asked.

Charlie hesitated. "I need to break a blood pact."

"You didn't!" Glinda hissed.

"Yes, she tricked me into it. She told me she had captured Maryjane. I followed her to the Emerald City, where I was ambushed and put in the pit of no return. That's when I met Emma. She told me if I did what she asked, she would have Scarlet release me and return Maryjane home.The only thing I had to do was a blood pact. It was the only way to save her. It was an instantaneous removal of memories. She filled me with hatred toward you and anyone else I cared about. She filled my head with false memories of Emma and me. In my head, I was shown I loved her, but it wasn't the image of her face I loved. I didn't know it at the time, but it was because she looked so much like Maryjane. I don't know how long they kept me from people while they brainwashed me. It had to be long enough for them to completely wipe me clean of any aspects of good versus evil, and to annihilate any lingering feelings or thoughts of Maryjane. They turned me into a monster," he said, crying.

"Son, I don't know if I can remove the blood pact, especially with none of her blood. When you do a blood pact, it's forged like a contract and hard to break. I don't know if any power on earth can break it," Glinda stated sadly.

He reached into his shirt and pulled out a vial on a necklace. Inside the vial was a reddish liquid. "She gave me this to wear so she could 'be with me at all times.' It's her blood. Take it. Do what you must with it. If you cannot break this blood pact, then Maryjane and I fight to the death," he said, breaking off with the last word.

"You are sure of this?" Glinda asked, taking the vial in her hand and looking at it in the moonlight. "This is definitely just her blood and not hers and yours combined?"

"I watched her prepare it. She only placed blood from her hand in it," he said, staring at the vial Glinda held.

"It's funny. Once I decided to go against her rule, my memories returned along with my own self-will. Maybe the blood pact is a fake...but better not take any chances."

Glinda watched her son's face. "I will call upon Goddess Hecate to undo the blood pact," she said. She placed the vial in a pocket hidden in her dress. "In the meantime, you need to guard yourself. She is going to be sending everything your way. She knows your weakness. She will try anything and everything to hurt you, including sending more and more henchmen after Maryjane. She will try to find a way to get to Maryjane and use her against you," Glinda said, standing up. "Once the pact is broken, I will let you know, and I will tell the others as well. We will get this whole mess sorted out," Glinda said, smiling.

She was acting odd. He shrugged it off. He did try to slay her earlier in the day. "Momma, thank you." He smiled at Glinda. He truly meant it, too. He felt ashamed for what he had done.

Glinda looked at him, and her eyes melted. She walked over and hugged him. "You are welcome, my son." She reached into her pocket once more and fished out a necklace. It was a heart-shaped gold locket. She handed it to him. "Here, this belongs to you. I have been saving it for three years. Now is the best time to give it to you."

He took the necklace and looked at it. It was a quaint little necklace, and it seemed so familiar. He looked up to ask his mother where it came from, but she had already turned into her mists.

"I love you," he said as she floated away in the wind of her mist.

Suddenly, the ground began to tremble again, and he looked to the sky as a fiery essence lit the sky up at Emerald City. He knew Scarlet knew of his disobedience. All he could think of was Maryjane, and he pushed aside the temper tantrum Scarlet was having.

He lay down, resting his head against a tree. The ground was soft and spongy, and the sounds of Oz were beginning to return. Wherever she trekked, she had truly healed the earth beneath her feet. He smiled at the thought of the two of them being king and queen together. He turned the locket over in his hand and opened it. Inside was a single picture. It was a picture of her. The other side was engraved with, *Love Always*. He remembered the day she gave it to him. She told him it was a gift to remember her by. He thought back to the day he cast it away.

He had held onto the hope that she would return to Oz and see him again. He waited every day. When the second year since her departure had passed, he gave up on her return. He took the necklace off and threw it as far as he could. It was his fault she hadn't returned. He was heartbroken. Never again would he love anyone the way he had loved her.

He went walking that day outside of Munchkin Land when he ran into the Red Sorceress again.

"Why, hello again, Charlie," the Red Sorceress snickered.

"What do you want now?" He wasn't in the mood to be toyed with, and his gruff voice showed his annoyance.

"Have you spoken with your little friend lately?" she asked sincerely.

"No, but that's none of your business anyway." He glared at her.

"Oh, you haven't, you say? Well, well, do you have a message for her or anything to tell her? I can see that she gets it," she said, grinning.

"What do you mean?" Charlie asked, eyeing her.

"Oh, well, since you two weren't talking, I didn't know whether to tell you of her arrival back in Oz or not. She has been back for a while and has been the dearest friend," she said, grinning. There was something about her grin that sent shivers down his spine.

"Let her go," he said, glaring at her and balling his fists up.

"How about a trade? You become my subject, my slayer, my slave, and I will let Maryjane go," she said. *Her evil eyes pierced through his. He didn't know what to do. He had no choice but to go with her. He couldn't let her keep Maryjane locked away in Emerald City.*

"What do I have to do?" he asked her.

"Oh, not much. I just need some of your blood. Come with me, and she will be released as promised," she said, smiling.

He jumped up from his lying position. *I can't just sit here,* he thought. *I have to follow her and make sure nothing else happens.*

Chapter Eight

THE GROUP WALKED at a slow pace. They stopped for a breather every so often to catch their breath and for Maryjane to rest her leg. It had been a few hours since they had left the cave, but it seemed like it had been an entire day. Everyone was tired and drained from the hike through the woods. When they came to a creek bed with some old tree stumps sitting near the edge of the stream, they all sat down.

"If we follow this creek, we will run into another nesting area of the Lion," Nick said, easing Maryjane to the ground.

She was silent. She removed the bandage from her leg to see her wound. The herbs were not helping at all. It was starting to get infected, and she knew if she didn't get it to heal, it would go septic. She fished her spell book from her bag and thumbed through it.

"There has to be a spell in here I can use to heal this up," Maryjane said as she flipped through the whole book, not finding anything. She shut the book and shoved it back into her bag.

"I have a thought," Dorothy said, looking at Maryjane. "Remember how you healed the earth? Maybe you can use that power and heal yourself?"

Maryjane thought about this for a moment. Even though she had healed the earth, it returned to the same dismal look it had before she walked through. "It's worth a try," she huffed. "It may or may not work like we hope for. I know the magic was just a temporary relief from me on the land. It returned to the same dull shades of gray and black."

She looked down and found a small bloodstone lying on the ground. She remembered what Glinda had said about crystals and their healing powers. Bloodstone was used to protect and remove impurities from the blood. She held the crystal in her hand, placed her hand over her wound, and closed her eyes. She gathered the energy within her and felt the power envelop her whole body. She imagined the purple rays of her power penetrating her wound and healing it from the inside out. She concentrated hard on her leg healing. Her hand grew hot, then went cold. She opened her eyes and lifted her hand from the wound. The wound had disappeared and left bare skin visible along with a scar. She moved her leg left to right and lifted it up and down. She stood and tested it. It had worked.

"No pain," she smiled, "It worked," she said, looking up at her mother. "Maybe there's a little witch in you as well."

Her mother chuckled. "No, just age beyond the years."

Nick was staring off into the distance, holding his axe as if he were in defensive mode.

"What is it?" asked Maryjane, walking over to him and looking in the direction he was staring.

He stared a while longer then shook his head, "It's nothing. I thought we were being followed, but I haven't seen any movement in the woods," he said, resting the axe on his shoulder. "We rest a little while longer, and then we should start moving again. I don't like sitting in one place for long," he said, easing down on a log beside the creek.

"Of course, you wouldn't," Scarecrow said, laughing.

"You're afraid you will rust again."

The whole group joined in with the laughter. Just then, a mist descended down from the sky to the group.

"Well, I see I am missing all the fun," Glinda said, smiling. She looked at Maryjane, "I see your wounds have healed nicely and not by herbs alone." She winked at her, giving her some encouragement

"What's the special occasion?" Maryjane asked. "What brings you to our neck of the woods?" The whole group laughed once more together as their moods lightened in contrast to how their day had started.

"I had an interesting chat with one of Scarlet's minions of destruction," she said, looking Maryjane in the eyes. "I don't know if it's a trick or the real deal, but it seems as if the glamour that she has cast on Charlie is wearing off."

Maryjane's heart fluttered. "So, he's back to the old Charlie now?" she asked enthusiastically.

"Not quite yet. It seems as if our red-headed temptress and her mini-me have tricked him into a blood pact. If he doesn't willingly battle you and kill you, then she will make Emma use her mind control on Charlie and do it herself," she said sympathetically.

Maryjane was once again crushed. "So, what now?"

"I am working on a spell to break the pact. It will take a lot of magic and help from the Goddess, but I think it will work," she said.

"How will we know if it worked?" Maryjane asked.

"I assume based on Scarlet's reaction when they lose the bond. I imagine a lightning storm would ensue after," she said, smiling.

"So, if we run into Charlie again…" Maryjane asked, trailing off.

"All is well for now," Glinda said, smiling a halfhearted smile. "Now, I must be off; there is much work to be done." She walked over to Maryjane and lifted her chin, so she could face her, "Do not fret, child." She smiled and stepped away. She was enveloped in her mist and floated away.

"Well, that's partial good news," Dorothy said cheerfully.

"Yes, yes, it is," Maryjane said, staring off after Glinda. She returned her gaze to the group. "Everyone ready to continue the journey?" she asked.

Everyone in the group stood up and began their way up the creek. Who would have thought the forest would be so beautiful when everything else in Oz was shambles? They passed by a cliff where you could see that a rock slide years ago had caused the face of the cliff to look so wonderful. They walked for miles, climbing over fallen trees and boulders. The sun had risen high in the black sky, and midday was upon them. Even though it wasn't as bright as it should be and dimmed by the dark clouds that hung in the sky, it was still warming as if it were.

"How much further to the next nesting area?" Maryjane asked. "It's getting hot and humid."

"Not much further," Nick replied, stepping across another fallen tree. They heard a snap, and Nick was hurtled straight up in the air by his foot. He had stepped into a hunter's trap. He was up too high for any of them to try to cut the rope.

"Get me down from here! Get me down!" he cried, swinging side to side.

Right as Maryjane was going to climb the tree, a ferocious roar erupted in the area. The roar was non-stop and deafening to the group. Maryjane looked around with her hands on her ears to find the source. She looked to the base of the mountain range and saw a hideous beast emerge. It was twice the size of any normal animal. Its fur was matted and tinged black. It had razor-sharp claws that cut through the logs it walked across. It had a large mark across its face, dripping with blood. She was petrified.

"Quick, you two, come here," she said, motioning for Dorothy and Scarecrow. They ran toward her, and she used her powers to levitate them into the tree out of harm's way. When they were set safely in the branch, she looked back to where the beast had been. It was gone. She was terrified. She turned in a complete circle and could not see the beast. "Where did it go?"

As soon as the words escaped her mouth, she was pushed to the ground from behind by two, unimaginably, large paws. She scrambled from beneath the beast and popped out behind it. However, no sooner was she out from under it, it was turning to face her. It let out another howl that tore through her bones as fear and anxiety crept in. She backed away slowly, trying to think of something to fend it off with. It struck at her with a claw, and she jumped back in time, with it just grazing the top of her dress, ripping it, and her falling to the ground. She was now crawling backward, not taking her eyes off the beast. It got within inches of her face and let out another ferocious roar, and without realizing it, she was screaming back at it.

She looked to her left and saw something silver smack on the ground.Nick had thrown his axe for her to use in her defense. She lunged for it and grabbed the handle with both her hands. When she rolled around, the beast opened its mouth with its large fangs protruding as it roared in her face again and lunged downward at her, trying to strike her. She thrust the axe handle in its mouth, trying to block its attack. It bit straight through it, breaking it in half. She looked at the snapped axe in horror. She was out of options.

An arrow whizzed through the air, striking the lion in its hindquarters. It momentarily distracted the beast so that she could wriggle away out of its reach. She looked to where the arrow came from as the beast tore the arrow from its backside with a smack of its paw. Her eyes lit up.

"Charlie!" she screamed.

"Run away, Maryjane! Get out of there!" He jumped down from the tree he had been standing in while the beast ran to him, roaring and circling him, ready to attack. He drew his bow and arrow, and it angered the beast even more. It smacked the bow from his hands, grazing his skin with its razor-sharp claws.

"Charlie!" Maryjane screamed again. She was running toward them.

"No! I told you to run away!" he yelled as the beast smacked at him again, barely missing him.

What to do! What to do! She thought. *What do I have that can help him?* She was scrambling through her bag. She came across some flowers she had picked outside of Munchkin Land.

"Poppies!" she breathed in relief. "Charlie, run!" She started smashing the poppies to release the toxin in the flowers. She had watched once before as some baby cougars were playing in the poppy field, and what happened when they released the poppy toxin. She threw the balled-up flowers at the beast as a bomb. The toxic smell hit the beast immediately, and it began to sway and lose its footing. It roared, and the roar got quieter and quieter. It took a step toward Charlie, but with unsure footing. It let out one last roar and collapsed.

She ran to the beast and kicked the balled-up bomb away from everyone. It was still breathing but had fallen asleep. She looked up at Charlie. He was still sitting there looking at the creature. And then he looked down into her eyes. The spark between them radiated through the forest. They didn't take their gaze off one another. Their breathing got heavier as their hearts thudded in their chests.

A voice interrupted them, "I know you two just fought the beast and are very tired, but could one of you

PLEASE cut me down!" Nick begged.

Scarecrow and Dorothy chuckled in the tree at Nick's begging. Maryjane looked at them and smiled. She glanced at Charlie and then walked over to the tree. She levitated the two out of the tree.

"Do you think you can hit the rope with an arrow and cut it for him to be released?" Maryjane asked, looking at Charlie.

"I think I can manage that," he said, boasting.

"Please!" Nick cried. Everyone laughed. He shot the rope with the arrow, and Nick came crashing down.

"Oh, what, no easy let down for me?" he said jealously.

"Sorry, it happened too fast for my reflexes," Maryjane chuckled. She looked at Charlie's hand. It was sliced open good.

He shoved his hand in his pocket. "Don't worry about it, it's fine."

She looked at him as if seeing him for the first time in years.His face had the shadow of a beard growing back in place. His hair was a mess, like it had always been when they were kids. His eyes had turned a marvelous bluish green hue. They were stern in their gaze at her, but smiled at her at the same time. She broke her focus on his face. She blushed and looked over to the animal lying in a heap on the ground. She started to walk back over to the beast. Charlie grabbed her shoulder.

"What are you doing? Don't go near that thing. It nearly killed you!" he said in his protective tone, which he always had with her.

"It's ok. I know what I'm doing. I'm not a little girl anymore, you know?" she said, flashing him a smile.

"Little girl or grown woman, you're not going near it. I need something to finish it off, an axe, a sword…something before it wakes up!" Charlie cried out, looking around for a weapon to kill the beast.

"No!" Maryjane defiantly placed herself between him and the beast. "Don't hurt it."

"Why not?" he asked with that familiar tone of annoyance.

"Because it's not a beast, it's my mother's friend, and at one point, it was my pet," she said, reaching for the creature to touch it. She had always known that the kitten she had been given as a small child was really Lion in the real world. The cowardly lion was shifted into a harmless house cat in her world. She loved him to death for staying by her side. When the wall had gone up, he disappeared as well.

"Don't touch it!" he demanded.

She whirled around, "Look, just because your memories are returning, along with your same annoying protectiveness, it does not mean I haven't battled enough battles to know what the heck I am doing. Back off!" she snapped.

He stood speechless. She turned back around, reached down, and touched the creature. The matted black fur turned into a beautiful golden mane. The scar on its face healed, and its lustrous color returned. It opened its eyes and looked around. Charlie grabbed Maryjane's hand and pulled her backward.

"Was I dreaming, or was I just a courageous killing machine?" the beast laughed, looking at the group. He began to lick his paw and clean his face with it.

Dorothy was the first to speak and step forward toward him, "Hello, Lion. It has been years since we have seen each other," she said, smiling.

He looked from her to Nick and Scarecrow. "Is it true? Has she returned to us? Or was I killed by the children?" he asked the two.

They exchanged glances, and Dorothy walked over to Lion and gave him a hug, laughing. Maryjane watched the group huddle together, and everyone exchanged hugs.

She was happy they were all together once more. Her mother needed their presence one final time. She looked over to Charlie, and he was staring at her as she sat on the ground. Even after having a spat, his eyes still glowed, looking at her as if it was for the first time. She turned away, blushing once more. It was so awkward being around him. When she was younger, she didn't care if he knew how she felt. She's older now, and it's frightening to think of talking about how they feel about one another. It had been five years, and she held onto those feelings without him ever saying he felt them back. He didn't know what it was like for her in her world. She hated being stuck there for five years without an escape to Oz. The boys were horrible to her. She thought back to the previous day when the one taunted her. She cringed, thinking of how she had been treated.

She stole another glance in his direction, and he still sat there staring at her. He looked mesmerized and in awe as he stared at her. He had half of a goofy smile plastered on his face. She bit her bottom lip and returned her gaze to the group of laughing hyenas chattering away. *Do I want to be alone with him right now? Will I be safe? I don't think he will try to hurt me, but can I trust him?*

Maryjane was deep in thought over a decision. Someone jostled her from her thoughts. "Hmm?" she replied.

"Do you want to sit down with us and catch up?" Dorothy asked.

Maryjane glanced at Charlie for her answer. He was still staring at her. "No, I think I will leave you four to catch up alone. It has been a while since you four have talked and caught up with one another," Maryjane said, standing up from the log she had been sitting on.

Lion looked at her, "Hey kid, no hard feelings, right? I mean, I wouldn't have eaten you."

She smiled and laughed, "Of course not, you big

pussycat," she said as she scratched his underbelly, and he purred away. Everyone laughed. "Your claws were sharper as a house cat. Momma is still mad about that couch you clawed up, though," she laughed.

Lion lowered his ears and hunkered his head as he looked over to Dorothy. She smiled in return, showing no hard feelings over her furniture. She scratched at his head, and he purred in compliance.

Maryjane looked at Charlie, who was laughing at Lion rolling around on his back while being scratched like a kitten would. It felt so good to have him back with her. He would have never understood how she would've felt if she had to fight him, and worse, kill him. "You want to take a walk with me?"

He looked over at her and stared deep into her eyes. He stood up and walked closer to her. "I wouldn't miss it for the world," he murmured, brushing a strand of hair from her face.

Chapter Nine

"THAT BOY is so disobedient. It's not the right time to completely take charge of his mind, not yet, that is," Scarlet hissed as she spoke with Ashe and Emma.

"I told you, my Queen, that he was too inferior to have ranks in our court. He is too, what shall I say, compassionate. For God's sake, he grows flowers for a power," Ashe jealously ranted.

"You are just jealous because all of the girls bow at his feet for love," Emma retorted, rolling her eyes at Ashe.

"You would know best, wouldn't you?" Ashe sneered and grinned. Emma started walking toward him with her eyes glowing.

"Not now, Emma," Scarlet cooed. "You will have your chance for revenge on the rightful person who deserves it."

Ashe looked at Emma nervously as her eyes went from glowing yellow to normal. She spat in his face and walked to sit down in her usual chair to the right of the throne. Ashe took his seat ten feet from her. He watched her and eyed her as she sat there, throwing an energy ball back and forth between her hands.

"Ah, my right hand of power," Scarlet said, tipping her head to Emma in her seat. "Now to get my left hand of power back."

Scarlet paced the floor as she thought deeply to

herself. She came to a stop and looked over at Ashe, who sat haphazardly in his chair with his feet propped up on the table, still watching Emma.

"I have a marvelous idea that I'm sure you would be more than willing to take," she said, smiling insidiously.

Ashe hesitated to speak when he saw the smile. "What kind of idea?" he asked.

"They believe our strike will be to the heart of Charlie, which is his precious little witch, Maryjane," Scarlet said, flustered.

"Yes, we should take the wretched brat out of the picture, then, Charlie would come crawling back to you," Ashe said, smiling proudly as if he had the most brilliant idea imaginable. Emma snorted as she let out a small laugh. Scarlet shot her a look of disapproval, and she straightened up.

Scarlet returned her gaze to Ashe, and she smiled. "I like the way you think, but you're a little far from the thought I had," Scarlet said, sneering. "We strike Maryjane where it hurts the most," she said, smashing the goblet to the floor she had been drinking from.

Ashe, confused, protested, "How do we do that? Take out Charlie? That's nearly imp…"

"You're not thinking of the bigger picture here! Yes, the two love each other. We get that!" Scarlet screamed as Emma scowled at Ashe. Ashe was frozen in his seat with fear. "But there's something more important to Maryjane than just foolish love for a boy. When I strike at her, I want to cut her deep!" Scarlet said with her eyes burning deep into Ashe's eyes. "You leave at dawn!"

Ashe, bewildered from the look in her eye, knelt to the floor and bowed his head, "Yes, my Queen. Whatever the task is, it shall be done," he looked up to meet her eyes still full of fire. As if there were a silent command uttered between their minds, he replied, "Understood."

"Good!" she said, walking over to her throne.

He stopped at the bookcase, pulled the dagger from the wood Charlie had thrown, and left the room to gather a few men to go on the mission she had just assigned.

Emma stood to go with him, and Scarlet shooed her back into her seat. "Let the boys handle this one. This task is so simple that if they screw it up, I will personally eat their hearts from their chests," Scarlet scoffed. Emma took her seat. Light was beginning to cut through the twilight of night as the emergence of dawn quickly approached.

Scarlet sat down on her throne, picked up another goblet setting on a table beside her, and chucked it across the room. She let out a furious, blood-curdling scream, and the room filled with a fiery essence that sprouted through the top of the tower of Emerald City. It swirled in the sky, looking as if it were a small whirlwind of furious power. The torrential storm of power came crashing back down into the room, blowing all the furniture to the sides of the room, toppling over statues and bookcases. Emma sat unfazed by the outburst as if it weren't the first time she had seen her lose her head. Scarlet composed herself and picked up the silver goblet that had toppled over. She filled it with a greenish liquid from the bottle Ashe had brought her and took a drink from the cup.

"Now, we will see who is more powerful," she snickered. "By hurting her, it hurts him, the grandest plan of all!" she said, laughing maniacally. "He will be your slave forever, my dear child! If you cannot have him, I will make sure no one does," she said, taking another drink from her cup. "Glinda thought she was the only one with a magical prodigy. Well, let's see how she fares against you after I develop your powers even stronger."

She stood and sauntered off to her empty bed in the next room. "How I hate the light. Soon, and very soon, there will be nothing but utter darkness," she said, closing the door behind her.

Emma sauntered off upstairs to her room, which Scarlet had given her when she first appeared six years ago. Emma lived a hard life in the orphanage in her own world. She was given up at birth and bounced from home to home. No one could understand or come to terms with the special gifts she had. Even as a baby, she could levitate objects, and when she didn't get her way, electrical storms would roll through the plains and surround the house. She grew up without any friends or family to call her own. She was more than just an outcast. No one wanted her, and no one wanted to be around her.

When she arrived, Scarlet stood before her at a strange building that was turning from a beautiful green into a dull gray color.

"My, my child. Tell me, what is your name?" Scarlet asked as the terrified twelve-year-old girl stood before her. "Do not be afraid. I wish you no harm," Scarlet stepped forward to touch the girl. A lightning bolt came shooting from the sky, nearly striking Scarlet.

Scarlet looked to the sky and then to the girl. "Did you do that?"

"I'm sorry. I didn't mean to, honest. I don't know why these things happen around me. Please, please don't be mad at me," the girl begged.

"Oh, I am not mad in the least. You and I will be the best of friends." Scarlet's mouth widened in a sinister grin. "Tell me, child, what is your name?"

"My name...is Emma," she squeaked out.

"Do you have any sisters, Emma?" Scarlet asked, circling her and looking her over.

"No, I'm an orphan. I was given up at birth," Emma replied.

"Where do you live?" Scarlet asked, taking her face in her hands and giving her a hard look over. It amazed her how much she looked like Glinda's apprentice.

"Kansas," Emma replied.

"Kansas, is that so? Well, I know of another girl who you look

undoubtedly so much alike to, who is also from Kansas. You're an orphan, you say?"

Emma nodded.

"How would you like to live with me forever? You would never have to go back to Kansas ever again," Scarlet said, bending down to her. "I will treat you as if you are my real daughter."

"I would like that," Emma said, smiling.

Scarlet was always telling Emma how she despised the other young girl. She would pace the halls of Emerald City late at night. One night, Emma walked downstairs after being woken up by a terrifying scream. Scarlet was angry and throwing things.

"That brat thinks she owns Oz when she doesn't," Scarlet scoffed.

"Why do you dislike her so much?" Emma asked.

Scarlet looked over at her and smiled, "One day you will learn the truth of everything, including the truth of who Maryjane is. Right now, we must continue your lessons, so you will be strong enough to battle her in the end."

She took Emma under her wing and taught her what she needed to get by with at the time. Emma gained control over her powers with Scarlet's lessons. She tested the strength of Emma's powers when she had her create the wall barring Maryjane's re-entrance back into Oz. Scarlet loved Emma as if she were her own daughter.Emma had never seen any children with Scarlet.

"Scarlet," the twelve-year-old Emma spoke, getting her attention. They walked around the outside of the Emerald City while Scarlet used her powers to kill any flowers that bloomed in the field.

"Yes, my child."

"Where are your children? Do you have any of your own?" she asked.

Scarlet was silent for a few moments. "No, I do not."

"Why don't you have any?" Emma said, stopping and sitting down at a tree.

"Many years ago, my mother became so enraged with this land

while pregnant with me that the rage seeped into her womb. The rage took away any chance of me ever having children of my own." Scarlet stared off into the distance as she spoke. Silence fell between the two of them.

"I will be your daughter if you wish me to," Emma offered. She looked up to see a single tear fall from Scarlet's eye that she rapidly brushed away.

"I would love that, my child."

Scarlet truly loved Emma to the point where she would give Emma anything she wanted. Right now, she needed a friend of her own to grow with and be happy. So, Scarlet decided to give her a friend, a friend she knew would instantly take a liking to her, considering how she favored his one true love. It would take some work, but she would eventually convince him, whether it be through persuasion or by spell.

Emma sighed as she thought back to the day she met Scarlet. How different would things be right now had she not accepted learning under Scarlet? She knew one thing: she would fight to the death with this Maryjane girl to keep Charlie by her side. Charlie was her friend, her love now, and no one was going to take that away from her. She went into her room, but not to go to bed. She walked to her potions table and began brewing two potions. One for hatred and one for love. They didn't need to be drunk; all she had to do was scry for them in her mirror, and the damage would be done as she poured it over the mirror. She cackled as she went through her herbs, calculating the perfect blends for her spells to work.

Chapter Ten

MARYJANE AND CHARLIE walked silently through the dense trees. Small bursts of light from the sun cut through the leaves and branches in patches. Butterflies fluttered in and out of the light while birds danced in their nests. The forest was becoming alive once again with creatures that had long since disappeared. Just her presence in Oz was breeding new life. Even the animals could feel it. Peace was mounting in the air, and the animals emerged unafraid of the darkness that had raptured the land. Rabbits and squirrels darted in between Charlie and Maryjane's feet. Maryjane giggled as she bent down and petted one of the woodland creatures before it scampered off to the others. There was a silent, mutual understanding between her and the creatures that had existed prior to the Red Sorceress' arrival in Oz.

Maryjane and Charlie trudged through the thicket of the forest. He helped her climb over some logs, even when she insisted she could do it herself. The longer they walked in silence, not speaking of the day five years ago, the more the anxiety and anticipation of conversation mounted in Charlie's mind. Charlie thought silently to himself., *Just ask her why she never came back, why she left without a word, just why?*

"Why what?" Maryjane asked, confused.

He hadn't realized that last why had come out in words instead of thought. His thoughts still plagued him, and the more he thought, the more the anxiety turned into anger toward Maryjane.

"Why didn't you ever come back? Why did you

110

abandon me here?" he blurted out.

She looked stunned for a moment. She stopped walking and sat down on a log beside the creek.

"WHY!?" he yelled.

"I tried to! I tried every day for five years, Charlie. Someone put a wall up that completely encircled Oz. I walked for miles on each side, trying to find a way in. I searched for years for a trap door or opening in the wall. I couldn't find one.It took me five years to learn that I could take it down with my own mind and powers." She looked at him, then looked away.

"What?" He stopped her in her steps and stood in front of her, trying to get her to talk to him.

"You were the only reason I kept returning to Oz. That last day..." she started and went quiet for a moment, staring at the ground, "That last day, you really broke my heart. I was completely and without a doubt in love with you. You cut me with a knife, saying we'd never be together. I had always felt destined to be with you, but I respected your wishes. I didn't want to become the reason you and your mother fought. I didn't want you banished or anything that the Elders may have done because you were with me. I didn't want to be the reason for your troubles anymore. I just wanted you to be happy, and if that meant letting you go, I was prepared for it. I'm still as much in love with you as I was then..." she said, trailing off. "But, I understand you have to uphold the laws of Oz. I'm ok with that now," she said, looking at him. A single tear had rolled down her cheek. She turned her face away from him, so he wouldn't see, and refused to look him in the eye.

He stopped pacing and turned her to face him. He wiped the tears from her eyes. "Nothing will keep us apart any longer. Our love is not forbidden in the eyes of the Elders. My mom was angry with me over that fight. She told me the Elders smiled upon you and blessed you because of how your mother helped Oz when she was a teenager," he said, smiling. She did not. "Why aren't you happy with this news?" he asked, confused. "I thought you would be delighted that we can be together without having to hide in secrecy."

She stood and walked away from him and on further into the woods. Her walk turned into a sprint, and he found himself chasing her down. He tackled her to the ground. She tried to roll out of his grasp, but he pinned her arms down.

"What the heck? What is wrong?" he asked.

"Everything is wrong!" she screamed at him.

He didn't know what she meant, and his face showed it. She placed a hand to her forehead in aggravation. "What do you mean?" he asked, still not catching what she meant.

"You want to go back like nothing has happened in the past five years since I've been gone. Every day I woke up, I thought of you. Every night, I dreamt of you. You don't know what it's like to have your heart shattered over and over in your dreams. That's what happened every time I recounted what happened that day. You crushed me! You pulled my heart out, held it in your hands, and just tossed it aside. Every day we were together. Every day we got closer to each other. Every day, we were within kissing distance. Every day, you never once told me how you felt about me, even though the passion and intensity were evident. Now, five years later, I run into you once more, and you're in league with the enemy of Oz. Finally, you profess your love for me, you tell me everything is ok, that we can be together, and that everyone won't be mad about it. Love isn't about following the rules. Love is falling without looking and without caring what others may think. I loved you with all of my heart, without a single thought about it. I loved you for you. I didn't care you were a magical being, even when I still thought I was just a human girl. I loved your ferocity in protecting me. I loved your concern for me when I was in danger. Not to mention, a day ago, you were trying to kill me! You had no clue who I was, had a new toy you were playing with, and now want to be in love with me. You shot me with two arrows!" she said, practically yelling at him.

He sat quietly. What could he say? She was right. He was a jerk to her when it came to their feelings for each other. "So, my siding with Scarlet is the priority of this argument right now?" he asked. *Stupid, you shouldn't have said that,* he thought.

Her eyes burned into his, "I'm sure you just didn't 'side' with her. I'm pretty sure there was more going on behind closed doors with the girl who looks surprisingly the same as me, or is that just a figment of everyone's imagination?"

"Are you done ranting yet?" he asked. She didn't answer. She remained quiet. "I take that as a yes. Now it's my turn. You are *not* the only one who spent each and every day thinking of us. Yes, I was an idiot. I know I broke your heart, but I broke mine as well. I was completely and utterly in love with you. I wanted to hold you, kiss you, and make every dream I had with you come to life. I waited for two years for you to return before I gave up hope. I thought you weren't coming back because of me. I was devastated. I was going to profess my love to you, whether it was against the Elders' rules or not. Any guy would be an idiot to pass up the chance of loving you. Scarlet tricked me into siding with her. She said she had YOU. My one weakness, and I fell for it. She removed every memory I had of you. Whenever I tried to recall memories, a haze filled my head, but once I saw you and had the dream of us, she could no longer keep what I felt for you under wraps anymore. She could no longer hide my memories of you. I chose you over her and

Emma," he said, looking into her eyes.

She had started crying when he started talking. He wiped the tears away with one hand. "And no, nothing went on behind closed doors with either of them. I do have standards when it comes to women the age of my mother, under mind control or not." She laughed. "Emma means nothing to me. It was all mind control and spells. They had replaced my memories of you with memories of her. I figured it was easy to do since she does look like you. I haven't understood what that means yet." He looked down at the ground, then back at her. "And at long last, and long overdue," he said, leaning in close to her, "I love you, Maryjane."

His mouth found hers with ease. She invited his mouth openly. Both of them shuddered from the pleasure of the first kiss shared between the two of them. Their mouths trailed from one another and were roaming each other's bodies. He ran his hands through her hair while she kissed his neck. Her lips found his again, and they were kissing madly. He ran his hands up and down her back and down her arms. His hand ran across the scar from where he had pierced her with his arrow. He couldn't look at her because of the shame he felt for his actions. He ran his hand along her leg and came to where the hole in her dress was from the second arrow. The dress had been ripped open for the wound to be made visible, and a bandage was applied to the wound. The scar was much larger and rose from her skin. He remembered her limping from the cave and winced from the thought of how he had hurt her. He looked at the scar, bent down, and kissed it.

"I will never hurt you again," he said, looking deep into her eyes.

"I know," she replied back.

His mouth was back at hers again. He laid her back in the grass. They kissed each other hungrily. He pulled his

114

shirt off, and she ran her fingers along his bare chest. He dove in, stealing another kiss, and they rolled in the grass intertwined together. They lay there forever. She ran her fingers over his chest. He took her hand in his, interlaced their fingers together, and kissed her hand.

"Mm," she said, sighing, "I don't ever want this to end. It feels too much like a dream to be real. I'm afraid I'm going to wake back up in the cave, or worse, at home."

He rolled over to his side, looked at her, and asked, "Would you stay with me?"

"What do you mean?" she asked, turning her face to look him in the eyes.

"Would you stay with me, forever, here in Oz?" he asked again. She didn't know how to answer the question. Her silence brought worry to his eyes. "Do you not want to be with me forever?" His face showed the same amount of concern that his voice had when she hadn't answered..

"I want to, I do," she said sitting up, "but I have my mother to take care of now. There was a time if you had asked me that question I would've without a doubt have said yes. Things have changed now though," she said, glancing over her shoulder at him. His eyes did not look back at her. Instead, they stared down at the ground. "Of course, I would return every day," she said, trying to sound reassuring. It didn't work. He was still staring at the ground. He sat up, put his shoes on, and then stood to put his shirt back on. "Are you angry with me, Charlie?" she asked, peering at him harder, waiting for an answer.

He didn't respond to her. She began to feel the same panicky feeling she had always felt with him when they had talked around their feelings for one another. She searched his face for some type of answer, but it was like looking at a wall.She never knew what was rolling around in his mind, and his stern face didn't make her feel any more reassured than if she couldn't have seen his face at all.

"We need to get back to the group and continue forward." He had no emotion in his voice or reassurance in his actions.

That was all it took for her to crumble. He would never understand what she was going to go through. Just those few simple words felt like a knife plunged into her heart. She stood up without facing him. "Just go back to Emma," she blurted out and pushed past him. She ran. She ran as if someone were hunting her down. Instead of taking the same path back to the group, she veered off and took off through the woods. Her lungs were beginning to ache from her quick gulps of air. She didn't care. Pain seemed to be her only release from the drowning of her heart.

She saw a bright light atop the hill she had been climbing. The sun peered through the edge of the forest. She topped the hill and was at the crest of the mountain range. She fell to her knees, buried her face in her hands, and released all of the emotions she had held onto for five years.

Charlie had tried keeping up with her pace, but she ran so fast down the path that he couldn't keep up with her. He was angry and hurt. He had finally professed his love to her, shared the experience of a lifetime with her, and she refused to stay in Oz with him. It was like a smack in the face and a smack to his ego.

He wasn't planning to apologize for his actions. He didn't think he did anything wrong. He had every right to be angry at her. He topped the end of the path where the group had been left. The four of them sat still, talking and laughing with one another. Maryjane was not there.

Dorothy looked up at him, smiling, "Did you two have a nice walk?" He didn't answer. Panic filled his body. Dorothy's smile faded. "Where's Maryjane?" Her eyes searched his face in the absence of his words. "Where is my daughter?" she demanded.

He found his words, "She's not here? She's really not here?" he asked, stumbling over his words.

Dorothy stood up, "No, she's not. She was with you!"

"We— we had a…disagreement, and she ran off back in this direction. You're sure she didn't come back?" he asked, looking around in all directions in the woods.

Dorothy didn't even answer his question. She began to yell, "Maryjane! Maryjane!"

To no one's surprise, she didn't answer. Charlie turned around to face the path. His head was spinning from the adrenaline of anxiety taking over his body. *What have I done?* he thought to himself. *I have to find her. I have to apologize. I have to find her…before someone else does.* His thoughts flashed to Emma or Ashe, and his jaw tightened. He hadn't realized he had started running back down the path. Ashe is ruthless and willing to do anything to get Scarlet's attention. Emma would just torture her from spite.

I swear I will kill them, he thought to himself running beside the creek. He was eyeing his surroundings trying to find a trail that she may have left behind. He came around a bend in the path and saw a footprint that had stepped off in the curve. *Why hadn't I noticed it while walking back the first time?* He had been too wrapped up in his anger and ego even to think she might have run off somewhere else. It would have been the walk of shame. Running from the woods, probably crying, just to have a bunch of questions asked. Especially when every question she would have been prodded with would have been his fault. *Why did I have to react so childishly toward her? She was reaching out to me, and I threw it back in her face.*

He took the mountain in large bounds as he ran up. He barely felt the ache in them from the steep climb. He pushed forward and saw the light at the edge of the forest. It was the tree line. He hastened his pace as fast as he could and pushed through the edge of the trees.

"Maryjane!" he yelled breathlessly as he toppled from the tree line and into the light. He had tripped on a root sticking out of the ground. He lifted his head to look around. There had been no answer to his yell. She was not there. He didn't see any tracks to show where she had gone either.

He rolled from his stomach to a sitting position. He was without any ideas and out of options. He couldn't track without any trace of her footsteps. He climbed to his feet and surveyed the top of the mountain. To his right, there was a waterfall cascading down the side of the mountain. He walked to the river that formed the waterfall. Where it flowed over the edge was a boulder big enough to stand on. He climbed on it and looked out across the valley.

I screwed up, he thought, shaking his head. A reflection of light hit him directly in the eye, and he looked around to see where the source came from. He looked down, and his body was filled with dread and terror. The reflected light was the sun bouncing off one of the enchanted silver slippers she had been wearing. His mother had shown him once before how she cloaked the magical gifts she gave to people, so no one would know what they truly were. It was barely hanging on a tree branch right below the boulder. He fell to his stomach to reach for the shoe, but it wasn't within arm's reach. He scooted closer to the edge of the boulder so that he could peer down further. He saw a leg lying on the ground.

"No, no, no, no, no, no!" he cried out. He was beside himself with panic and fear. "Maryjane! Maryjane! Can you hear me? Please sit up! Please, answer me!" he said, trying to yell over the roar of the water crashing down.

She didn't respond to the yells. She still didn't move.

He sat up on the boulder and rocked as he cried. *My love...* "I shouldn't have gotten angry with her. I shouldn't have..." he trailed off, talking to himself.

He surveyed the area, looking for a way he could climb down to where she was. There were no trails that would safely get him there and back. His heart was completely shattered. He suddenly felt nauseous, jumped up, and ran to the edge of the trees. He vomited for what seemed like forever. He wiped his mouth and collapsed against a tree.

"What have I done...?" he whispered, crying to himself.

The reflecting light seemed to haunt him with his eyes closed, for he still felt the light upon his face. He would never be at peace again. He wiped his eyes and opened them. The light was not haunting him but was annoyingly glittering in his eyes. He was lightheaded and dizzy from all of the adrenaline coursing through his body.

Through blurry eyes, he could see the shoes were in the hands of a fair-toned person. His eyes drifted from them, doing a complete look from the feet upward. He couldn't see the face of the woman because the sun was directly behind her. His eyes were blurred with the tears that kept coming through, and the wave of dizziness that left him on the ground. The figure knelt down from the sun to where he could see the person's face, however, it was the voice that made the smile come to his lips. The voice sounded like it was in a tunnel.

"Charlie! Charlie!" the voice said, barely audible. And then there was a pain to his face as the figure slapped him across the face. His hearing regained its normality. His eyes came into focus. "Charlie!"

"You..." he whispered. Maryjane stood before him with her shoes in her hands. He stood and wrapped his arms around her tightly. He had begun crying again.

"What is wrong?" she asked, slightly confused.

"I thought you had fallen over. I saw your shoe and your leg protruding from the side of the mountain," he said, not letting go of her. "I thought you were gone forever..." he trailed off.

"Why did you think I was gone forever?"

"You didn't move when I called your name. I came looking for you, thinking something or someone had gotten to you."

She pulled away from him. "So, this has nothing to do with you treating me the way you just did?"

He just looked at her, baffled that she was still angry over their argument. "I thought you were dead, and you're still hung up on the argument?" he said in disbelief. His eyes went stern, "Why did you veer off the path anyway? It's dangerous to separate yourself from everyone."

"Oh, now you want to be the fearless protector. I can't do this, Charlie!" she said, stepping back from him. "Nothing has changed. You haven't changed. You're the same dominating person you were at thirteen. You can't make up your mind whether to love me, be mad at me, or hate me! I can't do it! I never know when you're going to blow up over something I have said or done. My heart can't do this anymore!" She was crying and took another step back. "You don't know what it's like for me back home, what I go through from day to day. I would stay with you because it's so miserable there, but I have to help my mom!" she pleaded with his eyes.

She could see that he still didn't understand her reasoning behind not staying forever. She took a deep breath and closed her eyes tightly. "When the Red Sorceress is defeated, and Oz has returned to normal...I'm leaving, and not returning," she said, looking away from him.

His eyes widened in disbelief. "You can't be serious," he breathed, trying to hold back the heartache washing over his body.

"I am. Charlie, the only time you seem to love me is when I'm in danger. When I'm not, we're fighting over petty things that shouldn't get in the way of our relationship. You used to be the one who wanted me to go home so I would be safe. When I tell you I can't stay with you, you get mad. I'm lost around you. I never know what to say or what not to say. My mom needs me, and you were selfish with your reaction to my staying. My mom is dying! She's sick, and I can't save her! No one has the power to save her!" she cried.

He finally understood everything. The whole reason for her mother being here. Everything. He walked over to her and lifted her face to his, "Whether you return or not…I'll be right here waiting for you. No one will ever take your place in my heart. I love you and always will."

He leaned in and kissed her mouth. He lingered for a moment and then stepped back hurriedly. "Let's catch up to the group," he said, turning around quickly so she wouldn't see the tears flowing from his eyes. He brushed them away and trudged back down the mountain with her on his heels.He now understood the wave of emotions she had always felt when it came to her wanting him. He had always chosen his mother over her, just to save her reputation in the community. She was choosing her mother over him to help her live her last days out with someone who cared for her. He wasn't going to stand in the way of her doing something that would have been the same choice he would have made, or, for that matter, still would make.

Chapter Eleven

THEY WALKED in silence down the mountain. Both of them were too bruised to argue or talk anymore. They loved each other, but it seemed as if fate wanted to keep them apart. Instead of fighting fate, they were embracing it. They would forever love each other, but not be with one another. It shattered them both in two.

Charlie walked a couple of paces ahead of Maryjane. She wished she knew what was going on in his head. Did he want her decision? Did he want to fight her decision? Why didn't he protest her leaving? Everything inside her wished he had fought back for them to be together, to plead with her to stay here instead of returning with her mom, a reason to stay with him forever, but he hadn't protested. He only said he'd be waiting for her return.

He wanted to protest everything she told him, but he respected her wish. He's lived his whole life trying to control her life, and for once, he's going to let her live it the way she wanted. It was too selfish for him to still ask her to stay after he knew her mom was dying. He would do the same for his mother. He's done worse to her for the sake of his mother.

They made it to the bottom of the mountain and turned the curve to continue on the path back to the group when they heard a scream. It froze them in their spots. "Who was that?" Charlie asked.

Maryjane's eyes widened, "My mom!" she yelled, running back to the group now.

Charlie was hot on her trail. When they reached the edge of the path where the group had been, they caught the last glimpse of a band of men pulling Dorothy onto a winged creature. Maryjane remembered the creature from her nightmare. It looked over at her and squalled in anger. Maryjane was frozen to the core from fear.

Ashe sneered at Charlie, "Looks like your number two now, Charlie. I hope you don't mind, but I'm borrowing your dear mother-in-law for the evening. We're going to have so much fun," he said smiling a hideous grin at Dorothy and rubbing her face with his hand that clutched the knife Charlie had thrown at him. He was the first to fly off while the rest of the crew Ashe had assembled ambushed the five left behind.

"Mama!" Maryjane yelled as she tried to push her way through the men. Charlie grabbed her and pulled her back. "Let me go!" she howled at him. "I've got to go after him. I've got to save her! It's my mom!"

"I know. We will get her back, I promise!" he said, pulling her back to him and away from the hands of the rest of the henchmen. The men who had been his brothers in arms for the past three years surrounded them, ready to make a kill.

Scarecrow had been disassembled and tossed about. Nick was strung up from a tree. Lion was under a hunter's net, weighted down around his feet. The crew circled Charlie and Maryjane. All of the men were saying snide comments to Charlie.

"Traitor."

"Deserter."

"No wonder he left. Look at that catch!"

"Hey, Charlie, feel like sharing?"

Maryjane and Charlie were back-to-back. "Whatever happens, you stay behind me. If something happens to me, I want you to run as fast as you can," he said while the men circled around them, getting closer with each step.

Maryjane jumped in front of him, "No, whatever I do, you stay behind ME," she said, planting her feet. The men laughed. "Back up, Charlie. Things are going to get a bit out of hand."

They all drew a weapon. Maryjane drew her sword. It began to glow along with her hands that wrapped around the end of it. Charlie ran to the others caught in the snares of the henchmen to help free them. He looked over to Maryjane as she began to battle the others.

The first one lunged at her with a club. She swung her sword, blocking it. The energy that erupted from the sword left the man dazed. She kicked him in the stomach and did a spin around, slicing through his midsection. Another was right behind her, swinging a sword; she turned and blocked it. The force from her sword knocked the sword from his hands, and she caught it midair. She plunged it deep into his stomach. The next one came at her from the side with a whip. The whip caught the end of her blade and tore it from her hands. He cracked it again, and it wrapped around her arm.Her entire arm began to glow. She grabbed the end of the whip, gave it a hard yank, and he lost his footing. She yanked it hard once more, turning when she did, bringing the whip over her shoulder, and he went flying in the same direction, landing ten feet away. He stood up, ready to charge. She drew her athame from her boot and flung it across the way. It struck him square in the chest. Another man came at her with a club from behind her that she wasn't prepared for. She blocked the blow with her arm, and it sent her falling to the ground. Her arm felt shattered. He came at her again. She was within reach of her sword. She picked it up and plunged it deep into the henchman just as he lifted the club to bring it down on her again. The club fell to the ground, and she stood, yanking the sword from his torso as he toppled back.

It seemed like twenty more of them were coming out of the woods. "Charlie!" she yelled for help as she stood defenseless with her shattered arm.

Charlie was busy helping Nick, Lion, and Scarecrow. They were encircling her once more. She could hear Charlie yell out her name as he realized what was happening. She couldn't take it any longer. She lifted her fist to the sky, and a bright gold energy surrounded her hand. She brought her fist down to the ground in a downward thrust and gave it a hard pound. The earth shook, a blast ricocheted from her fist, impacting the earth, blowing the group surrounding her away into trees, rocks, and other landmarks. The land began to crack, and all in the path of it fell into the trench spreading through the forest. The men who had poured in from nowhere through the trees stood to one side of the trench, while Maryjane stood with the others in her group on the opposite side.

"This isn't over, little girl," the one man said. "We will be waiting everywhere for you. You can't win. There are too many of us," he said, backing up.

"I'm not the one running away," she said in a thick, malicious tone as the men retreated.

Once they were all gone, she collapsed to the ground holding her arm. The blow of the club crushed it. Charlie was at her side. "Let me look at it," he said, trying to take her arm from her other hand.

She jerked away. "It's broken. There's nothing you can do," she said heatedly. She was still upset they had taken her mother and were possibly doing ungodly things to her.

"Just give me your dang arm!" he yelled at her, annoyed, trying to pick her arm up once more.

"Just leave me alone, Charlie!" she yelled at him, jerking away from his touch.

"Why are you mad at me for?" he countered.

"Because if it weren't for you, my mother would still be here, and not captured by that witch!" Maryjane roared at him. "I don't want or need your help anymore, Charlie! Just leave!" she yelled again.

A breeze blew, and a faint singing could be heard in the wind. The wind picked up speed and circled around Maryjane and Charlie. "Fine," he said, standing up. He looked down at her, "I should've just stayed with Scarlet's troop and Emma," he growled, picking up his bow and arrow.

She glared up at him, "You two are made for each other."

"I don't know what you want from me! I can't do anything right in your eyes! You want me to love you, you don't want me to love you. You want to be with me, you don't want to be with me. You want me to stay, you want me to go. It's all a game to you! I will leave! Don't expect me to save you anymore. Don't expect me to protect you anymore. You're on your own from now on. I'm done! Scarlet, I'm coming home to you, my Siress! Emma, my love, I'm tired of child's play. I want a real woman!" he yelled, stalking off.

The wind exploded from the area. Maryjane sat watching him walk away. At that very moment, her love for Charlie melted away and turned to a dark hatred...and so did his.

Not long after he had stalked off, Glinda appeared. "What happened?" she asked, concerned. "Where's Charlie?" she asked, looking around.

Maryjane did a half laugh, "Charlie. Charlie! Charlie is the only one you care about!" she screamed at Glinda.

Glinda took a step back. "What's wrong, child? What's happened in my absence? The blood pact was nearly broken, and all of a sudden, it blew up and became untouchable," she said, walking slightly to her left, closer to the remaining group.

Maryjane scowled at Glinda, "The only person you notice gone is your precious son, the only person you give a crap about right now."

Glinda glanced at Nick, and he looked to the ground. She looked at Scarecrow, and he looked away as well. Lion stared back at her without flinching away as the others had.

"Well, are you going to answer her question?" he asked, licking his paw and cleaning his face.

Glinda was uneasy. She looked between the four of them, and it dawned on her. "Where's Dorothy? Where's your mother at?" She looked at them all, waiting for them to answer.

"Ding-ding. Ding-ding. We have a winner!" Maryjane yelled sarcastically. She stood up and winced as her arm was jostled. "Can I have the Red Sorceress category, please?"

"She was taken by the Red Sorceress? When?" Glinda asked.

Maryjane glared at her hard. "Do you honestly think she came herself to take her? Her henchmen came, and we battled for a good bit about twenty minutes ago. Come to think of it, Charlie didn't do anything to help fight them off either. He wouldn't let me go after them to rescue her. I faced roughly thirty men alone," she said, resting on the fallen tree, the other three were leaned up against.

"What happened that reversed the blood pact removal?" Glinda asked, looking Maryjane in the eyes.

"What's wrong, Glinda? Are you afraid the Red Sorceress is going to use him against you again? I don't think you have to worry about that anymore. You're no longer his target," Maryjane hissed.

"What did you say to him?!" Glinda demanded.

"I told him to leave me alone, that all he had done was cause my mother to be captured by that red-headed witch," she said, pausing with a look of defeat on her face.

"And?" Glinda urged on.

"I said Emma and he were meant for each other. He stalked off back to Emerald City," Maryjane said, looking to the ground, so no one could see the tears forming.

"I'm sure there was more magic behind the scenes than this, but you have no idea what you have done," Glinda said, stepping back away from the group. "I can't help you anymore. You've drawn a clear line as to who you want or need help from. Now, I have to undo what you did once again," Glinda said, turning away.

Just before she floated away, Maryjane called to her, "And you say you're a good witch. You only have one priority, and it's a selfish priority. I have been fighting selflessly for two days to destroy the person you asked me to. Your son nearly killed me with the arrows he shot at me. Did you help? No! I had to help myself just like I had to help these three while you hid away in your castle. The Great and Powerful Glinda has no magic of her own to wield against evil, so what does she do? She trains a teenager to do her dirty work. I have been the one saving Oz while everyone just stood around. And when my mother is taken, everyone turns on me? You know what? Defeat the Red Sorceress yourself. I'm taking my mother, and I'm leaving Oz in the shambles it's in. You can clean up the mess. I'm done. You act as though you are the highest power that I report to, and you're not! I report to no one! So, go ahead and float away like you always do. I don't care anymore. I hope your throne is as comfortable to you as Scarlet's is to her because you are no different than she is." Anger and hatred flashed over Maryjane's face. Glinda stood with her back turned to them for a brief moment and then floated away. She turned and faced the three left in the group. They all looked at her in awe.

"Are you with me, or do you wish to return to your lives before you met me?" she asked, looking the three all in the eye.

The three exchanged glances, and Scarecrow spoke, "Do you honestly think this is the first rescue mission to save Dorothy from a tyrannical, power-driven witch?" The three of them took and bowed before her. "You have our allegiance, young one. We will follow you to the ends of the world."

They all stood back up straight, and Nick spoke next, "You remind me so much of your mother, but there is one difference between the two of you."

"What is that?" Maryjane snorted.

"You are much fiercer than she. Your heart is much larger, and no matter what, in the end, you are the selfless love that Oz has needed to reign as Queen. I hope you do not leave because I would serve you as a loyal subject," he said, bowing once more.

"Well, it's a long walk, maybe you three can change my mind," she suggested with a smile. "You three are good friends. I can see why my mother loved you all so much, more than me even," she said, looking off into the woods, planning a trail.

"That is where you are wrong. Your mother loves you more than life itself," Nick said, laying his hand on her shoulder. "And I can see why." She teared up, turned around, gave him a huge hug, and cried. The other two walked over, and they huddled together, hugging each other.

"Don't cry now. You'll rust me," Nick laughed, choking back tears.

Maryjane pulled back from them, "Let's go save my mom," she said, and the three of them started off through the woods heading toward Emerald City's red glow.

Chapter Twelve

"Let me go!" Dorothy yelled as she was dragged through the rooms of Emerald City.

The more she struggled, the tighter Ashe's grip became on her arm. She struggled to rip her arm from his grip again, and he spun around and smacked her across the face, bloodying her lip. They reached the throne room, and he threw her to the floor in front of the Red Sorceress. Dorothy jumped up in a defensive manner and backed away. The Red Sorceress and Emma looked at her and smiled.

"Ma' Lady," Ashe said, kneeling before Scarlet, "the task is completed. Here is the bounty you sought," he said, motioning to Dorothy.

Scarlet stood from her throne and walked to Dorothy. She picked up a tissue and offered it to her to wipe her mouth. She then turned to Ashe and smiled, "Excellent work," she said, smiling at him.

He looked up, smiling back, and she backhanded him, knocking him entirely to the floor. "I did not say for you to lay a single finger on her," she hissed at him as she walked back to her throne.

He wiped his bloodied nose and began to protest, "She was trying to slip away from me."

Scarlet stopped in her tracks and turned to face him with a demented look on her face. Her eyes caught fire, and so did his entire body. He screamed as he was engulfed in flames. You could smell the stench of searing skin. She closed her hand, and the fire ceased. He still screamed from the pain the flames had caused. He realized he was no longer engulfed in flames, and his body was untouched by the fire. Emma chuckled at his inferior state of mind.

He immediately bowed in obedience. "I'm sorry, my Queen, for my insolence."

"Get out of my sight," she sneered, and he quickly ran from the room in shame and fear. She turned to Dorothy and said, "I apologize for the behavior of my subjects. I can assure you it will not happen again. You will go unscathed while in my fortress. You have my word," she said, smiling at her.

"What do you want with me?" Dorothy hissed, backing up.

She had no weapons and no chance of escape from the Red Sorceress's powers. Dorothy looked around the room that she had made her throne room. It was rearranged, but she could still see the remnants of what used to be the Emerald City. She knew her way around the city as if it were yesterday she was there. If she could distract her long enough, she could make a break for the gates.

"You? Nothing. You're just a pawn in my game," Scarlet laughed. "You see, I devised the perfect plan, and it worked. I kidnap you, and Maryjane would blame Charlie. The two had a nasty little falling out, as my sources tell me," she said, waltzing to her throne. Emma snickered as she sat to the right of the throne. Scarlet sat down and smiled at Dorothy. "They tell me he's on his way back to me to crawl back into my good graces and has abandoned your daughter." She picked up her goblet and took a sip. "Excuse me, where are my manners? Would you like something to drink? Eat?"

Dorothy scowled at her.

"Fine. Suit yourself. I offered," Scarlet smirked. "I understand that you are sick and not even Glinda can heal you."

"Yes, but how do you know? How do you even know she is my daughter? The only people who know are Glinda and my friends," Dorothy asked, narrowing her eyes at her.

"Dorothy, Dorothy, you still don't get the picture, do you? You still don't recognize me," Scarlet smiled.

"Who are you?" Dorothy questioned her.

"In due time, my dear, in due time you will learn. For now, I'm waiting on Prince Charming to show up at my palace so we can get business finished, starting with the destruction of that little brat of yours. My duo of evil has taken down so many innocent people together. They really are a match made for each other," she said, winking over at Emma. Emma sat with her back straight in her chair to show her superiority to Dorothy. Dorothy didn't budge in her expression or stance.

"But, in the meantime, I have a proposition for you. Like I said, I understand that you are sick and cannot be healed by Glinda. She doesn't have the power to heal you," she said, taking another drink from her goblet. "But I do. See, what dainty little Glinda doesn't realize is that in order to heal someone, you have to know how to throw a curse as well. We both know that is my specialty." She grinned from ear to ear. "I can have you fixed in a few minutes, if you do what I ask for in return."

"You know he will never hurt her, and you can't make him," Dorothy said, ignoring her attempt to lure her in.

"Oh, you see that's where you are wrong. Their little fight strengthened the blood pact Emma and he share. Not to mention my little minion has learned well from me, and not saying she did or didn't, but may have nudged the two apart with a spell. The blood pact is now untouchable. It cannot be removed unless someone offers themselves up to me and is a more suitable candidate for my reign of evil. He will do what I want when I want him to," Scarlet snickered.

"He loves her too much to bow to your will. You will see," Dorothy said flatly.

Scarlet laughed maniacally, "Aw, but you see, that's the thing. The two lovebirds called it off already. He's making his way back to his Siress and the love of his life right as we speak. Maryjane hates him because you were captured. He hates her because she refused his love. Add in a dab of black nightshade and pepper oil, and the two started fighting like cats and dogs. My plan worked." Scarlet laughed. "Oh, Emma, doll, you better get back to work on that love spell of yours to ensure Charlie wants to be betrothed to you. Run along," Scarlet said, motioning walking with her two fingers.

"Yes, Siress. I will gladly *love* to finish it," Emma smirked, walking from the room. "Oh, and don't worry, mother dearie, I won't hurt your daughter...too much." She cackled and left the room.

"All plans can be spoiled," Dorothy said, watching the girl who looked like she could be her daughter's twin walk up the staircase. She looked to Scarlet and stared her down, "Especially yours, Gulhimer."

"Ah, so we're on the same page now," Scarlet said grinning. "Now about that proposition…"

Chapter Thirteen

CHARLIE MADE HIS way hastily back to Emerald City. He was still enraged from their argument and the way Maryjane had treated him. After they spent time together talking about their futures with each other, she tells him she won't stay. After he nearly loses his mind thinking she was dead, she blames him for his mother's capture. He had stopped walking and was now pacing back and forth on the brick road.

He didn't know how he felt anymore. He felt anger boiling beneath his skin when he thought of her. She was a snot-nosed little brat. She was immature, and he realized he was way out of her league anyway. Emma was more of a woman than what she was.

He couldn't feel his love for her anymore. He remembered her; his memories were untouched, but the love that had bubbled to the surface had sunk back into darkness. Emma had filled his heart and his thoughts. He was impatiently traveling back to Emerald City so that he could profess his love to her. An overwhelming feeling of love and a marriage proposal clouded his mind as he walked the road alone. He heard a noise trailing on the road behind him and hid in the bushes. Footsteps were maybe fifty feet out, and the sound of voices talking. He peered out of the wood line as the group he had left in the woods caught up with him in record time.

Here's my chance, he thought, raising his bow and

arrow. *I can take all of them out without them even knowing where the arrows are coming from, starting with her,* he thought, drawing back the arrow and directing it at Maryjane. He waited until they got closer.

"So, I know you really don't want to talk about Charlie right now," Nick started, "but take some advice from the love doctor, you two shouldn't break up over something small and stupid. He wasn't the cause of your mother being captured. He didn't even know it was going to happen."

He's defending me? Charlie was baffled by the strangers rooting for him and taking his side in the situation.

"I know it's not his fault for her being captured, but if I hadn't been frolicking in the woods with him, I would've been there to protect her," Maryjane replied.

No, if you hadn't taken off on your own and scared the heck out of everybody, making us believe something happened to you, THEN she wouldn't have been captured, Charlie smirked to himself. His bow was still drawn and pointed toward the group.

"Yes, but you two needed the time together," Scarecrow said, "and so did all of us."

"I understand what your mind and heart are going through," Lion stated.

"Oh, you do?" Maryjane chuckled.

"Yes, you need a little courage," Lion said, chuckling back.

"Courage to do what?" Maryjane asked

"Courage to give yourself completely to him. I know why you haven't. He's broken your heart once before, hasn't he?" Lion asked, looking at Maryjane, already knowing the answer.

Maryjane was silent. *Oh, no answer to him?* Charlie snickered in his head.

"When we were younger, Charlie and I went everywhere together and did everything together. He wouldn't let me out of his sight. He never once told me he loved me. He would simply say, 'I care about you.' Where I come from, that's just a nice way for a boy to tell you he's not interested in you. He would look at me in the dreamiest way, as if he had never seen anyone like me, as if I were beautiful or something. None of the boys back home ever gave me a second look. Actually, no one back home ever paid me attention unless they were taunting me. I was one of the least liked in school. Even though I was born and raised there, I was treated like an outsider.

"You can imagine how easy it was for me to fall for him. I went off by myself one day. There was word in Munchkin Land of some new beast that lived on the outskirts in a field. I wanted to see what kind of beast it was. I was nearly there by myself when he came running up behind me. He was always protective, always telling me what I should and shouldn't do. He told me then we would never be together. It broke my heart. I went home that day and was unable to return because either Scarlet or Emma was throwing up a wall that blocked my reentry to Oz.

"When I return five years later, he is in league with the same monster that he tried to protect me from. He has a girl by his side that he treats with the same respect he used to treat me. I could tell they were together just by how she wrapped her arms around his waist. Also, for that matter, she looked nearly identical to me. I'm still wondering what that is all about.He shoots me with arrows and vows to destroy me. He later professes his love to me that we can be together forever and asks me to stay here. He didn't understand how much had changed in the past five years. I cannot leave my mother. She is too ill to take care of herself. I tell him this, and it makes him mad. He was mad because I wanted to help my mother through her dying days instead of abandoning her! Then, she is captured by the same men he used to walk these roads with, enslaving people for Scarlet. That is my answer to your question," Maryjane said, walking straight ahead, never removing her eyes from the road.

Charlie put his bow down. *How could boys not find her attractive? She is gorgeous! I never thought of her being self-conscious about herself. I thought she knew she was beautiful and flaunted it. Why wouldn't anyone like her or even want to be her friend?* He thought to himself. *That makes the people in Oz her only friends...*

"You cannot blame yourself or him for the capture of your mother. We lost her once too in this forsaken forest," Scarecrow said, grabbing her hand to slow her pace.

"It's not so much as blame that I place on him," she said, flinching away from his hand. "I put my trust in him that while he was with us, we would all be safe. That he would protect us all, not just me."

The group was silent as they continued down the road. Charlie followed them along the wood line, making sure not to make any sound. He wanted to hear her speak more. He wanted to know why she was as crazy as she was to him. They came to a fork in the road. The group looked down both paths.

"Which way is Emerald City?" Maryjane asked the group.

"Umm, I'm not sure," Nick replied, still looking up and down both paths. "I don't remember this as part of the road."

Charlie came up behind them, still in the wood line. *That's funny, neither do I,* he thought to himself as he gazed upon the same decision as the others were. A bright white light descended from the sky in front of the group. A woman dressed in a white and blue robe stood before them. Well, she could hardly be called a woman. She didn't look any older than fourteen or fifteen. She smiled at the group.

Maryjane was too tired to go into defensive mode, so she simply asked, "Who are you?"

"I am Ozma. I was once the princess and ruler here in the Land of Oz. Now, I am one of the Elders who oversee the laws of Oz. You must be Maryjane," she replied, smiling at her.

"How do you know I am Maryjane?" Maryjane asked sarcastically, rolling her eyes.

"You wear the tiara specially crafted just for you. Now tell me, young one, where is Charlie?" she asked.

"Oh, not you too. I guess you're a Charlie fan as well and only worried about his safety," Maryjane blurted out.

Really? Charlie thought.

"Charlie and you have a grander purpose than this quarrel between the two of you," Ozma said to Maryjane.

"Yea, yea, yea, I know. We're supposed to rule Oz together," Maryjane said sarcastically.

"It's much more than that as well. It goes beyond your mother, his mother, and the Red Sorceress," Ozma said, still smiling.

"Then what is this purpose? If it's not about love, not about the people we love, not about saving Oz from the Red Sorceress, then what is it?" Maryjane asked impatiently.

"With the joining of the two separate worlds in love, the veil between your world and our world disappears. This is only foreseeable if you stay and become our Queen of Oz. If you do not stay to be our Queen, when you leave, you will never be able to return again," Ozma said with her smile fading.

Maryjane didn't know what to say. She couldn't just leave her mom, but she loved Oz as much as she did her mother. This was an unfair course of action they were asking her to take.

"The decision doesn't have to be made right now. It

would've been unfair to you not to let you in on the whole situation, and you leave without being able to return without a clue as to why. Charlie and you were hand-chosen by us to be blessed. He is the last witch of his family bloodline and the last one to remain in Oz once his mother is gone. The last of his kind. We blessed you at birth because your mother did so much for Oz while it was under my rule; we wanted to return the favor. We gave you your powers because we knew you had the same will and fight that your mother did. You were born the same year as Charlie. It was perfect. We just didn't expect your mother to become as gravely ill as she has. We are sorry about that," Ozma said, bowing her head to Maryjane. "Glinda has brought to our attention another young sorceress who has been apprenticed under the Red Sorceress."

"Who is she?" Maryjane asked, hoping for an answer.

"We know who she is, but I have been informed not to tell you," Ozma replied.

"Why not?" Maryjane asked, annoyed.

"The others feel it would be better heard from your mother, and that's all I can share," Ozma offered.

Maryjane stood there taking all of the information in. What does my mother have to do with Emma? Even with that bit of information floating around, it was still overpowered by the much larger picture at hand. She was going to have to choose between her mother and Charlie.

"How long after I become queen will the veil disappear between our two worlds?" she asked Ozma.

"That I cannot answer. We are hoping immediately, if not, we have much work to do to open the gateway," Ozma replied.

"So, if they don't open immediately, my mother will be all on her own to battle her sickness alone." Maryjane sneered.

"If you stay, we will do everything in our power to

help your mother and her illness," Ozma offered to Maryjane.

Maryjane stood there thinking everything over.

"We're trying to look at the positive side and believe it will open at the consummation of power. Nothing is ever easy in life, Maryjane. Everyone always has heartbreaking decisions to make. Look at Charlie, he gave up his free will because he thought it was saving you, but you can change all of that!" Ozma said, walking toward Maryjane and placing her hands on her shoulders.

"I don't know what to choose!" Maryjane exclaimed. "I'm no sorceress, there is no guarantee that I can even defeat Scarlet!"

Ozma lifted her hands above her head. Another white light enveloped her in a flash and was gone. Within her hands, she held a wooden staff.

"This staff is crafted from a great source of power. It holds not just one tree within its creation, but a plethora of powerful trees. It is adorned with a multitude of power crystals for protection and defensive magic. Use it wisely, my child," she said, handing her the staff.

Maryjane looked at the staff, turning it over in her hand and gazing at the beautiful structure. "How does this make me more powerful?" Maryjane asked.

"The staff does not hold the power. The only thing that holds power is you. Each of the items you received from Glinda was just items to amplify your power or to centralize it, such as your wand. The staff is just a symbol of your declared status as a sorceress, just as your wand symbolized you as a witch. Your powers are mounting. You are no longer a simple witch, you are a sorceress, and your power has surpassed any that we have seen before," Ozma said, bowing. As she bowed, Maryjane was encircled with dancing lights. Her torn, dirty, white dress was replaced with a pink flowing gown. It was the same style as the one she had on before, but more dazzling.

"This decision…it's one that I cannot make in a day," Maryjane said, looking back up to Ozma.

"It's all up to you to decide your fate." And just as fast as she had come, she was gone.

The weight of the world on her shoulders, Charlie thought, bowing his head in shame for his actions. *They cannot ask this of her. It's unfair. It was unjust for me even to ask. I'm sure when she said she was never returning when she left, she didn't mean it. Now, it's set in stone.*

Once Ozma had left, the road returned to normal. Maryjane didn't know what to do. Lion, Nick, and Scarecrow just stared at her. She was afraid to give herself to Charlie completely. All of this scared her, the unison of both worlds, her powers growing, defeating the Red Sorceress, and marrying Charlie. It was all too much for her to handle and take in.

Charlie sat contemplating what to do. His festering, ill feelings toward her were subsiding. The spell Emma had cast was wearing off faster than she had anticipated. His head was clearing, and he had gained his wits back. No matter what happened, no matter what Maryjane chose to do, no matter who tried to step in between the two of them and their love, he would never stop loving her. If she decided to go back to her world, he would ask the Elders to send him with her as well. It seemed right. After all of the sacrifices she had made for Oz, it was time for Oz to sacrifice something for her. If that meant giving up his right to the throne, giving up his powers, giving up his way of living, he was ready to make that sacrifice for her.

A deafening clap of thunder came from the center of Emerald City as Emma realized her spells had backfired and were no longer working. Charlie shook off the remaining feeling of hatred for Maryjane and the love he had begun developing for Emma. He looked to Emerald City as a storm began to swirl around the tower, alongside the thunder and lightning. Charlie was getting ready to emerge from the wood line and show himself to her. He was going to show her he was with her when they all heard a noise up the road.

"There she is! Grab her!" It was Ashe giving the command. The group was immediately swarmed by a troop of the Red Sorceress' men.

Maryjane was still in an ill mood. "Leave us be or suffer the same fate as the others did," she hissed at the men. She hadn't seen the one sneak up behind her. He grabbed her hands, throwing her staff to the side of the road, and tied them together, facing each other so she couldn't use her powers against them. She screamed in pain from her broken arm. Ashe snickered, walking up to her.

"Look at the catch Charlie got for himself. Too bad he abandoned you for our Siress," Ashe said, pulling her close to him. He sniffed her hair. "Mm, you smell delightful." He pulled her close, ran his hand through her hair, and down her face. "This will be fun," he said, smiling an evil grin. "Tie the rest of them up!" he ordered the troops. "I have business for Emma with this one."

He grabbed her arm and towed her into the woods, fighting. The others watched in silence. He got past the tree line and out of eyesight of the others. He smacked her across the face, and she went careening to the ground. She landed on her arm and let out another yelp of pain. He walked over to her and kicked her in the ribs. She felt at least two of them break as the pain took her breath. He bent down and weaseled her sword away from her.

"My Siress wants you alive. She will get you alive even though you may have a few broken bones. It will please Emma to see you broken into bits," he said, lifting her face to his by the hair of her head. He then planted his lips on hers. His lips were dry and cracked. "Mm, you taste as good as you smell. This will be most satisfying. It's been a long time since I have had anyone," he said, removing his satchel of weapons from around his neck.

It dawned on her what he meant. "Don't touch me! Do you realize what will happen to you? Charlie will kill you!" she screamed at him.

He laughed in her face. "Charlie doesn't care about you anymore. He's on his way back to Queen Emma. She is so infatuated with him. She doesn't pay any of us attention, just him. So, if I can't be with her, I'll take the next best thing in line," he said, forcing his lips on hers again.

"Stop!" she said, kicking him in the stomach.

He picked his foot up and came down hard on her leg, shattering her shin. She howled in pain.

"I love a woman with some fight in her," he sneered, climbing on top of her. With her good leg, she kneed him in the groin, and he fell over, grabbing himself.

"You witch!" he yelled as she tried to squirm away. She rolled to her stomach, and the pain was excruciating. She pushed through it using her one good leg to move her body. She was just a few feet away when he grabbed her by the hair and yanked her back.

"You will pay for that one!" he hissed. He climbed on top once more and placed his hand around her throat, cutting off her oxygen. She was utterly defenseless. She closed her eyes and waited for it all to be over. She heard a whirring noise in the air. Ashe screamed out in pain as an arrow hit his shoulder. He looked over his shoulder to see who his challenger was.

"Charlie!" he growled and stood up.

She sucked in a breath coughing, struggling for air. Charlie was standing there with another arrow trained on Ashe's chest.

"Oh, do you plan on fighting an unarmed man?" Ashe asked Charlie as the two walked in a circle around each other.

"You are not a man. You are far from it," Charlie

said, tightening his bowstring. He hadn't realized that Ashe had picked up a rock from the ground when he stood.

"Aw, now is that how your mother taught you to treat your friends?" Ashe asked mockingly. Ashe saw his chance and thrust his hand out against Charlie's head, catching him square in the jaw. Charlie went down, and the arrow flew, missing Ashe by inches.

"Charlie!" Maryjane screamed, trying to worm herself over to him. He didn't move. *No!*

Ashe was already on his way back over to her. "Now, where were we?" he said, grabbing her by the jowls.

She spat in his face. He backhanded her once more, sending her careening to the ground in pain. She tried to get away again, moving on her stomach, and he pulled her back by her feet.

"Now this looks even more fun," he said. He placed a rope around her neck and pulled it tight.

"Don't fight, or it will get tighter." He showed her his point by tightening it enough so she could barely breathe.

She was tired, in severe pain, and suffocating from lack of oxygen. She was giving up. She quit struggling against him and just closed her eyes, hoping it would all be over soon. She lost consciousness.

"You always were an asshole, Ashe," Charlie said, sneaking up behind Ashe and swinging Maryjane's sword. Ashe had enough time to look at Charlie as the sword took his head off. Charlie pulled the headless body off of Maryjane and hurriedly untied the rope around her neck. She wasn't breathing.

"No, no, no. You're not doing this to me. I already thought you had died once today. You're not going to die. I won't let it happen," he said, bending down and blowing air in her mouth into her lungs.

He gave two puffs and started to do chest compressions. He gave another two puffs, and she began coughing. She was gasping for air. He set her upright, and she howled in pain from her ribs. She hadn't even looked to see who it was. She began to struggle and fight. She started kicking. "Get away from me!" she yelled, trying to squirm away.

"Maryjane! It's me. It's ok," he said, pulling her to him.

She started crying, and he swallowed her with his arms. "I thought he killed you with that rock," she cried in between gasps.

He untied her wrists and hands. She screamed in pain again as her arm hit the ground. He grabbed her up and pulled her in closer to him.

"Everything is ok. He can't hurt you anymore. I would've been here sooner, but I was helping the others. I should've been here sooner. I shouldn't have left you alone. Everything always happens when I have left you alone."

She was crying into his chest. He looked her over. Her face was bruised, and her lip was bleeding. Her arm was broken. He assumed her ribs were broken. He looked at the bone protruding from her leg. He pulled her closer and cried with her.

"I should have been there to protect you. My greatest fear has always been this. You would get hurt in my absence. All of those years, I protected you, and I let one silly argument get in my way. I will stand by your side from now on. When it comes down to it, if you choose to go home, I will go with you," he said, caressing her face in his hands as she shut her eyes out of exhaustion.

He bent down and kissed her. He felt a sharp pain in the back of his head, and everything went black.

Chapter Fourteen

SCARLET WAS SITTING on her throne as the fleet of troops carried Charlie into her throne room unconscious. She looked from the troops to Charlie. "What happened?" she growled.

"We were in the middle of capturing the group when he ambushed us. He freed Lion, Nick, and Scarecrow. They took off into one of the fields. He then ran to the woods where Ashe was with the girl…"

Scarlet cut him off mid-sentence, "Why was Ashe in the woods alone with the girl?" she asked him, eyeing him suspiciously.

The henchman was uneasy. "We're not sure. He told us to stay with the other three and wrangle them, that he had unfinished business with the girl."

"Where is Ashe now?" Scarlet asked, standing from her throne and walking to the henchman.

He stood before her, petrified. "Charlie killed him," he replied, shaking in his boots.

"Why did Charlie kill him? What did he do to the girl?" she asked him, getting closer to him.

"We don't know what he did to the girl. Whatever it was, it was bad enough for Charlie to behead him," the henchman replied.

"Well, where is she? Where's the girl? I can ask her what that unfaithful beast did to her," she hissed in his face.

His voice couldn't find balance, "She's dead, Siress," he croaked. "We found Charlie crying over her body. Ashe did a number on her," he said, backing away slightly.

"She's dead?" she asked in disbelief.

"Yes, her face was bruised and puffy, and you could see the trace of a rope tied around her neck. Her arm was broken, and her leg was broken in half with the bone protruding. Whatever he was trying to do to her, she fought him with tooth and nail," the henchman said as he reached the doorway. He was prepared for her to strike him down from the news.

"Put Charlie in Emma's room on her bed. Then, you may all leave," she said in a dream-like voice.

Scarlet stared at him as he turned and left the room. They all shuffled past her, carrying Charlie, and she smiled at them.

There's no way she could be dead. She was powerful. She grinned. The grin turned into a laugh. She stood there laughing menacingly as the henchman carried Charlie from her throne room to the stairs. Once they got to the stairs, they hustled up them and out of sight.

"I win," she said, sitting back on her throne. "I win!" she yelled. "I beat you, Glinda! Your little prodigy has died!" she screamed in joy. "Emma!"

Emma came bounding into the throne room. "Yes, Siress?" she asked as she knelt before her.

"We won. We won! Maryjane is dead, and Charlie is in your room," Scarlet walked around the throne, dancing.

"I don't understand. My spells backfired. What happened?" Emma asked, sitting down in her chair.

"Apparently, Ashe took it upon himself to get rid of the brat alone," Scarlet snickered.

"I didn't tell him to kill her! I told him to teach her a lesson!" Emma exclaimed.

"Ah, I figured the order came from you. Either way,

he did us a favor. There is no power now to dispute our power. You shall rule Oz alongside Charlie as king and queen. Why aren't you excited?"

"I don't know. It just feels anticlimactic," Emma sat slumped in her chair, brooding. "She didn't even get to find out who I truly am."

"Never mind all of that. We skipped a couple of steps. You should be celebrating, not brooding." Scarlet was becoming frustrated with her.

"You're right, Siress," Emma said, smiling. "This does call for celebration. Can you have one of the men bring up some wine and strawberries to my room, so I can make an offering to the Dark Goddess for granting my successful spell?"

"Of course, my young one," Scarlet smiled.

Emma started out of the throne room and remembered that Charlie was placed in her room. She ran to her room and shut the door behind her. She climbed into the bed next to him. He was so handsome when he slept. She unbuttoned his shirt, and he stirred a little.

"My love, are you ready to be with me forever?" she asked, whispering in his ear.

He mumbled something under his breath. She couldn't understand him. She took it as a yes. She kissed his lips. They parted slightly, and she took the invitation.

"Mm, this is what I have wanted for so long. You, me, together at last. A joining of phenomenal power," she said, licking his ear. He was still in and out of consciousness, but he kissed her back, and it delighted her. She blew the candle out, the only source of light in the room.

It was morning when he awoke. He grabbed his head. He had a killer headache. He had dreamt of Maryjane and him back in the woods while unconscious, and it felt so real. He looked around his surroundings and realized he was in a bedroom.

148

Where am I? He looked down at himself and realized he didn't have any clothes on. *What the-?*He looked at where he was lying and realized he was in a bed. His eyes trailed from the blanket wrapped around him to the person lying in bed with him.

Maryjane? All he saw was red hair. He pulled the covers back a little further and nearly fainted. *Emma! No, what happened? How did I get here?* He put his face in his hands. He couldn't undo what had happened while he was out. This would crush Maryjane. *Oh God, Maryjane! Where is she? Did they take her too? Did they-?* He couldn't even finish the thought.

He climbed out of the bed as quietly as he could and began to get dressed. Emma felt the shift in the bed and rolled over. Her eyes popped open, and she watched him as he got dressed.

"Now, where are you going, my love?" she asked all childish.

He panicked; he didn't know what to say. "I'm famished. I'm going to find something to eat," he said, lying.

"Don't be gone too long," she said, smiling at him.

He cringed. He walked from her room and throughout the fortress. He stopped in the dining area. Maryjane's mother sat there looking at him.

"Playing both fields, I see," she said, eyeing him suspiciously.

"It's not what you think. They knocked me out and brought me here," he tried explaining as he looked at her unfazed face.

"Save it. I don't care if you love Emma or not. All I care about is you hurting my daughter," she said with heat behind each word.

"I don't want to hurt her. I will never hurt her, not willingly. I love her," he said, looking at her, searching her face.

"You know, the one thing I hate about castles and fortresses is that everything echoes throughout every room. So, when you're on one side and someone is on the other, they can hear everything that goes on behind closed doors," she said, sipping her drink from her teacup.

No, she heard what happened? She would never believe me if I protested, he thought.

"The noises I heard were unmistakable. But please, do tell your side of the story," she said, placing the cup back on the saucer.

He sank down in a chair. "You wouldn't believe me if I told you," he said, putting his forehead down on the table.

"Try and see," she said.

He told her everything. He explained the fight, his leaving, the ambush, and Ashe. "When I got to her, he was...he was trying to...it angered me so much. I was angry with him and myself. It's my fault. Everything happened once I left. He knocked me out with a rock and went back to her. When I came to, he was back on top of her, holding a rope around her neck. I picked up her sword and cut his head off," he said with tears rolling down his face.

Dorothy sat there with her eyes closed. She looked at him. "She's dead. They said she was when they found you with her," she said, looking down, letting the tears flow.

He looked up at her, "No, she isn't. I resuscitated her right before I was knocked out again. She was alive when they took me," he said, eyeing her.

She looked up to him, "She's alive?" she asked with hope brimming in her eyes.

"Yes, she was," he said, standing up and walking over to her. "She had broken bones, but she was alive. She fought Ashe with every ounce of will she had," he said, hugging her.

"You must go to her. She needs to be healed, then. She does not know how to heal broken bones. She barely healed the arrow puncture on her leg," she said, pushing him away to stare him in the eye. "It's up to you to restore her."

"I don't know if I can. I've never tried healing people before. I'm good with fighting and growing plants, but I've never really tapped into my own power," he said, sitting down.

"You must try! She needs you right now. Scarlet believes her to be dead. It's the perfect opportunity to finish what was started," she pleaded with him.

"I'll see what I can do to get back out of the palace," he said, kissing her hands.

He walked from the dining area and back through the halls. Scarlet was up and dressed, sitting on her throne. Emma sat to her right in an emerald green gown that hugged her body in all the right spots.

"Hello, love, did you find anything good to eat?" Emma asked.

"Yes, Charlie, did you have a nice sleep? Get something good to eat." Scarlet grinned

Her smile was different than before. She actually had a nice smile when she wasn't being evil. Of course, this smile was from where she thought Maryjane was dead when she really wasn't. He could just imagine the temper tantrum she would throw when she found out.

"Yes. Siress, I must go find the other three. I'm sure they still plan to rescue Dorothy," he said, watching her eyes for any type of suspicion.

"That is a marvelous idea! Do you need any of the men to help you?" she asked.

"Or would you like me to come along and help?" Emma offered.

"No, they trust me. If I find them alone, they won't run from me," he said, trying to sound as honest as he could.

"Ok. Leave at once," Scarlet said. He wheeled around and started for the door.

"Charlie?" Emma asked. He stopped and turned around. "Be careful. I wouldn't want to lose my best man," she said, smiling at him.

He shuddered. He took a knee and bowed his head, "Yes, my love." He stood, turned, and walked through the door.

Once he was gone from the room, she motioned for one of the guards to come closer. "Tail him and find out where he's heading. Make sure he does as he said he would. If he doesn't haul them in when he finds them, report back to me. That's an order."

"Untrusting of your future husband, daughter?" Scarlet raised an eyebrow.

"He's betrayed us once, I'm not so sure he wouldn't try to again," she replied, gulping down her drink.

Charlie made it through the doors of Emerald City and headed for the gate. He walked past the guards, and he heard the murmurs under their breath: "Traitor." "Two-faced." He didn't care what anyone thought of him. He had to get back to Maryjane before something more terrifying found her in the woods. *I'm coming, my love, just hang in there.*

Chapter Fifteen

"WHAT ABOUT THE GIRL? Do we take her body to the Red Sorceress?" asked one of the men.

"No, just leave it. I'm not lugging a dead carcass back to them for them just to want us to bring it back," another answered as they hauled Charlie up on their shoulders.

"Well, what about Ashe's body? Do we leave it here too?"

"How many times do I have to tell you? We're not taking any dead bodies back with us. I don't care if it was Oz himself, we're not doing it. It's not in our pay grade." The two men shuffled off with Charlie, leaving Ashe and Maryjane in the exact spot they had found them.

Maryjane had lain as still as possible as they dragged Charlie off. If she moved or breathed, she knew they would hear her and take her as well or do something even worse. She cringed at the thought of Ashe and what he had tried to do before Charlie stopped him. His body lay a few feet from her, but it was his head that lay within view that bothered her. She lay there for hours, not moving. She was afraid they had scouts still watching her to make sure she was dead.

When she knew there was no one else around, she sat up. The pain was intense. *How am I going to get out of these woods? I can't even walk, and I can barely breathe,* she thought, sitting there. She tried to stand with her one good leg and arm. The jostling of her broken limbs sent her back to the ground in pain and strained wheezing, trying to catch a breath. She couldn't go anywhere. She lay back down on the ground and curled into a ball, listening to the sounds of the forest.

Great. I'm stuck here in the woods for any wild animal to come and eat me alive. She heard a noise to her left and snapped her head in that direction. She strained her eyes to see through the woods, but it was too dark to see anything. *See, there it is. There's the animal that has come to eat me.* The footsteps got closer and closer. She lay as still as possible. Charlie taught her the basics of survival in the wild. He taught her not to move, not to make a noise, and if you can't get away, lie on the ground like a baby. If it were a bear, and she played dead, it would go away.

"Maryjane?" a familiar voice called out. "Over here, guys! She's over here!" Lion roared as he ran closer to her. He bent down, nuzzled her with his snout, and cleaned her face with his tongue.

"Boy, am I glad it's you! I thought I was going to be some bear's dinner," Maryjane breathed once she realized it was her friends.

"What happened?" Scarecrow cried as he got closer to her on the ground. She looked like a crumpled doll. "What did that savage do to you?" he asked.

"He was following orders from his dear Emma. I don't want to go into details," she grimaced as she sat up and doubled over in pain.

"What's wrong, Maryjane?" Nick asked, bending down on one knee to examine her.

"He broke a few of my ribs and my leg. With my one arm already shattered, I couldn't get anywhere. I've been stuck down here," she said, sucking in deep breaths.

"Where's Charlie? He was running down here to help you after he freed us from that mob," Lion said, nuzzling her again.

"They knocked him unconscious and carried him off with them. I played dead, so they would leave me be. They bought it," she said, wincing again as another sharp pain took her breath away. They all looked at the body lying a few feet from her and the head right beside her.

"Did you…" Lion started gulping in fear.

"No, Charlie did that. If he hadn't shown up when he did, I don't know where I would be right now," she said, looking up to them.

"Well, we need to get you up and off the ground. Scarecrow, help me stand her up. Be careful with that arm, too," Nick ordered. They hoisted her up, and she let out a howl of pain.

"I can't walk anywhere, and you can't carry me without dislocating my shoulders," she said, dangling in the air between the two.

"Put her on my back. I can carry her," Lion said, and they hoisted her up on his back.

She lifted her good leg over his side, and pain shot through her body. She put it back and sat on his back like an old-fashioned pony ride.

"If you run or gallop, I'll fall off," she told Lion, leaning down to his mane where she lay her head.

"It's ok. I laugh in the face of danger now," Lion joked back, eyeing his surroundings.

"Here's some rope. Do you want us to secure you on his back so that you won't fall off?" Scarecrow asked, walking over with the rope.

She eyed the rope that had been around her throat hours before. "Yes, and leave a handle for me to hold onto," she lay down on Lion's back.

She rested her head on his mane and rolled to her good side. They tied the rope around her waist, around the belly of Lion, carefully around her broken leg, and secured her leg by tying the rope off.

"There, your leg won't slip off and cause any more

pain, neither," Scarecrow said, smiling.

"Thank you all so much," she said, drifting off to sleep.

"She needs to sleep," Nick whispered to Scarecrow. "That poor child has been through so much these past few days. She is a warrior," he said in awe. The three of them walked back up the hill and back onto the road.

"Here's Maryjane's staff," Nick said, bending down and picking up the staff that had been cast aside by the men who grabbed her. He picked it up and tied it to Maryjane's side with what little rope was left hanging.

"We need to camp somewhere," Scarecrow said, looking around.

"I agree," Lion chimed in as he looked around as well, but with more frightened eyes.

"You're such a big wimp!" Nick said, laughing. "There should be some sort of building up ahead for us to hide in. I don't think any patrols are going to come back through. Especially not this late. Besides, they did what the Red Sorceress wanted. They 'think' they've killed Maryjane," Nick said, walking in the direction of the old, run-down shack.

It was just maybe a mile up the road when they arrived at the abandoned building. Nick and Scarecrow checked around the perimeter and then carefully went inside to scout out any danger. They popped their heads out the door, "The coast is clear."

Lion walked into the building with Maryjane still fast asleep on his back. He lay down on one of the beds in the corner. All three of them looked at each other. "So, what now?" Lion asked the other two as he looked back at Maryjane, who was asleep on his back. "The kid can't fight in her condition. She can't even walk."

"I have an idea, but I don't know if it will work," Scarecrow said, walking to the window of the building.

"What's the idea?" Nick asked him to follow him to

the window.

Scarecrow turned around and looked at the other two. "We could summon Glinda to help," Scarecrow replied.

"Are you crazy? If Maryjane were to wake up and see us consorting with Glinda, it will be war," Lion hissed at the two of them. "I don't know about you two, but I'm rather fond of this kid. It's not every day you see a teenager take on a raging beast and live to tell about it," he chuckled to himself, thinking back to the showdown the two of them had. "Besides, she gives good back scratches too," he said, flexing his claws as he remembered his days as a house cat.

"Then what do we do? How do *we* heal her? I don't know about you two in the past couple of years, but gathering magical powers was not one of my gifts from Oz," Scarecrow said sarcastically.

Nick walked over to Lion, "Scarecrow is right. She needs to be healed, and none of us can do it. We have to call Glinda," he said, looking at Maryjane strapped to Lion's back.

Lion nuzzled Maryjane in her sleep. She didn't stir. Lion lay his ears flat back on his head and looked over at Scarecrow and Nick. His eyes had worry written all over them. He straightened up and growled. "Well, if she wakes up, this was you two's hair-brained idea, not mine. I'm keeping this buddy in case a lion comes around fiercer than me," he chuckled again.

"Quit joking about everything. This is a serious situation," Nick scolded.

"Without humor, I'm not fearless. It replaces the fear. I have to have humor," Lion squeaked, laying his head down in shame.

"So, we're all agreed on summoning Glinda," Scarecrow said to the other two, looking each of them in the face.

Nick nodded. Lion let out a low, grumbled roar. "I

take that as a yes," Scarecrow said.

He grabbed a piece of chalk lying near the table and drew a circle on the ground. "Since we don't have special powers, we can't just summon her like Maryjane can. We have to use a summoning circle," Scarecrow said, finishing up the circle. He stepped back and looked at his masterpiece.

Nick walked up beside him, "That is the most horrid circle I have ever seen. A baby sloth could have drawn it better than that."

Lion laughed. Scarecrow huffed and scowled at the two of them, grumbling something under his breath. He walked to the center of the circle, "Glinda, my good witch of the south, we need your assistance. We summon you to this circle of protection."

A flash of light lit the room up. Glinda stood in the center of the floor.

"What do you need?" she asked Scarecrow in an irritated voice.

"Maryjane needs you. We were ambushed on the road by the Red Sorceress's men. Their leader dragged her off into the woods and did…things to her. She has badly broken bones. She can hardly breathe, so I assume her ribs are broken too," he said as everyone heard the wheezing coming from her body as she lay there sleeping.

"Why should I help her?" Glinda asked cynically.

"Because that's what you were trained to do. You were trained to help those in need," Nick said, eyeing her suspiciously.

She laughed, "I was trained to help no one but the people of Oz. She is not a person of Oz."

"A lot has happened in your absence, Glinda. The Elders wouldn't want to hear that after they told her she was going to be Queen, you refused to help her," Lion said, rustling his mane.

"What do I care if she is Queen or not. As much as I

have done for Oz, they repay me with nothing. After the wizard left Oz, did they come to me to rule over the land? No, they left you three hair-brained idiots in charge. Then Ozma came along, and everyone bowed to kiss her perfect, fairy feet. It's all rubbish!" she scowled.

Lion, Nick, and Scarecrow exchanged glances. "Are you ok?" Scarecrow asked. "You don't seem yourself. You seem…off."

"I am no different than how I was years ago. As a matter of fact, I feel liberated," she said with her eyes glinting in the dim light.

"You would help Maryjane if you weren't any different than years ago," Lion growled. "Charlie would want you to help Maryjane."

"Charlie is the Red Sorceress's pet now. He and Emma will be the ones to rule this land, not he and Maryjane. Emma's little spell I speculated over seemed to have enough power to pull through and keep them separated. Now she has a love spell in the works. His feelings on the situation have no bearing. Maryjane made sure of that when she sent him off on his own, and Emma is fortifying it with her love spell," Glinda hissed.

"No, Charlie was the one who saved her from being captured. He was the one who slayed the man who did all of this to her. He was captured afterwards and dragged unconscious back to the Emerald City," Nick said, standing up, holding his axe. He looked at Scarecrow, and Scarecrow seemed to read his mind.

"Well, I cannot help you. She will have to finish rescuing her mother with broken bones. That's if she can make it through the septicemia setting in. I'd say she has around a day to live, if that," Glinda said with her voice full of malice.

"You didn't do it, Glinda. Did you?" Scarecrow asked.

"Do what?" she asked.

"Take Charlie's place with the blood pact? You didn't offer yourself up to her in exchange for Charlie to be free, did you?" Nick asked, walking over toward Lion to shield Maryjane from any type of attack.

Glinda laughed cynically, "Oh, so smart, Scarecrow, with that brain of yours. Without that brain, you wouldn't even understand the circumstances of anything that has happened. I despise the day the wizard gave it to you," she said, zapping him with her finger. He hit the floor.

She looked to Nick, "And you, with your heart of gold. You wouldn't give two thoughts about this girl without that heart! The only reason you care is so Dorothy and you can ride off into the sunset," she hissed, walking over closer to him.

She eyed Lion, then moved her eyes to see behind him, where Maryjane still lay perfectly asleep. "So, are you going to defy me, too?" she asked, walking right up to Lion. Nick stepped in her way, pushed her with his axe, and tackled her to the floor.

"Run, Lion! As fast as your feet can carry you without her toppling from your back!" Nick screamed.

Lion wasted no time. In a single bound, he was out the door and running through the woods on the opposite side of the road. His night vision made it look like daylight outside. The kind of daylight that existed before the Red Sorceress tore the land into shreds. He raced through the trees, dodging and dipping. He ran forever. The daylight Oz had grown accustomed to was beginning to peek above the horizon. He jumped onto a large boulder and hopped from one to another. He made sure he didn't jostle too much to make the child fall from his back. She lay there still out, maybe unconscious, who knew? They hadn't even thought to check that.

He came to one of his caves behind a waterfall and ducked behind the raging falls. This one, no one knew where it existed. It was hidden well behind the raging water that fell into the river below. He climbed the slippery slopes with ease and ducked inside the cave. He ran to the very back and huddled in the corner. He faced the entrance, so the child was hidden behind him.

He lay there and waited. He didn't know what he was waiting for, but he felt it coming, that feeling in the pit of his stomach. Whatever came, he was ready to fight it off. He was willing to die for this child just as the other two were. This is the gift that the wizard gave him. When the wizard gave him courage, it wasn't courage to act like a lion all the time. It was the courage to stand up against benevolence. He fought when necessary. It didn't matter much when it was his own life on the line. The lives of his friends were a different story. He would fight to the death to protect them from harm. He would die for them to live and be free from danger.

His eyes needed no adjustment to the cave, even if it was as dark as the forest in the pitch dark of night in there. His ears were fine-tuned to the noises of nature. He could distinguish little critters from other beasts of the wild. He crouched in a lunge position. He would be ready for whatever stepped through the entrance of the cave and tried to hurt the girl. This was his territory. This was his child.

Meanwhile, back at the abandoned building, Nick lay in a mangled heap on the floor. Scarecrow still hadn't stood back up. Glinda had done a number on the two of them. The powers granted to her with the blood pact fed her ego. She was no longer Glinda the good witch of the South. She was now Glinda the bad Sorceress, something the Elders never cared to explore with her. No one could stop her now, not even that little brat would be able to when she awoke from her coma; that is, if she ever did. She had hours before she would die. She walked from the building and stood outside in the morning light. She looked down at the pink gown she was wearing. She flicked her fingers, and it changed to a black, slinky, leather dress that wrapped around every inch of her body in just the right spots.

"That's better," she said, smiling. She had never felt so alive with all the power that surged through her body. "This is what my dear sisters felt," she said, thinking of her wicked sisters. It was liberating to be bad for once instead of always trying to please the Elders with her actions.

She snapped her fingers, and a small fire started in the building. She turned toward the Emerald City, and instead of floating back in her pink mist, a black mist grew around her. "You should've picked me to be your queen," she sneered, and she disappeared into the mist.

Chapter Sixteen

CHARLIE WATCHED a black mist disappear into the clouds above Emerald City. *What was that?* He went on alert for any other surprises lurking near the path. He saw an old, abandoned building that was engulfed in flames. He ran to the building as he heard someone screaming for help. He busted the door down and found Scarecrow on fire. He quickly put him out and dragged him outside. He ran back in and fished the heap of metal on the floor that he assumed could only have been Nick. He coughed and strained his burning eyes through the smoke to find Lion, but he wasn't in there. He walked over to Scarecrow, lying on the ground, to try to wake him and see if he was okay or if he knew where Lion was.

"Scarecrow. Scarecrow!" he yelled. His eyes opened and looked over at Charlie. "What happened to you two?" Charlie asked breathlessly. The building caved in, and a loud echo of the crash sounded throughout the valley.

"You wouldn't believe me if I told you," he said, standing groggily to his feet. "Oh, no Nick!" he yelled as he walked over to the heap of metal on the ground. He grazed a few pieces of the metal, and they heard a mumble come from the heap of twisted metal.

"I'm alright," Nick barely managed to say, "I just need... put back together," he strained out, grimacing in what seemed like pain.

"You need more than just put back together. It's not like your arm fell off, you're in pieces!" Scarecrow shrieked. He was pacing, mumbling inaudibly under his breath. He was throwing his hands in the air with ideas, and then swatting them away. He looked like a madman. He stopped and looked at Charlie, "You."

"What?" Charlie replied.

"You can use your powers and put him back together. You've done it before," Scarecrow said.

"I don't know how to use my powers, if I have any at all. My mother never sat down to develop them. The only one she developed was Maryjane. I have never done that before," Charlie said, looking at Scarecrow.

"Yes, you have! I just remembered! I knew Maryjane looked familiar after we first met. It didn't dawn on me until right now. You two helped us. We were being attacked by some vicious animal that had moved to the field right outside Munchkin Land. The same vicious animal that was Ashe's winged creature that he swooped Dorothy off on. Charlie, you are a very powerful warlock. Hasn't your mother ever told you that before?" Scarecrow asked him.

"No, she's never spoken of my powers, only of Maryjane's. She was always working hard to expand her powers. She never bothered with mine. I assumed it was because I had none beyond the facet of growing things," he replied, bending down to examine Nick closer.

He thought back to his dream and remembered how he couldn't quite grasp the familiarity of the place where all the skeletal remains were. He still couldn't recollect what had happened there any time before the day they met Scarlet, or even if the dream was interlaced with two different memories.

"Well, I know you can do it," Scarecrow said cheerfully. "Do what Maryjane does, hold your hands out in front of you over top of Nick and will him back

164

together."

Charlie looked over at Scarecrow. He didn't know what to believe. He didn't remember them being in the field that day. He sighed, "Well, here goes nothing, it can't hurt to try it," Charlie said as he placed his hands on top of Nick and closed his eyes. He went through the exercise of channeling his energy through his hands like he does when he grows his plants. He concentrated on Nick reassembling. He sat there for a few moments with his eyes closed.

"Charlie," Scarecrow said. "Charlie!"

His concentration broke and he opened his eyes. Nick stood before him in one solid piece. "It worked," Charlie breathed.

"Like I told ya, you've done it once before," Scarecrow said. "You're the last witch, Charlie. Of course, they gave you powers. It would be senseless for the Elders not to give you any powers of your own to wield to protect this land. Maryjane may be a powerful sorceress, but she needed someone of equal standing at her side to protect the land. She's not supposed to do it on her own. Both of you are to rule Oz as the leaders."

"I can heal Maryjane's broken bones, then," Charlie jumped to his feet and started for the woods.

"Whoa, where are you going?" Nick asked, grabbing him by the shoulder.

"Going to where I left Maryjane. She needs to be healed," he said, tugging loose from Nick. He went to walk for the tree line again when Nick grabbed his arm a little bit harder than the last time.

"She's not there anymore," he said, pulling Charlie back to the group.

"Well, where in the world is she?" he said, looking around at the two of them standing there with stupid looks on their faces. "Speaking of, where's Lion?" He looked at the two and watched as they exchanged glances.

Scarecrow shook his head, "Huh-uh, I ain't tellin' him."

"Tell me what?" Charlie demanded, becoming impatient with the hidden innuendos. "Where's Maryjane?" he hissed, pacing.

"She's safe. She's with Lion," Nick replied.

"Why did you separate the group?" Charlie asked, glaring at the two of them.

Nick sighed, "After you two had your little spat, your mom showed up. Maryjane and she had words and said some things that are hard to take back. Glinda was angry that she couldn't remove the blood pact; she thought there may have been a spell at work, but wasn't sure. Maryjane told her what she thought of the whole situation of her saving Oz, and made Glinda mad before she floated off. Well, while Maryjane was passed out, we summoned your mother to help Maryjane. We told her she needed to be healed…" Nick paused and looked at Scarecrow.

"What?" Charlie asked, getting impatient. "Did she heal her? What happened?"

"Your mother is no longer the good witch of the South. She took your blood pact with the Red Sorceress. She is the one who set Scarecrow and the building on fire and chopped me up. She disappeared right before you walked in the door. She changed her entire attire and turned into a black mist," Nick finished watching Charlie for a reaction.

My mother is in league with the Red Sorceress now? Impossible! He realized what he had done. Scarlet said that until she found someone who was more powerful and willing to take his pact, he was hers forever. His mother knew that was the only way to erase the pact between Scarlet and him. She put the fate of Oz over her own fate. She would die at the hand of the Red Sorceress, but he would not be bound to her any longer. He sat down on the ground.

What can I do now? Everything is messed up.

"Where is Lion at now? Where is Maryjane?" Charlie asked, realizing the imminence of her being found. Panic took over his body when he snapped from his daze and remembered his mother had not healed her.

"We don't know. I tackled Glinda so that Lion could get the two of them out unharmed, and he bounded off into the woods. He has various nesting areas all over Oz and many, many caves. It will take us forever to find him, who knows which territory he went to," Nick replied, looking off to the side of the road where he watched Lion disappear.

"Well, we're wasting time. Let's go," Charlie said, walking to the tree line once more.

"Where are we going?" Scarecrow asked, confused by Charlie starting for the woods again. "Nick just said he doesn't know which nesting area he went to."

"We're going to find them," Charlie said, straightening his bow on his back.

"But, we don't know how to track Lion. We don't know how to track period," Nick protested.

"I do," Charlie said, walking from the building and across the field into the wood line.

Scarecrow and Nick trailed behind him. He stopped at the entrance to the trees and bent down. In the dirt was a fresh paw print. Far too large to be a normal animal. He saw more than twenty feet apart in distance.

"I'd say he was running," Charlie mumbled. "It's going to take us forever to find them with him running at that pace and taking steps that far apart. We have no clue how long he ran, or how far he ran."

"When it comes to protecting those around him, he does it with all of his might. He knew he couldn't defend Maryjane against Glinda's magic. The only thing he knew to do was to get to familiar ground and fight from the offense stance as opposed to a defensive stance,"

Scarecrow explained as they started through the woods.

They walked down the path and followed the leaping footsteps. They walked for hours, and the sun rose high in the sky. Sweat dripped from Charlie's brow, and he wiped it away, keeping his eyes to the ground for any sign of Lion stopping.

"Look out!" Scarecrow yelled as a tree came crashing down toward Charlie. Charlie jumped out of the way as the tree smacked the ground.

"We are definitely getting close to Lion's lair. These are his booby traps," Nick said examining the tree. "See the claw marks on it." Charlie peered over at the tree where it had splintered and fallen from the stump.

"Everybody tread carefully. Who knows what other surprises are going to pop up at us," Charlie urged as he climbed over the trunk of the fallen tree. They continued on in silence, eyeing the terrain for more surprises from Lion. Charlie halted them and blew dirt away from the noose of a rope.

"A spring trap. Nick, you remember what that felt like, don't you?" Charlie laughed.

"Oh, yeah, let's pick on the one who was dangling from the tree," Nick muttered.

They passed by two more spring traps, a pit with stakes at the bottom of it, and a handmade rock slide.

"Lion really wanted to stay hidden, didn't he?" Charlie asked as they walked over the rocks that nearly carried Scarecrow away on the slide.

"He lived in fear his whole life. When the Red Sorceress put a bounty on all of our heads, he told us to seek refuge in one of his nesting areas, that they were well protected. We decided against it because of being too close to one another and getting caught," Scarecrow replied.

They came to large boulders, and the footprints disappeared. Charlie walked to the left about twenty feet out and came back. He went the other way another twenty feet, and walked back. "The footprints stop here. There's only one thing I can think of in that case," Charlie said, bending down to the ground and peering at the last set of prints. The prints were dug deep into the ground.

"What do you see aside from them ending here?" Scarecrow asked.

"He jumped to those boulders and hopped along them," Charlie said, peering up at the boulders. Charlie turned around and walked back the way they had come.

"Well, apparently, he doesn't think we can climb these rocks. He's going back," Nick said to Scarecrow.

They turned to follow and were met with a gust of wind as Charlie ran past them and leapt to the top of the boulder. He landed gracefully like a cat. Scarecrow and Nick looked at each other, and then the jump he made.

"Yeah, I ain't doing that," Scarecrow said, walking toward a stump to sit on.

"There's no way I can do that," Nick said, shaking his head and smacking his metal stomach to exemplify why.

"You two are big babies. Here, take the rope," Charlie said, throwing a rope down to them he had fished from his bag to hoist them to the top.

Scarecrow was the first to be hoisted up. He got to the top and nearly lost his footing. Charlie caught him by the shirt before he fell forward and yanked him backward.

"You have great dexterity," Scarecrow said to Charlie.

Charlie laughed, "It's a gift."

It took the two of them to hoist Nick up. All that metal was heavy, even with him being simply tin. Once they were on top of the boulder, Charlie peered out across the stone passage. There was a five-foot gap in between each boulder. The boulders stopped at the base of a beautiful waterfall.

"He wanted to make sure no one could get to his

home, didn't he?" Charlie asked, leaping across the one boulder to the next. They all followed suit.

"He's kind of a private being," Scarecrow said. "He did live his whole life in fear," Scarecrow jumped, nearly losing his balance. Charlie straightened him up.

"Not to mention, he was running from danger. He chose the best hiding spot. I don't think normal people could have found this place," Nick said as he balanced himself and jumped to the next boulder. They had six more to jump across, and they were all tired. The next few boulders were slightly farther apart than the first few.

"Good grief, Lion. I'm going to chop you into pieces," Nick said, eyeing the fall in between the boulders.

"Don't look down, it will psych you out," Charlie said, heaving himself through the air. He landed with precision.

"Too late," Nick cried. He took a run and start and jumped across the boulder, landing on the top of it. He began to flail his arms as he lost his balance. Charlie grabbed him and pulled him forward, nearly knocking him face down. "You sure are strong."

"Another gift," Charlie said, watching Scarecrow jump across.

He landed easier than Nick. They proceeded like this for the last two boulders. They then walked across the rock bridge to the waterfall and peered up at the top. Charlie saw only one path up there, and it looked dangerous. It was barely two feet in width, and where it slinked up the side, you could see it was wet from the waterfall.

"Do you two want to wait down here? This is a bit more dangerous than those boulders," Charlie said, turning to face them.

"We wanted to wait back at the base of the boulders," Scarecrow said, flopping down on the ground.

These two are a case, Charlie chuckled to himself.

"Alright, I'll be back. If you hear me screaming, please tell Lion he ate me, not an intruder," Charlie said, starting up the rock path.

It wasn't so bad at the bottom. It was when you got higher up the side of the mountain that it started getting trickier. He turned his back to where it faced the mountain and slinked up it sideways. Some parts of the path had fallen due to erosion. He tested each step he made before he firmly planted his foot. He was nearly to the entrance of the cave when his foot slipped on the water, and he toppled forward. His hand grabbed the ledge, and he hung there for a moment. He pulled himself up and slung a leg over the narrow base of the ledge. He hoisted his body back up on it and lay on his stomach. He didn't stand up. Instead, he crawled to the entrance of the cave. He stood up and brushed himself off. He then peered into the dark cave. He couldn't see anything. He couldn't hear anything.

"Lion? Are you in here?" he asked, walking through the entrance. The cave was icy from the chilly wind from the cascading waterfall. He took slow steps past the entrance. He looked around, but from the darkness, it was useless. "Lion?" he asked again, walking further inside the cave.

He didn't hear it coming, and he didn't see it coming. All he felt was weight as something pinned him down to the cave floor. He couldn't reach his bow and arrows, so he had nothing to defend himself with. "Help!" he cried out as the creature in the dark growled in its throat.

"Who dares enter my lair?" the beast roared, pushing his claws into Charlie's chest more.

"It's me, Lion, it's Charlie!" he yelled as the beast growled again.

"How do I know I can trust you? How do I know you haven't turned like your mother?" he growled, pressing harder down on Charlie's chest.

Charlie could barely breathe from the pressure. "Please...Lion," he said, barely choking the words out, "I have...to heal her. You're just...gonna...have to...trust me," he choked out as the walls began to close in on him.

Lion roared in his face, pressing harder down on him, and when he nearly passed out from the lack of oxygen, the pressure was gone as Lion walked to the back of the cave. Charlie took in deep gulps of air as he tried to stop the room from spinning. He sat up easily and looked around. His eyes had finally adjusted to the dim lighting of the cave. Where Lion had placed his paws, his shirt was shredded. Aside from the ripped shirt, he did not inflict any other damage. Charlie stood up and walked toward the back of the cave where Lion lay.

"Where is she?" Charlie asked, rubbing his chest.

Lion looked over at him and said, "Right where the other two put her." He stood up and turned to his other side so Charlie could see. There, lying tied to his back, was Maryjane fast asleep.

"You mean you didn't wake her when you pounced on me?" Charlie asked, running to the Lion's side and untying the rope. Her staff fell to the ground as he cradled her in his arms.

"No, she's been asleep ever since they put her on my back. She hasn't woken once," Lion said, stretching his now freed body and sitting down.

Charlie eased Maryjane to the ground. He brushed the hair from her face, which had fallen when he picked her up. "Maryjane? Are you ok?" Charlie asked, hoping she would awaken to the sound of his voice. She did not. "Maryjane, wake up," he said flatly. Her eyes didn't budge. "Wake up," he said more heavily. Nothing. "Wake up!" he said, slightly shaking her. No response. He checked her pulse, and it had a steady rhythm to it.

"Well, what's wrong with her?" Lion asked Charlie as he nuzzled her with his snout.

"I…I don't know," Charlie said, cradling her in his arms. He put his hand to her forehead. "She's burning up with fever. She must have an infection from the broken bones," he said, laying her back down on the ground.

"Glinda did say that she had maybe hours left to live if septicemia set in." Lion began pacing the cave floor. He stopped and looked at Charlie. "Well, are you just going to sit there, or are you going to heal her. You said that's what you came here to do," Lion flopped down beside Maryjane and licked her hand. Charlie looked at Lion and then back at Maryjane.

"I've never healed anyone before. I don't know if it will work or not," he said, brushing his thumb along her jawline.

He closed his eyes and centered himself. He didn't lie her down on the cave floor, but held her, and willed her broken bones to be healed. He put all of his emotion into the working. The cave started to grow bright as Lion watched dancing lights swirl around the two. The lights got more colorful, swirled faster, and then swarmed the two. The cave was illuminated like the sun, and it looked like an explosion out of the cave, then it was all gone.

Charlie opened his eyes and looked down at Maryjane, still asleep. "Awaken, my love," he begged her. She did not budge. "Maryjane, you have to wake up. This land needs you, your friends need you, and I need you. Open your eyes," he pleaded with her. She didn't move. He hung his head and softly said, "It didn't work. I knew it was too good to be true. I'm not as almighty and powerful as everyone thinks I am or can be."

He laid her body down carefully on the cave floor and walked over to the entrance. He peered out at the light in disappointment. He didn't know how much longer she had to live, and there was no one to turn to who could save her.

"Charlie? Is that…you?" he heard a soft voice float

from the back of the cave.

He wheeled around on his heels and ran back to the far end of the cave. She had begun to sit up. She no longer screeched in pain. She could move both arms and legs. He ran to her and scooped her up, swinging her around, kissing her.

"You had me so worried. I didn't...I didn't know what to do," he said, squeezing her.

"You healed me?" she asked, pushing from his arms to look at him.

"Yeah, I healed you. I never knew I had it in me," he said through deep breaths of excitement.

"While I was in and out of consciousness, I overheard Nick and Scarecrow talking about summoning your mother to help me. What happened? Why didn't they do it?" Maryjane asked Charlie, and then looked to Lion.

Charlie hadn't even sat down and thought about that situation yet. He backed up to one of the walls in the cave and slid down it, sitting with his hands to his head.

"Charlie, what happened?" Maryjane asked him again.

Charlie looked at Lion, and Lion sighed. "I guess I'll tell her," he said, and he began to recount the entire situation once more. When he finished with Charlie coming to rescue them, she stood up and walked over to Lion.

"You are so brave, Lion," she said, hugging him tightly. "Thank you for taking such good care of me."

"Aww, shucks," he said, looking down at the floor in embarrassment. "I couldn't let anyone hurt my favorite kid. Besides, you give the best back scratches," he said, nuzzling her face.

She walked over to Charlie, who hadn't moved from the floor. She kneeled before him and lifted his face to her face. "We will get her back, Charlie. I promise you," she said, interlacing her fingers with his.

He leaned in to kiss her, when Lion roared a

ferocious roar, and took off out of the cave. No sooner was he out of the entrance than he came flying right back in the cave, and thudded against the wall.

"Well, well. Isn't this a lovely moment? Maryjane, it's a nice surprise to see you alive. Last I heard, you were dead," the voice sneered in the dark. "I guess we will have to fix that now, won't we. Charlie, be a dear and tame the Lion. I don't want my dress ruined with cat hair."

Charlie pushed Maryjane behind as the face emerged from the darkness. "I'm going to have so much fun with you two. It's like playing with rats in a cage."

Chapter Seventeen

THE ENTIRE GROUP was led away through the forest by the Red Sorceress's henchman, in particular Emma. She didn't believe the reasoning behind looking for the girl's three friends. This time, however, she joined the hunting party. What a surprise it was to come across the girl still alive and in the arms of Charlie. It sent fire through her spine. She could've struck the two dead right there, but what fun would that be? She wanted to make them both suffer.

Everyone walked in silence. They were not tied together, but no one dared to retaliate or run away. They pushed through the edge of the trees, and there it stood, Emerald City. Charlie was aware of the ghastly condition it was in. The others stared in shock at the City that had once been so beautiful. Maryjane remembered her first trip to the City before darkness started to fall across the land. The grace of the City fell away with the crumbling wall of bricks. Its lustrous green emeralds had lost their sparkle and faded. All of the colors it radiated had been long replaced with black and grey walls. The sky that was once so blue and bright was black with blood red clouds circling the tower. A pillar of smoke rose from the center of the city as the enslaved people worked hard around the clock to facilitate the Red Sorceress. The fields of poppy flowers had long since died and now were just rotting shrubs. The yellow brick road was devastated the worst here. Instead of gray and crumbling, chunks of the road were missing from the electrical storms that swirled the city every day.

Standing at the gates was Dorothy, as she watched her friends and family march along as if it were an execution line. Maryjane saw her mother, and her face brightened. Her smile was quickly replaced with confusion because her mother did not have the same reaction to seeing her. They were marched right past her as Maryjane looked her in the face. She saw no love in her eyes.

"What have you done to my mother?" Maryjane demanded as they walked into the next room, where the Red Sorceress stood with her staff.

Scarlet snickered, "Why, I've done nothing, child, but open her eyes to the truth of Oz." Scarlet sauntered before the group, and Emma bowed in response. "Excellent work, my child."

"The scrying mirror worked perfectly. They were holed up in the very cave it pointed to," Emma smirked.

"Make sure Dorothy is comfortable after you lock them up," Scarlet said, turning to go to her throne room.

"You've brainwashed her!" Maryjane hissed, and Scarlet whirled around to face her.

She was within inches of Maryjane, and fire burned bright in her eyes. "I have done no such thing. Before you accuse me of doing wrong, why don't you ask your precious lover what he has done wrong?" Scarlet chided. She looked him square in the eye, and he shook his head, pleading with her eyes. "Go ahead, Charlie, tell her what you've done. Tell her about your betrayal," she said, smiling. Charlie looked from Scarlet to Maryjane, who peered at him with confusion and suspicion.

"What is she talking about, Charlie?" Maryjane was meek with apprehension.

"What she's talking about right now isn't important. What's important is…"

"What is she talking about, Charlie?" Maryjane

demanded once more. Charlie took a deep breath. How can he tell her what happened without losing her trust and love? "Charlie!"

"Emma seduced me in my unconscious state," Charlie blurted out. "I thought I was back in the forest with you, and it was her I was with. I awoke the next morning, undressed in her bed with her lying next to me," he confessed, looking into her eyes, pleading with her eyes to believe him. She just looked at him. Her eyes were full of love and despair.

Scarlet laughed, "Why, Charlie, you just broke her heart. How cruel of you."

Maryjane's eyes dropped from his to the ground. She didn't want to be around anyone right now. Her whole world was crashing down around her. She looked up to see Glinda float in on a black mist. She descended beside Scarlet. She looked so different than her usual self. Her normal, bubbly self was replaced with an odd aura of darkness. She was dressed in a slinky black outfit. It wasn't like her at all. Glinda glared at her as her feet touched the ground.

"Oh, Maryjane, have you met my new best friend? She is so wonderful," Scarlet said, smirking.

Maryjane did not respond. She just wanted to be thrown in a cell or cast into a pit of fire. She didn't want to be in the crowd of eyes that surrounded her, judging her, mocking her. Nick, Lion, and Scarecrow looked at her in sorrow. Charlie didn't look at her at all. He knew what he had done to her. When Maryjane didn't respond to Scarlet, her smile turned into a scowl.

"Take them to the tower, chain them up separately, and put a muzzle on that cat," Scarlet ordered. "And give the girl a dress or something. She's halfway naked!"

Maryjane looked up at her and then to Glinda as one of the men pulled her arm to lead her up the stairs. Charlie ripped his arm from their grasp and glared at

Scarlet and his mother. They were led upstairs to a small chamber. They chained up Charlie and the Lion first, getting rid of the immediate threats. Charlie pulled on the chains, wondering if they would budge. To his dismay, they did not. They didn't even budge for Lion, who was fighting against the chains with all the power in his body. They then chained up Nick and Scarecrow. They tossed Maryjane's staff into one of the corners. One of the soldiers brought her a green gown that resembled Emma's attire to change into.

"Can you leave the room, please?" she asked with her eyes to the floor.

"How do I know you won't make a run for it after you change?" the one hissed at her.

"You have my word, I promise," she again pleaded.

"No, change in front of us, or not at all," the other man said.

She turned around to face the wall. She slipped the shredded clothes from her body, and they landed in a heap on the floor. Maryjane could feel the eyes of the men staring at her. Charlie kept his eyes trained on them. They didn't watch her undress. They had turned around to face the door. Once Maryjane had the dress on, she cleared her throat, and they turned around. They led her over to where the last set of shackles hung. When they placed her hands in the chains, they rubbed her face with their hands, and one of them grabbed her jowls to make her look him in the eye.

"Mm, what a piece of meat," the one said while the other man chuckled.

"Don't touch her!" Charlie growled through his gritted teeth.

She said nothing. She didn't flinch away from their touch. She didn't speak to them. She just sat there, chained with a look of shock on her face. The two men left, and Charlie tried to get her attention, to get her to talk to him. "Maryjane, you have to believe me. I didn't do it intentionally. She had me tell you, so you would be mad at me. Look at me, please!" he begged, trying to get her to look at him.

She did not. "Have you ever had those feelings where you wish you had never existed to begin with, or you just wish you were dead. You know no one would ever be one hundred percent in love with you, so what's the point in living through a life already full of grief? Do you know the feeling?" she asked, not looking up at anyone. No one answered.

"Well, that's what I have felt every day of my life. I'm not special. I'm no different than any other girl. I'm not beautiful. I'm plain and ordinary. I can't even talk to guys at school, let alone date one of them. All the girls remind me each day that I will never be liked or loved. So why would any man want to give me his heart fully and completely? There are so many other people in the world. If I fight for one person, it's selfish, because I hold them back from someone who could be better than me, prettier than me, more powerful than me," she said, looking up at Charlie. "So, I'm done fighting. I'm done trying to be something I wasn't cut out for. I'm tired of arguing and making up. I'm tired of fighting and having to be saved. I'm just tired of everything. I officially give in," she said, staring off into space.

"Kid, you can't mean it," Lion said through his chained mouth.

Everyone was looking at her. She looked at no one. "I can't fight forever," she said, looking up at Charlie. "Especially only to be disappointed and find out that being special to just one person isn't enough. They will always want more."

Charlie just stared back at her. There was no argument to be made. No matter how much he protested, her mind was made up. She really was giving up. She was giving up on them, on her powers, on survival. Whose fault was it? His. This whole situation was his fault. If he had only listened to his mother five years ago, they wouldn't be in this predicament. His mother wouldn't be enslaved to the will of Scarlet. Maryjane would not have gone through hell and back.

"The only existence in this life that was pointless was my existence. I have done nothing but mess up everything. This whole thing is my fault. I never listened to my mother when I should have. I let my thick-headedness get in the way of how things were supposed to go," Charlie said, looking to the floor. "I'm sorry," he said, looking up at Maryjane. "This whole time I've been trying to protect you from being hurt, and I turned out to be the one who hurt you the most, even when I promised you I would never hurt you again. I wish for myself a fate much worse than death. I will partially receive it when you leave me forever. I wouldn't blame you for leaving forever," he said, looking her in the eyes and then back to the floor.

The room remained silent for the remainder of the day. Everyone had slumped against the walls when Glinda walked into the room. No one uttered a word as she strode in. She looked at everyone directly in the eyes. She walked past Nick, Scarecrow, and Lion. She looked from Charlie to Maryjane.

She turned to Maryjane, "Maryjane, your mother would like to see you." The chains around her fell to the ground. Maryjane looked at Glinda, who smiled back at her. She was reveling in her newfound power. "Follow me."

Maryjane looked to Charlie, who had stood to his feet. She followed Glinda to the door, and Charlie pulled on his chains. He rattled them and tried to break them. Glinda spun around, "Now, Charlie, behave. I'll be back for you soon enough."

She smiled at him. He didn't like the smile she gave him or the unknown meaning behind it. Maryjane gave him a tentative glance and walked through the door. Glinda shut it behind them. Maryjane followed her down the spiral staircase. When they reached the bottom, Glinda veered to her right and opened a ballroom door. She motioned for Maryjane to walk in. Maryjane stepped through the door, and there, sitting at a table, was her mother.

"Mama!" Maryjane said, running over to her and throwing her arms around her. "Did they hurt you?" she asked her mother, pulling away and looking over her.

Her mother sat there. "No, they have treated me with respect the whole time I have been here," Dorothy said, looking at her daughter.

"Mama, what's wrong?" Maryjane asked, taking a step back from her mother. "Why are you acting so funny?" she asked.

"Maryjane, how much do you love me?" her mother asked her.

"I can't tell you in words," Maryjane said, smiling. Her mother did not smile back.

"Would you do anything in the world to make me well again?" She looked at Maryjane, peering deeply into her eyes for the answer she sought.

"Of course, Mama, but I don't quite understand what you're asking," Maryjane said, looking at her mother confused.

"I have found a way to be healed of my cancer," Dorothy said to her daughter.

"But Glinda said that you cannot heal cancer," Maryjane said, shaking her head in confusion.

"That is because Glinda cannot heal cancer," Dorothy said, looking down at the floor, "But Scarlet can."

Maryjane shook her head, "No, Mama, you can't trust her." Dorothy looked up at her daughter and smiled at her.

"You are so brave, yet so naïve," Dorothy said, patting her hand. Maryjane jerked her hand away from her mother.

"Well, if she can heal your cancer, then why hasn't she already?" Maryjane asked defiantly.

Her mother looked her in the eyes, "Because she wants something in exchange for the gift of life." Dorothy said, staring hard into Maryjane's eyes.

"Well, if she wants Charlie to be married to Emma, she can have him. They can rule Oz together, I don't care anymore," she said, looking at her mother. Her mother shook her head and chuckled a little bit. "What's funny?" Maryjane asked in a shaky voice.

"It's much bigger than that, child. She said I can be healed and return to my healthy old self if..." Dorothy paused, "If you relinquished your powers to her, for Emma." Dorothy said, staring at her. Her eyes looked so tired. She had battled back and forth over this deliberation.

"Mama...you're...you're asking me to give up what sets me apart from everyone else. I was given these powers as a gift, as a blessing for what you did for the Land of Oz, and you want me to hand them over to the very power that has wreaked devastation and havoc upon this once beautiful land. What has she done to you? How did she swindle this thought into your mind? If I give up my powers to her, we cannot save Oz, and our two worlds will never combine. Don't you understand? This is bigger than you and me. This is about everyone. This isn't just my choice. This would be everyone's choice because it affects everyone. Think about your friends upstairs right now in chains. Think of what will happen to them if I give my powers up to her. She will destroy them! My powers were not meant for Emma. If the Elders wanted her to have powers like mine, they would have blessed her with them. They are too powerful for her. They are too powerful for me! I'm still learning how to use them. Emma will destroy everyone, and they will cease to exist. I will probably cease to exist. Once she has my powers, she can destroy me without any hesitation."

"No, Scarlet has given me her word that once you relinquish your powers to her, she will send us home. We will not have to fight for the farm anymore, and I will be around forever," Dorothy said, looking at her daughter. "Please, Maryjane. I have never asked you for anything. I ask this one thing of you. Save me from my destined fate," Dorothy pleaded.

"You're on a first-name basis with her now? Do you even know what you are truly asking me to do? I never imagined you would be so selfish, Mama. No, I will not give up my powers to her," Maryjane said, turning from her mother and walking to the door.

"Then I guess I will just give her this, then," Dorothy said, holding up Maryjane's Book of Shadows.

Maryjane patted her bag. It was empty. "How did you…"

"It's easy to take from you when you're so vulnerable, and hugging your mother," Dorothy said, standing.

Maryjane ran to her, and two guards stepped in front of her. "Mama, you have to give me that book. Glinda said not to let anyone read it," Maryjane pleaded.

"I know what Glinda said. Why would I protect you? You're a selfish child who wouldn't do this one thing I asked of you. You are no daughter of mine. Emma, however, is. She came up with the idea for Scarlet to present me, but of course, you won't do it. I knew you wouldn't," Dorothy said, walking out of the opposite door with Maryjane's Book of Shadows.

"What are you talking about?" Maryjane asked, confused.

"It hasn't dawned on you at all how she looks so

184

similar to you, and why. When your father died, I had no one to help me. The baby I was pregnant with turned out to be twins. I couldn't take care of both of you by myself, or the farm's upkeep. I was struggling as it was just keeping the farm healthy and thriving, let alone an additional baby I hadn't planned on. It would have been too much for me. So, I gave her up for adoption. I gave the wrong one up for adoption. It took Emma a while to figure out how to get to Oz. She wasn't graced by Glinda on her first visit. She was met by Scarlet, who took her under her wing and treated her more like a daughter than anything. Two prodigies similar in looks and powers. Yes, Emma knows how to wield your powers because her powers are similar to the ones you were given. You were twins, so when they blessed you, they blessed her. From my understanding, she knew how to use her powers at an earlier age than you. She has been using her powers since she was a baby. She is far more powerful than you. Everyone has been focused on you and your triumph over Oz. How about letting your sister take your place instead? After she reads this, she won't need your blessing to do it," Dorothy said, continuing on through the door.

"Mama, no!! Please! How could you possibly think I don't care for you? There is a bigger picture than you and me that I have to fight for. It's not selfish! Mama, please don't!" Maryjane screamed, pleading. Her mother kept walking. The guards pushed her out of the ballroom, and Glinda grabbed hold of her arms.

"Back up to your room, little one," Glinda said, pushing her up the stairs.

Maryjane was in tears. *My own mother has turned against me. She* cried silently within. Glinda towed her up the stairs and back into the room, sobbing. Charlie stood up, looking at Maryjane for any sign of abuse. Glinda restrained her in the chains. Her features softened toward her.

"I'm sorry it happened this way to you, especially finding out about Emma. Even I had no idea who she was. I don't even think the Elders knew she existed," she said for a moment, returning to herself. "Cloaking yourself won't help, but if you erase it from your mind's eye, it will work," she said to Maryjane.

Maryjane didn't understand what she meant. She turned on her heels and was out the door. Maryjane broke down in a fit.

"What happened?" Charlie asked her.

"My mom, she's...I don't know. She's not under Scarlet's control, but she's not herself," she said, choking back the tears.

"What happened?" Scarecrow asked. The three of them peered at her.

"She asked me to give my powers up to Emma. If I gave them to her, then Scarlet would cure the cancer eating away at her insides," Maryjane said with tears still freely falling down her face.

"What did you do?" Charlie asked in alarm.

"I..." Maryjane started breaking down in tears again. "I told her no. She told me I was selfish for wanting to keep my powers instead of saving her. When she stood up to leave, she had my spell book to give to Scarlet. She...she told me Emma was my twin sister, that she gave up for adoption at birth because she couldn't take care of both of us, that Emma was far more powerful than I and had been using her powers longer than I." She stopped to breathe through her tears. "She told me she wished she had kept her instead of me because I was selfish. She said Emma was her daughter, not me anymore. I... I don't know what to believe anymore," Maryjane said, sniffing and trying to wipe the tears off her face.

"Is it selfish of me not to give up my powers to save my mother? It's either save my mother or save Oz. I thought choosing to stay or leave was a hard choice, but I just made a choice of a lifetime. I chose a faraway land where my mother was committed to an insane asylum for believing in over healing her, and ridding her of any cancer," Maryjane said, fighting back the tears again. "Now she has the very book that will lead to my destruction, and I don't think she even cares anymore. Why would she care? I would hand the book over to Scarlet if my snot-nosed, little brat chose anything but to save me from an excruciating death. Emma is probably consoling her right now, saying I never deserved her for a mother, that she gave the wrong one of us up for adoption. Did I make the right choice? Would you have chosen Oz over your mother, or would you have saved your mother and say screw everyone else?" Maryjane cried out in hysterics. Everyone was silent. She cried and cried. She felt as if she had just betrayed life itself.

"I would have chosen my mother," Charlie said guiltily. "I do not have your strength or your courage either, but that makes me selfish choosing my mother. Choosing one life over thousands is selfish. You may have saved your mother for her to live another day cancer-free, but what if tomorrow she were murdered, or had a heart attack, or fell off a cliff? The deaths of those thousands of people would have been for nothing. The true gift of life to your mother is you staying true to your destiny. You are destined to do great things, Maryjane. These things are beyond life, beyond love, beyond family. These things will eventually lead to your ascension as a warrior priestess, as a magus mortem. You are the strongest person I have ever met in will and faith. I would follow you as my queen any day," Charlie said, looking into her eyes.

"I agree with Charlie," Nick said. "I love your mother, but I would have chosen Oz over her. It's selfish of her to ask you to do the opposite," he said, bowing his head in shame for her actions.

"It doesn't matter what my decision was. She's handing my book over to Scarlet. Emma will know every secret to my powers once she reads it," Maryjane said, slumping against the wall.

She thought back on everything that had happened in the last few days. She thought of Glinda and how she had been turned into a mindless slave. She thought of her last words to her just now. *Cloaking yourself won't help, but if you erase it from your mind's eye, it will work.*

Erase it from your mind's eye, Maryjane thought to herself. "Of course!" Maryjane yelled out loud. Everyone looked at her, confused. "Erase it from your mind's eye," Maryjane repeated aloud.

"Umm, what does that mean?" Lion asked through the chains tied around his mouth, looking around to see if anyone else understood it.

"What are you talking about? That's what my mother told you before she left," Charlie said, and then the realization hit him as well. "Of course!" Charlie exclaimed as well. Nick and Scarecrow joined in on the excitement of what to do.

"Will someone please clue me in on what's going on?" Lion growled in muffled tones.

"Book of Shadows; Book of Light; Shelter thy words from her mind's eye; Hide my spells; Hide my power; Hide it from her within the hour; From her eyesight it shall flee; So, as I will it, so mote it be!" Maryjane exclaimed.

Chapter Eighteen

DOROTHY WALKED THROUGH the halls holding her daughter's spell book in her hands. *Should I do this?* she asked herself. She felt horrible for what she had said to her. She just wanted to live longer than what was in store for her. She had gone back to her room and thought about it for a while. She knew she should've broken the news about Emma more easily than she had, but there was no time. She still wanted to sit down with her longer and talk about things as to why she had to be given up for adoption at birth. The time would come later for that. She had decided it was for the best to hand over the spell book and descended to Scarlet to give it to her. She rounded the corner and entered the throne room. Scarlet was sitting on the throne, drinking from her Goblet. Glinda was sitting on the armoire to the left of her, and Emma was to the right in her chair.

"Dorothy, what a nice surprise," Scarlet said, setting her cup back on the table. "What do you have for me, my dear?" she asked, smiling at her.

Dorothy hesitated again, thinking everything through once more. She walked forward and held the book out. "I thought you might like to use this as a gift instead of her relinquishing her powers to Emma. If I give it to you, you will remove my cancer," Dorothy said, testing the sorceress.

"What is it?" Scarlet asked.

Glinda watched the two from the armoire. She looked from Scarlet to Dorothy with a look of disappointment on her face. Emma sat beaming in her chair as she felt victory in the air.

"It's her spell book. It will tell you everything about her powers. Every spell she has learned or will learn. Everything," Dorothy said once more, shaking the book in her hand toward the Red Sorceress.

Glinda sat there and watched Dorothy hand over Maryjane's spell book, which she had presented to her a few days ago. Shame spread throughout her body as she looked at Dorothy for her selfish act. Dorothy didn't look the least bit ashamed of her actions. Who could blame her, though? She was dying of cancer and had found a way out.

Scarlet accepted the gift from Dorothy and smiled, "Thank you, my friend."

Friend? Glinda thought to herself, confused. *Since when are these two friends?*

Scarlet eagerly flipped the book open to the first page. She flipped to the second, the third, and she zoomed through the book. She slammed it shut and threw it across the room. "It's empty!" she shrieked. Dorothy backed up a step. "It's not the real book!" she sneered at Dorothy.

Emma ran to the book and flipped through the pages herself. She screamed out in anger and threw it a few feet from Dorothy, "I thought it would be filled with all she knows?!"

"I took it from her bag just an hour ago. She begged me not to give it to you...it has to be the real thing," she said, running and picking it up from the ground. She opened the book, and to her dismay, she saw what Scarlet did. Nothing. "I don't...I don't understand. It was just full of everything!" Dorothy yelled, flipping through the book backward as if there were a trick to making the pages show up. "This isn't fair!" she yelled, throwing the book to the ground and kicking it. "You have to believe me, Emma. I was trying to right what was wronged all those years ago!"

Emma flopped down in her chair and proceeded to play with a fireball.

"You're Maryjane's twin, aren't you?" Glinda asked, watching Emma throw the ball back and forth between her hands. "That's why you were so angry that I had Maryjane. You were hoping it was her instead of Emma who ended up as your apprentice."

"Enough!" Scarlet yelled. Emma heaved her fireball across the room, striking a statue. It exploded upon impact.

Dorothy looked up to Scarlet with pleading eyes, "You have to help me, Scarlet. If you have any heart left in you, you would help me. You're nothing like your mother," Dorothy begged.

Scarlet stood to her feet, "I told you not to call me that in front of anyone, that you had no rank to call me anything but the Red Sorceress in company's presence. No one needs to know anything more than they already know! If it weren't for you, my mother would be here! This is my revenge against you. Your daughter will age the same way I did. Without a mother! This is what I meant when I told you everything you love will be mine. Oz is mine. Your daughter, whom you gave away at birth, is mine, and soon, your other one will be mine as well! It won't take much to turn her. You keep someone chained up long enough, their will and spark will die. The fierce fight in her will dissipate, especially when she watches everyone she cares about die around her. You tried getting her to give up her powers to save you. Ha!" she laughed, thrusting her head backward.

"She was a smart one for not letting them go! You call her naïve when the one who is naïve is you! Do you honestly think I was just going to let her walk out of here and go home? Fool! She would have become my slave. She would have become just like me, just like Emma, an angry orphan! You took my mother from me, Dorothy, and I'm going to take you from her!" Scarlet said with the wind swirling around her.

"Scarlet!" Glinda exclaimed. It all made sense. Everything now made absolute perfect sense. "That's why you wanted Charlie. He is the last of my bloodline, as you are to the wicked witch of the West! How did she hide you?" she asked in disbelief.

"The same way that little brat came to Oz. She took me to the real world and hid me among them. A human family raised me. They gave me everything she had left me so I could learn. Once she was destroyed, I vowed to take down the people who helped her to her demise. Starting with this one," Scarlet said, pointing to Dorothy.

"It was an accident, Scarlet. I didn't do it on purpose! Honest!" Dorothy protested, backing up.

"Accident or not, you were still the reason she died!" Scarlet regained her composure and turned to one of her monkeys, "Bring Charlie down here and chain him to the wall," she said without batting an eyelash.

"What are you doing with Charlie?" Glinda asked, standing to her feet.

"Oh, he's going to want to witness this great power about to explode. You see, not only do I want to destroy Dorothy, which I will soon, I want to destroy anyone who will fight against me and try to save the pathetic, little Land of Oz that I wasn't good enough to be a part of. My mother hid me from the Elders because my father was a human, a mortal. She had gone against the rule of Oz, and they killed my father to teach her a lesson. The rage from the selfish actions of the Elders grew deep within her. She became wicked with anger. Her wickedness sank deep into me within her womb.

192

"When I was born, she carried me off to the human world. We lived there for a time. She left one day and never returned. She left her mirror with me for communication. She told me how Dorothy had managed to find her way into Oz. She had killed her sister, my aunt, and was heading to the wizard with the slippers of silver that YOU gave her. Betrayed by one of her sisters to protect a mortal girl. I didn't care too much for Dorothy growing up in that small town of Kansas. When I learned she had killed my mother, I was enraged. The rage is all it took to complete my power development," she said as the henchman dragged Charlie down the steps and chained him to the wall.

"Scarlet, it was not I who gave Dorothy the slippers. It was Lissandra. I did nothing but fight for your mother. Wicked or not, I would have never ended her life." Glinda was stricken with anxiety. Scarlet just glared at her, ignoring her words.

"And the final straw of my deep-centered hatred for that brat upstairs is the same as my mother's toward the Elders. They killed my father for being a mortal, but they blessed that child with powers, so Charlie doesn't have to suffer the same way. It's all bull," Scarlet yelled, her eyes glowing red with hatred and anger. "Hello, son. How are we today?" she asked vehemently as he sat down and glared at her. "Not in the greatest mood today, I can see. Well, neither am I," she said, stalking toward him. She grabbed his face in her hand at the jawline. He tried to shake her hand free, but she had an iron grip. "And I thought we were going places together with our reign of terror," she sneered and pushed his face away.

She sauntered to the center of the room where Dorothy stood. She grabbed her by the hair of the head and threw her against the wall. Her eyes went bright like fire. She gathered her energy in her hand and tossed a ball at Dorothy. Dorothy screamed and ducked away from it.

She repeated her action, playing a mouse and cat game with Dorothy. Dorothy was defenseless. She had no powers of her own, and she had no one to protect her from Scarlet.

"Stop!" Charlie shouted out to Scarlet. Scarlet stopped and looked at him.

"Are you talking to me? Are you dictating to me what to do? You are *not* in charge. I am," she said, tossing another ball in Dorothy's direction without even glancing over at her. Dorothy ducked the ball and hid in the corner.

"Oh, yeah, you're so powerful throwing energy balls at a mortal," Charlie chided her.

Her evil grin grew more insidious as she cocked her head to him. "Do you want to see power? I can show you power," she said, and lifted both of her hands upward.

Sparks flew around the room. She was summoning a thunderstorm inside the throne room. The wind coursed throughout the room, and the rain began swirling around everyone. Glinda stood from her chair and walked around the room, carefully watching Scarlet. Emma stood from her chair, frightened and confused. She had never seen her Siress explode in anger this way before. She looked over to Dorothy, huddled in the corner. She wanted to run to her and protect her, but she couldn't find the strength to do so. She was weak. Her sister was the stronger one.

Scarlet stood in the middle of the room laughing maniacally. "You think that is something? Now watch this," she screamed as the rain turned from water to freezing rain, and the temperature dropped below zero in a matter of seconds. Everyone was chilled to the bone as she stood in the center of the room laughing like a madwoman. "Still not impressed?" she screamed.

Fire replaced the water and ice on the floor. Everywhere, fire was popping up. Dorothy was trapped in the corner with flames wrapping around the area, trapping her in the corner. Emma glanced over at Dorothy, who pleaded with her through her eyes. She turned and ran from the room. It was Glinda who ran toward the corner and pushed a bookcase over to land on the flame, smothering it out. She reached out for Dorothy's hand to help her across the bookcase. She grabbed her hand, Glinda pulled her over the bookcase, and towed her across the room to the staircase that led to the tower.

"Go!" Glinda yelled at Dorothy as she whirled back around. Scarlet's attention was now on Glinda.

"You dare defy me?!" she shrieked.

Glinda stood in a defensive stance. Charlie knew what she was about to do. "Mom, no! She'll kill you!" he yelled.

"Remember what I told you years ago, sitting at that fountain?' Glinda yelled back at him as she faced Scarlet. "Never forget it, son. You are the rightful heir to this land. You and Maryjane were the ones chosen to rule over Oz. Everything you need lies in your soul. You can do this if you try. You have found yourself. You have found the power granted to you."

Scarlet whipped an energy ball at Glinda. She threw her hand up, and it exploded on the shield surrounding her. She then shot a ball of ice at Scarlet. She melted it in the air before it even reached her.

"Is that seriously all you have?" Scarlet asked mockingly.

Without hesitation, Glinda threw a bolt of lightning, and it struck Scarlet in the stomach. She doubled over in pain. She stood straight up and lifted her hands. It began to rain fire all around Glinda. The flames engulfed her. Scarlet cackled. Glinda was petrified as she jumped through the flames unscathed and shot a fireball at Scarlet. It struck her in the face, knocking her to the ground. She stood back up and glared.

"Enough games. It's time to finish you off," she said, stretching her arms straight out. Lightning rained down everywhere. Glinda dodged each bolt that fell from the ceiling. She deflected one that struck down on top of her, sending it toward Scarlet. She absorbed the bolt.

"Is that all you have?" Glinda asked, mocking her as she dodged the bolts of lightning. Scarlet snickered.

Glinda dodged two more bolts of lightning and stopped dead in her tracks. She looked at Charlie as he stood chained to the wall, trying to break the chain's grip on him. He couldn't break free to protect his mother. She looked down at her stomach. Embedded in the pit of her stomach was the handle of an athame with flames trickling from it. Scarlet stood still in the pose of the throw, smiling and cackling. Glinda hit the floor. She began coughing up the blood filling her stomach, and the flames engulfed her gown. The one weakness she had ever had was fire. She looked at Charlie. He was in tears.

"Be brave, my son, like you always have been. Never forget," she uttered, and the breath left her lungs. She lay there motionless on the floor.

Charlie stared in horror at his mother's body. Blood trickled from her mouth. "Mom?" he whispered, "Mom. Mom!" He got louder and louder with his plea for her to answer. No movement and no speech left her body. She was dead. "No. This isn't right. This can't be right," he said, talking to himself, searching his mind.

"Oh, but it is right, Charlie. Your mother was meant to die in this battle. Good never triumphs over evil. It's too wicked to kill," she said, doubling over, cackling. "Guards," she yelled through the hall, "Take the prisoner back to the tower and chain him back up," she said, gritting her teeth together. He looked from his mother's body to her, and anger ran through his body.

"You feel that surge?" she smiled enticingly, glaring at him. "Use it. It will one day be your absolution of power.

Feed from it." The guards released his chains from the wall, and he tried to run to his mother's side. Three of them pulled him back into place, dragging him from the room. "When you're finished putting him back in the tower, come dispose of this body. It's making me nauseous to look at and smell," she said with disdain dripping from her fingertips.

She walked back to her throne and sat down. *Not a bad day's work,* she thought. *I still have Dorothy to deal with, along with her brat I took under my wing. At the first sight of danger, she ran like a little kid. Well, I shall see to it that she is locked in a dungeon until her heart is back in my good graces.* She sat there planning how she would take Dorothy out of the picture next.

Meanwhile, Charlie was dragged back fighting all the way to the room with the others. The guards chained him back up, snickering at him. Charlie didn't look at anyone; he just stared at the floor. Maryjane stared at him. His face was flushed from the anger and sorrow swirling around in his chest.

"What happened?" Maryjane asked him, standing up, testing the strength of the chains.

"Nothing," Charlie mumbled, wiping away the trail of tears on his face.

"Something happened that upset you," Maryjane urged, staring at him.

He looked defeated. "Nothing happened!" he snapped at her.

"Whatever it is, you have to be strong and not let her get to you," Maryjane uttered quietly.

"Just shut up, Maryjane," Charlie yelled at her.

It startled her. She went silent and slumped back against the wall. She looked out the window. "I take it my spell worked. She couldn't read my spell book," Maryjane said, still staring out the window.

"Yeah, you're an almighty sorceress," Charlie said

snidely.

He glared over at her. She didn't look at him. "Why are you being this way, Charlie? We have to stick together,"

Charlie cut her off, "Stick together? If it weren't for you, none of this would be happening. She's doing all of this because of you. She wants your powers for Emma, and she will do anything to get them. Your powers cost my mother her life. Scarlet killed her for defending your mother. My mother was all I had. Does that sound familiar? Isn't that what you told me? Well, you still have your mother and the chance to leave and never come back. I'm stuck here forever. That's what you have never understood. You can leave if you want. I have nowhere else to go because this is my world. A world that has been turned upside down because of her hatred toward your mom. If your mother had never come here years ago, this would have never happened. So, excuse me if I'm not in the lightest mood right now," Charlie said through gritted teeth.

"If my mother had never come here years ago, we would have never met," Maryjane whispered, holding back her tears.

"That would have been fine by me. Since the day we met, I have experienced nothing but trouble with you. I wish you had never come here! I wish you would just leave!" he yelled.

"Is that what you want, Charlie? Do you want me to leave forever?" Maryjane asked, finally looking over at him. "Just say the word. Just say it! I will leave. I will leave forever!" she yelled at him.

"I don't know what I want anymore. All I know is I want my mother back, and that won't happen. Nothing can bring her back," he said, looking back down at the floor.

Everyone remained silent. Maryjane got antsy sitting

in the quiet. Thoughts were whirring through her mind. She didn't discuss anything with anyone in the room. "Guards!" she yelled. Everyone just looked at her. "Guards!" she yelled again.

"What are you doing?" Scarecrow asked, peering at her over his arm.

"I'm getting you all out of here," she said, standing. "Guards!"

"How are you going to do that?" Nick asked.

"I'm going to give her what she wants," Maryjane said, looking at the three in chains.

"You can't do that!" Lion roared, breaking the chains around his snout.

"It's my choice. I will give her what she wants on the condition that she lets you all go. If that's what it takes to set everyone free, then so be it," Maryjane said, waiting for the guards to come back to the room.

"Well, what if she kills you?" Scarecrow asked, looking from her over to Charlie, who didn't seem to be paying her any mind.

She followed his gaze and waited for him to acknowledge the question. He didn't look up or flinch. "Then so be it," she replied, looking back at her friends in chains.

"Maryjane, your purpose is much more than that here!" Scarecrow pleaded.

She looked at him. All the hope and will had drained from her. "A grander purpose. I've heard that since I was a little child. Look at me. Look at us. We are all here because of me. It's time I set things right," Maryjane asserted proudly, standing back up. "Guards!"

The door opened, and one of the guards stepped in. "What do you want?" he hissed angrily.

"Take me to the Red Sorceress. I have something she wants, and I'm ready to give it to her," she said without hesitation.

The guard walked over to her. He unchained her and then grabbed hold of her hair. "Don't try to run or I will drop you here," he said, pushing a knife toward her back. He walked her out of the room, passing by everyone still chained to the walls.

"Maryjane, no!" Nick cried out, pushing against the chains in futility, but it was too late; she was out the door with the guard, and the door closed behind them.

Scarecrow looked at Charlie, "I hope you're happy. That child was the best thing this land could have ever received as a warrior queen, a sorceress, a soon-to-be Magus Mortem! Now look, she's giving herself up to the very person who condemned us all, all because you are too selfish to care. She has risked her life the entire time she has been here, keeping everyone safe from the likes of her and the likes of you. You're always flip-flopping with your feelings toward her. No wonder the girl doesn't know whether to stay or to go. One minute you love her, the next you're pushing her away. If it were me, I'd leave forever, but that's me, not her. You are the one who made the final decision for her just now. You sentenced her to death, another person in your life whose life your arrogance takes.

"Your mother didn't die because of her. She died because of you. She took your blood pact that your stupid, hare-brained ass accepted and performed with Miss Red Sorceress. Whenever anything goes wrong in your life, you lash out at that girl. For once, be a man and take responsibility for your own actions. Right now, you are not a man in my eyes. You are still a boy. You're still the pretentious, little brat I met in the field years ago, and you will never change. No one can change you, but you. You have everything. You have power, you have a girl crawling on her knees begging for love from you, you have a kingdom ready to bow to their knees and serve you as king. You're throwing your whole life away. I don't

200

know if your mother ever told you that, but she should have. If she had, then you should have listened. Now, Maryjane is being led off to die. Another person that you supposedly care about is biting the bullet.

"What's it going to take to snap you out of this power trip you've had for the past few days? The death of her? Because it's going to happen and not within a couple of days, but a matter of minutes to hours. They may not have created me with a brain, but even people without brains have common sense, and the whole situation over the past few days has been a big smack in the face with a pie made from common sense. People without brains are not stupid. It's the people with brains that don't know how to use them that are stupid," Scarecrow muttered as he sat back down. He still muttered things under his breath, but no one could hear them, and the one person who could wasn't saying what he said.

Chapter Nineteen

MARYJANE DIDN'T FIGHT the whole way to the throne room, where Scarlet sat painting her nails. She glanced up at her. "What is she doing down here?" she muttered in disdain.

"She said she had something to give you that you want," the guard said, pushing her closer to Scarlet.

Scarlet was blowing on her nails as she looked at Maryjane. "And what would that be?" Scarlet asked sarcastically.

"My mother said you wanted my powers. Well, I'm here for an exchange. If I give you my powers for my sister, everyone is released, unharmed, and free to live the way they wish for the rest of their days," Maryjane said, looking at her. "Also, my mother's cancer is cured."

Scarlet stood up and walked over to her, "My, that is a proposal. Tell me, what's in it for me, though. You relinquishing your powers to Emma does sound awful nice, but without any rival power to fight, it wouldn't be any fun to possess," she giggled.

"To be so powerful, you sure are blind to the facts around you. The Elders will create more people with powers to fight against your reign. It will be a never-ending battle over Oz," Maryjane stated, looking her up and down.

"Hmm, it's a tempting offer that I will have to think about. In the meantime, you can go back to the chamber room with the rest of them," she said, gazing deep into her eyes. "You don't have to chain her back up. She won't run. She won't leave her mother here alone with me."

The guard pushed her back upstairs and into the room. He locked the door behind her so that she couldn't open it. Everyone glanced over at her.

"You didn't," Scarecrow started.

"No, she said she had to think about it. Now, let's get you all out of these chains," Maryjane said, starting with Lion. It dawned on the other two what she had done.

"Brilliant!" Nick yelled. "How did you know she wouldn't chain you back up?"

"I didn't. I hoped she wouldn't, but she was right, I wouldn't leave without my mother being here in danger," she said, releasing Nick from his chains.

She walked over to Scarecrow and was undoing his chains. He took her hand in his. "I will follow your rule to the end of the world if you stay."

His eyes pleaded with her eyes. She closed her eyes tightly in deep thought about what she would eventually do. She finished his chains and walked over to Charlie. He flicked her away with his hand.

"Just leave me. Maybe a few years chained up will teach me a lesson," he said, gazing out the window.

She glared at him, "One of these days, your pride is going to be all you have left. You're going to be angry and alone. I pity you," she said, standing back up. She walked to the corner where her staff had been left and made her way back over to the door where the others stood.

"Now what?" Scarecrow asked, turning to her, "He locked the door."

"All doors were meant to be opened," she said, waving her hand in a circle at the handle. They heard the tumblers turn in the door lock, she twisted the knob, and it opened. "See," she said proudly. "It took a couple of lessons to myself, but I no longer have to command my powers to use them," she smiled.

Lion went first, followed by Nick, then Scarecrow. Maryjane lingered in the room a moment longer. She looked over at Charlie while holding the door.

"I have always loved you, Charlie, and I will always love you. You were right, we were never meant to be together, maybe not in this lifetime…but we will be in the next. If you choose to be with Emma, so be it. I will be happy for you either way, because that's what love is about. Sacrifice," she said, walking out of the room, leaving him alone.

For once in his life, Charlie felt alone. He looked around the room at the empty space. He saw a mirror hanging on the wall and snorted. "Magic mirror on the wall, how did I end up so screwed up," he said bowing his head. To his surprise, it answered back.

"Your dang pride!" he looked up and saw his

mother's face.

"What the…" he stammered.

"Yes, Charlie, it is me," Glinda said, smiling at him.

"I saw her kill you," he stuttered.

"Yes, you saw her kill me. Yes, I am dead. Magic has many facets that can be used, and even from death, I can still speak with those who summon me. Why am I here? In the end, you still didn't listen to what I had to say to you, silly boy. You were supposed to use my death to fuel your hatred toward Scarlet, not toward Maryjane. You have put that girl through so much ever since you were teenagers. You never listened when it came to you two being together and being the elite power of Oz. Listen now!" she demanded. "I never developed your power because there was no need for it. Even as a baby, you were more powerful than I. The Elders knew there would be those to come forth and try to turn Oz into an evil pool of hatred. Your powers, along with Maryjane's, are what will bring an end to Scarlet's reign. All it takes is faith in yourself. Now, get yourself out of those chains and go help her fight Scarlet. It's not her power alone that will take her down. It's both of yours combined," she said, and disappeared from the mirror.

Through the open door, he heard a crash and a scream, along with a deafening howl. *Maryjane.*

With all of his strength, he pulled on the chains that bound him to the wall. The wall began to shake, and pieces of mortar began to crumble around the hooks that held the chains to the wall. He pulled even harder, and the chains broke free from the wall. He took the chains off his wrists and rubbed where they had grasped. A faint red mark was left where they had resided. He picked up his bow and arrows from the floor and hoisted them over his back. He looked to the door and heard another scream.

I need more than just the bow, he thought. A bright light

peeked from the ceiling. A sword descended to him. *Use it wisely,* a voice whispered to him. He glanced over the sword, and the words *King of Oz* were etched into the blade. When his hands touched the sword, it glowed a bright red color, and his entire body radiated the same color. He heard another scream that broke his gaze from the sword. He was out the door and ran down the spiral staircase toward where the cries for help had come from.

He found Maryjane and the other three trapped in a corner by an insanely large, three-headed dog. Lion stood before the three, smacking at the dog with his claws, like a pit bull and a cat fighting in a corner. Maryjane was shooting electricity from her staff at the beast, but it was to no avail. Charlie looked to his left, and there was a rope that tied a chandelier to the ceiling. The chandelier dangled straight above the beast. He pulled his bow from his back and shot an arrow where the rope met the chandelier. It sliced through the rope, and it came careening down on top of the beast, momentarily knocking it to the floor. It growled in annoyance, stood back to its feet, and looked for the source of its interruption.

Charlie stood tall, dropping the bow to pick the sword back up, drawing it in defense as the beast turned its attention to him. It charged at him, all three heads growling and snapping in rage. The head to the left reached out to lash first, and Charlie shoved the sword in its eye. It roared in pain as the two snapped at him out of pure rage. Charlie jumped back, his arm nearly bitten off by one of the monstrous heads. He lunged underneath it, slid behind it, and jumped to his feet. It whipped around to face him as he struck one of the heads with his sword again. The sword gashed open one of the faces, and the beast howled with pain. However, all of his feeble attempts weren't enough to slay the beast.

All three heads were now attentive to his sword. He

struck out with his sword as a razor-sharp claw came down hard on his arm, knocking the sword loose and breaking the skin open on his forearm. It was a deep gash, but it didn't stop the adrenaline pumping through his veins to save the others. He swooped and grabbed the sword from the floor. He ran with speed toward the wall, jumped on a chair, and from the chair, to the rope hanging from where the chandelier once hung. The rope swung over to the wall, and he used the wall as he would the floor, running full speed around the beast. He got close to it, coming from behind, and pushed off the wall onto the beast's back. He plunged the sword deep into the meat of the neck and spine where the three heads met. The beast let out a howl, a growl, and fell to the ground. It lay there whimpering for a few minutes, then went limp.

Charlie climbed from the beast and down to the floor. Everyone looked at him in astonishment. "Everyone ok?" he asked, picking his bow up from the ground. They all nodded yes, still mystified by his heroics.

"How did you get out of your chains?" Maryjane walked over to him and threw her arms around his shoulders. She picked his arm up from his side and ripped the shirt back from the gash.

"I broke them," he replied as she bandaged his arm with a clean piece of cloth.

"You broke them?" she asked in disbelief.

He looked around at the other three and replied, "Yeah."

"You could've gotten out of those chains this whole time! I risked being killed just so they wouldn't chain me back up, so I could free everyone," she complained and placed her hands on her hips in annoyance.

"Pretty much," he said, and she scowled. The other three laughed and crowded around the two of them.

"So, what's the plan?" Scarecrow asked, looking from

Dorothy to Charlie.

"We're not running from her. We're going to stand and fight," Charlie said, looking at all of them. "But, first things first, we need to find Dorothy and Emma, and get them both safely out of here."

"Why Emma?" Scarecrow asked. "She's part of-"

"Not anymore," Charlie said, interrupting him. "She fled from the throne room, scared when Scarlet began her attack."

"Besides, she is my sister. She was just swayed to the wrong side," Maryjane said, agreeing with Charlie. "She deserves a second chance with her powers." Everyone nodded in agreement.

"Scarecrow and Lion can come with me, and we can go find them," Nick offered.

"Sounds like a plan," Charlie replied.

"Well, what are you two going to do?" Lion asked, licking his paw and cleaning his face as if he'd gotten messy, smacking the dog heads away.

"We're going to find Scarlet and put an end to this tyranny once and for all," Charlie said. He locked his hand with Maryjane's, "It's time for the new king and queen to rule over Oz for a change," he said, gripping her hand tighter.

For the first time in a few days, she smiled at him. "Is everyone good with the plan?" Maryjane asked, looking around at everyone. Everyone nodded in unison. "Good, let's get going," she said, and they split into the two groups and took to different parts of the fortress.

Charlie and Maryjane rounded the corner and checked for any surprise guards. There were two that stood watch at the foot of the tower and were completely unaware of their presence. Charlie thrust his sword into the back of one of the guards, dropping him to the floor. The other was prepared to ambush him, but no sooner had he pulled the sword from the one guard's back than he plunged it into the stomach of the other. He grabbed Maryjane and towed her through the room.

"Where can we find Scarlet?" Maryjane asked Charlie as he ran through the rooms.

"Scarlet is so driven with power that she very seldom leaves her throne. She should be in there, more than likely waiting for the two of us," he said, gripping her hand tighter as they raced through all of the rooms. Every guard they came across, Charlie sliced with his sword and sent them falling to their deaths in heaps on the floor. They reached the throne room's door and stood hesitantly at it.

He turned to Maryjane and asked, "Are you ready?"

She turned to him and smiled, "As ready as I'll ever be." They busted the doors open and stepped through the doorway. Scarlet sat at her throne with her goblet in hand.

"You did it all wrong, Prince Charming. Don't you know the bride is supposed to be carried over the threshold, or it's bad luck?" she said, standing to her feet. She was dressed in a red gown fit for a queen. The back of the gown flowed like the train of a wedding dress as she stepped onto the floor and walked toward them. Charlie held his sword to a point at her.

"Oh, dear me, I thought this was a friendly meeting. It seems as if I've dressed for the wrong occasion," she said, snickering. She tapped her gown, and it transformed into a tighter-fitting, slinkier dress. She wore red high heels and stood with her staff in hand.

"So, are we going to chit chat first, or are we just going to battle this out?" she laughed, lifting her staff as a weapon. They heard rustling behind them and turned to see Nick, Lion and Scarecrow being led into the throne room with Dorothy and Emma fighting against the guards behind them. "Good, now we're all here," Scarlet said sarcastically. "You are such a disappointment, Emma. You could have been a powerful sorceress."

"After seeing you attack my mother the way you did, I would rather die than serve you," Emma spat on, spitting on her feet.

"Your mother? It saddens me that you would replace me in such a small amount of time. Oh well, in due time, my dear, you will die!" Scarlet snickered. She looked at Maryjane, who was being shielded behind Charlie. "Come forward," she said, motioning her closer.

Charlie looked at her and shook his head like he had done five years ago. Maryjane, not out of defiance, but out of bravery, stepped forward in front of Charlie and walked closer to the Red Sorceress.

"Things haven't changed one bit in these past five years. You will always be foolish to walk in front of the one who protects you as he beckons you not to," she jeered, descending the throne steps and walking to Maryjane.

"It's not foolish, it's called stubborn. I was given a task, and I intend to complete the task before this day is up," Maryjane declared as the Red Sorceress stopped inches in front of her. Maryjane did not shy away.

"Ah, so the brat thinks she's brave. Bravery is the death of many valiant soldiers who perished in wars. Tell me, Maryjane, are you ready to die to defend a land you were not born in?" the Red Sorceress said, bending down closer to her face.

"Life does not mean anything if what I love is destroyed by hatred and tyranny. If it is my fate to die here today, so be it, but I will die with honor, unlike you, who will die from vengeance," Maryjane hissed.

"Very well," Scarlet smirked, turning around with a scowl burning on her face.

She took a step forward, as if going back to her throne, when she whipped around, and a surge of energy lifted Maryjane from her feet, throwing her at a wall. She crashed into the wall and fell to the ground below. "I have been waiting five years to do that, and the fight is just beginning," Scarlet sneered as everyone backed away from her. Charlie ran to Maryjane to see if she was ok. Scarlet began to grow in height and started morphing into a hideous, fire-breathing dragon. Everyone gaped in horror.

Chapter Twenty

THE DRAGON OPENED its wings, flew to the top of the room, and breathed out a ball of fire. Maryjane tackled Charlie to the floor, wrapped him in her robe, and squatted to the floor as the fire hurtled at him. The fire engulfed them. Ice rained down in the room. The fire slowly died around them. The dragon breathed another ball of fire. As it came careening down, it hit a wall of ice, and the fire froze in its place. Maryjane removed the robe from the two of them, still holding her hand out, causing the ice to rain down harder. The dragon swooped down and tried to snatch her up with its eagle-like talons. Maryjane hit the floor on her stomach and rolled out of her reach. The dragon swooped down again, and its tail smacked Charlie into a stone statue.

Maryjane ran to him, but the tail lashed out again and threw her in the opposite direction, smashing her into a bookcase. It toppled over on top of her. Charlie ran toward that side of the room, but the dragon pinned him in the corner with a sheet of fire. He took his hands and clapped them together. The ripple from the mighty clap sent the dragon careening to the other side of the room and blew the ring of fire out that he was trapped within. The dragon smashed into the ceiling, revealing a large gap to the outside. Charlie grabbed a chain and ran to the dragon's feet while it was still discombobulated. He had its legs tied together when it shook its head, shaking off the attack. It thrust its clawed hand out at him, trying to grab him, and he ducked out of her reach. A simple tug to the chain, and it broke from around its feet.

Maryjane crawled from beneath the bookcase that had toppled onto her. She glanced around the room as it spun. Everything was a blur. When things started to focus, she saw Charlie dueling the dragon alone. It struck him, and he went soaring through the air, crashing into the throne in the middle of the room. It sauntered over to him, crunching the floor to pieces beneath its weight to finish him off. She didn't know what to do. Her staff was within her reach, and she grabbed it up. She looked at the group huddled in the corner, trying to stay out of harm's way. A thought occurred to her.

"Lion!" she yelled out across the room. Lion looked at her, acknowledging he heard her. "Are you ready to stand with me?" she asked. He looked around at everyone cowering from the dragon. He looked back at her and backed up one step with his ears flat against his head. She could see the terror in his eyes. "You are no longer the cowardly lion. You are a ferocious beast!" she yelled as he stood cowering beneath the stare of the dragon. "Lion, you can do this!" she yelled.

He looked at the floor and took a deep breath. He lifted his head, planted his feet, and roared a deafening roar in retaliation for the dragon! She pointed her staff at him as he walked toward the middle of the room. "Griffin!" she yelled, and light exploded from the end of her staff.

He began to grow impossibly large. Wings sprouted from his sides, and his fangs became like razor-sharp pillars. His head turned into the shape of an eagle with talons in his forelegs. He let out a bone-chilling howl. The entire building shook from the tremendous sound.

The dragon's attention was no longer on Charlie or Maryjane, but on the new threat that had presented itself. The dragon squalled back in response. The walls shook once more, and the ceiling cracked from the pressure of the sound. The dragon flew upwards and burst through the ceiling, and Lion was hot on her trail.

Maryjane ran to Charlie and made sure he was ok. He sat up groaning. "Quick, we have to get outside," Maryjane said, tugging on his arm. "Lion can be in trouble, and we are the only two that can help."

Charlie stood up, and they ran to the gates of the city with the others trailing behind them. Outside, it was a torrential fire pit. The dragon flew around, breathing a trail of fire at Lion. He dodged and zipped around every ball she sent at him. He got close enough to smack her with his claw. She howled in pain. She struck him with her claw, and it sent him flipping through the air. She was on top of the upper hand she had gained. As soon as he had stopped flipping, she was there again, knocking him to the ground, and breathing a wall of fire around him.

Maryjane threw her hand up, and an ice blizzard swarmed the two. The wall of fire was eradicated, and the dragon's attention was on Dorothy and the group now cowering at the base of the City. She blew a torch of fire at her as Lion tackled her to the ground. She clawed him across his face, and he howled with pain. She smacked him again, cutting his eye open. He flinched away, giving her enough time to whip her tail around, hitting him, and sending him hurtling into the City walls. He crashed with a thud to the ground. He didn't move.

The dragon returned her attention to Charlie and Maryjane, running toward her in the open field. Maryjane and Charlie were prepared to fight to the death. The dragon roared, sending a torch of flame skyward as if laughing at the two.

Maryjane looked at Charlie, and he returned her look. "Are you ready?" she asked.

He nodded. He walked a few feet from her as she raised her arms, wielding the staff to the sky. A wind began to blow lightly. The wind became fiercer and hard to stand in. Charlie grabbed onto a tree to keep his footing. The dragon was having a hard time staying suspended in one spot in the air. The wind got stronger, and you could see the dragon struggling. Maryjane began to spin the staff in a circle, slow at first, and then faster. The wind followed her movement. A whirlwind appeared down in the center of the field.

Dorothy, Nick, and Scarecrow had run to Lion, who had returned to normal size. In between the pillars of the city, they were sheltered from the suction of the winds. They all stood and watched in awe. Emma cowered beside Dorothy like a child as the battle ensued. She had no clue as to what she could possibly do to help out.

Maryjane spun faster, and the whirlwind grew bigger. A cyclone tore through the field. The dragon blew a fireball at Maryjane. The cyclone whipped it up, and it exploded into a fiery twister. Fire rained down everywhere. The twister grew into a monstrous storm, but no matter how big it got, the dragon was still suspended in the air, breathing fire down on everyone. Another twister popped down from the sky, and there were two circling the fields. Pieces of the city were sucked from the foundation along with trees and other natural landmarks. It began to rain and hail. Lightning erupted through the fields. The dragon dodged every bolt that struck at her. The water flowed into a huge crater in the ground to the back of the city.

Emma tore through the field toward Maryjane, dodging the debris flying around in the storm. "What can I do to help?" she asked as she reached Maryjane's side.

"Try to control her with your mind!" Maryjane yelled over the roar of the winds.

Emma began to concentrate on the dragon. You could see the dragon's face as she tried to fight the mind control. Emma had her fly straight into the side of the

City, toppling over one of the walls. The dragon shook its head and gained control back over its own mind. Emma's eyes glazed over as she began to walk into the middle of the storm.

"Charlie, stop her!" Maryjane cried out. It was too late. The storm swept Emma up into the center, and the dragon ripped her body into shreds. She roared and let out a stream of fire, celebrating her triumph of taking one more thing away from Maryjane.

Dorothy cried out in shock and hatred. Charlie turned his head just in time to miss seeing the body drop to the ground. Rage tore through Maryjane. A pillar of fire tore through the field and blasted the dragon in the center of the two pillars. Right after the fire dissipated, a pillar of ice tore through, freezing the dragon in an ice block. It lasted for only seconds as the dragon burst through the block of ice. She squalled in anger and let out a fireball of her own that blasted through the twisters, nearly hitting Maryjane.

"I can't stop her!" Maryjane yelled to Charlie. "She's too strong. I'm throwing everything I have at her!"

Charlie looked to the sky and saw the dragon dodging the cyclones and the lightning. The rain had begun to cool her down, so she couldn't breathe a field of flames anymore, just smoke. "Throw down another cyclone! I have an idea!" he yelled over the roar of the twisters.

Maryjane shook her head, and another twister tore through the fields. It slowed the dragon down, but it wasn't enough. The one cyclone was still lit on fire. One was full of water from the raging rainstorm. The other had debris swirling around in it from the surrounding areas.

"Drop just one more!" Charlie yelled, watching the dragon struggle with the three raging around it. Maryjane dropped one last cyclone, and the dragon was caught in the center of the raging twisters.

Earth, air, fire and water. It's the four elements. Maryjane thought. *To complete it, you need...* "No!" she yelled as Charlie ran across the field. "Spirit," she breathed.

Charlie ran to the raging twisters, unfazed by their gale-force winds. He looked down at his hands, and he had a purple shield surrounding him. He looked back at Maryjane to see that she was glowing the same color. She was bubbling him with her power so the magic of the storms didn't affect him. He got to the edge of the storm and leapt into the air. It carried him up in the air straight to the dragon.

He pulled his sword out from its sheath, glowing red from the power, and plunged it into the belly of the beast as he collided with her. The beast howled in pain. The sword melted into the dragon's stomach, embedding itself to prevent removal. The sword prevented the dragon from shape-shifting back into its original body. Enraged, the dragon grabbed Charlie with its sharp claws and threw him hard to the ground. Charlie impacted the ground and didn't move.

"You witch!" Maryjane screamed.

Maryjane looked around for a way to destroy the beast once and for all. The rain had filled the crater toward the back of the city. Maryjane slammed her staff to the ground to where it stood by itself. She clasped her hands around the staff as if grasping something in between them. The four twister bases collided together, completely trapping the dragon in the middle. She pulled the staff from the ground and swung her arms and hands as if holding a baseball bat. The four twisters started to follow her movements. The raging twisters combined into one monstrous-sized tornado. Fire, water, and earth swirled around in the wind in the pit of the storm. The dragon was careening out of control inside, flipping, and somersaulting. She swung her arms faster, and faster, and let go of the staff. The vortex went spinning to the sky, the staff flew a few feet from Maryjane, and the dragon went flying into the deep lake created.

As soon as the dragon hit the water, Maryjane ran to her staff and lifted it, turning the crater of water into ice. The entire body of the dragon was encased in the water, with its head and neck the only remnants left outside of the ice. It squalled in anger. Maryjane walked over to the crater. She got to the ice and sauntered right over to the roaring dragon. The roars and squalls did not affect her. She dropped her staff to her feet, pulled her sword from its sheath, and looked the dragon in its eyes.

In her mind, she could hear Scarlet pleading with her, "Please, don't do this. I'll change, I promise!"

"Go to hell, witch!" Maryjane yelled and swung her sword around.

The dragon squalled one last time before the blade sliced through it. Maryjane lifted her hand over the head, and it immediately caught fire. She stood there watching the head burn completely out. The Red Sorceress was destroyed. Maryjane dropped her sword and turned around. The valley was silent.

Charlie! She ran to Charlie, who still lay in the same spot the dragon had thrown him to. "Charlie! Charlie!" she yelled as she stooped over his body. He didn't respond... He didn't move... He didn't breathe... "No, no, no, no! You weren't supposed to be the one to die!" she said, crying, grabbing his head up. "Come on, breathe! Breathe, darn it!"

Everyone ran over to the spot where they were. She rocked back and forth, sobbing. "This isn't fair! It's not supposed to happen this way!" she cried out. Everyone bowed their heads as she screamed in grief.

"There's got to be another way!" Scarecrow cried out.

Maryjane ran her hands over Charlie's face. Blood had trickled from his mouth, and she wiped it away. She pulled his body up to her and hugged it with all of her might.

"You were always worried about me getting hurt, and look at you," she whispered in his ear. "Come back, my love. Come back to me!" she cried. "You can't leave me! We did it! It's over! It's our time to reign over Oz now!"

She buried her face into his chest. Dorothy walked over to her and put her hands on her back. They all saw a streak of light dancing through the valley. When the streaks slowed, they saw the most peculiar item before them. It was a wooden sawhorse, but unlike normal sawhorses to cut wood, this one moved like a real one. Upon the back of the sawhorse was Ozma; she dismounted and stood before everyone.

She walked over to Maryjane. "You can bring him back, you know. You have the power to do that," Ozma said, smiling at her.

Maryjane looked up in surprise. "You, you never told me this could happen!" she cried in breaths.

"I did not know this was going to happen. We Elders can only see so far into the future, and decisions always change the future. He made a decision we did not foresee coming. However, you have time to save him," Ozma urged. "You must do it quickly, though."

"How? I can't even heal myself properly," Maryjane said, sniffing back the tears and stroking his face.

"You have to use your heart and soul. You can't just want it. You have to need it. You can't just wish for it. You have to make it happen yourself. Now, grab deep within yourself, and place all of that power that resides in you, the good loving power, and you thrust it all at him," Ozma said, bending down, looking her in the eyes. "Love conquers all."

Maryjane looked down at Charlie lying there unmoving. He looked so serene. She closed her eyes and tried to think of how to will her power forth. She thought back to the first day they met.

She had walked through the mists and arrived in a strange little town. There were people running around, laughing and having a good time. She had never seen people who looked as they did. When they saw her make her way to the center of the town, they all fled to their houses.

"Who are you?" A young boy spoke to her, walking up to her from one of the piles of hay he had been stacking with one of the strange people. He looked at her weirdly.

She stepped back from him a few steps. "Who are you? Where am I?" she asked, looking around in fear. "This isn't my home! How did I get here?"

"I don't know how you got here, but this is Oz. I'm Charlie. My mother is Glinda, the good witch of the South," Charlie said, walking closer to the little girl. "I've never seen you here before, but I have heard stories of faraway travelers coming to our land. They never said any of them were bad people, so I guess you mean us no harm," he said, scratching his head.

"My name is Maryjane. What's a witch?" she asked, confused.

The boy smiled at her. "Maryjane. That's a really pretty name," he said, staring at her. "If you follow me, you'll find out what a witch is," he said, extending his hand out to her. "I'll take you to a castle of a witch."

"I don't want to get hurt," she said with fear in her eyes, drawing back from him.

He smiled at her again. "Don't worry, with me, that will never happen," he said as she took his hand.

Maryjane kept her eyes closed and thought of the day she gave him the locket.

"What are you dragging me off into the field for? You know Momma will tan my hide for us being outside of Munchkin Land," Charlie said, looking around to see if they were in hearing distance of his mother.

"I wanted to give you something," Maryjane said, reaching into her pocket. She lifted out a heart-shaped necklace.

"What is it?" Charlie asked, holding it up to the light, peering at it.

"It's a heart-shaped locket," she said, watching him turn it over in his hands, looking at it.

"What's a locket?" he asked as he continued to examine it in his hands.

"Here," she said, popping the door open on it, "it's a charm where you can put pictures in it," she said, showing him the picture of her in it.

Charlie stared at the beautiful picture of her in the mysterious necklace. He had never seen a picture before. "It's beautiful," he said, looking up at her. "Thank you. I'll wear it always," he said, fastening it around his neck. "Maybe it will bring me good luck," he said, smiling at her.

She smiled back at him and gave him a hug.

She thought back to the woods a couple of days ago. It was pure bliss being in his arms without him fearing someone would put a stop to their love. His hand was on her cheek as he kissed. It was a moment in time that no one would ever be able to take from her, a moment she had waited years to experience with him, a sign of how he felt for her was all she had ever yearned for. Her heart fluttered thinking of the two of them lying in the grass together, together for the first time, of many times.

She kept her eyes closed and concentrated on the white light within her. She thought of everything that had happened between the two of them over the years, all of the love they shared with one another, all of the good times, and all of the bad times, because that is what love is all about. Love isn't perfect. It's full of challenges and mistakes made by both people. It's about overcoming your problems and coming out together on the other side. Perfection doesn't exist in love because love is naturally flawed. One person will always love the other more. One will make mistakes that will forever break the heart of the other. Even when forgiveness is used, it's still hard to overcome the feeling that washed over them. When you love someone, though their mistakes may hurt, it hurts worse to think of them walking out of your life forever and never looking back. She had always feared that would be her and Charlie's fate.

A wise person once told her, though, that love conquers all. She wished with all of her heart that at this moment, that were true.

Maryjane sat with her eyes closed, and a bright white light enveloped her. Everyone stood back and watched her lift up in the air, holding Charlie. She hadn't even noticed she wasn't sitting on the ground anymore, but was levitating in the sky. A gift that only a Magus Mortem could possess. A divine white light descended from the sky and surrounded them. Her white light and the one from the sky grew brighter and brighter. Everyone had to turn their heads and shield their eyes because it was so bright. It lit the whole valley up.

Maryjane thought of one last thing he had begged of her:

"Stay with me forever."

"I will," she whispered.

The light exploded across the valley. The dark, black clouds that had covered the skies and hovered over Oz in hopelessness for the past five years disappeared. Emerald City's devastation was cleared, and it was returned to its previous, radiating state unharmed. The fields across Oz went from rotting shambles back to the thriving green plants they once were. The decaying trees sprang up with healthy roots and green leaves. The gray, somber color that had taken over Oz disappeared, and technicolor replaced the darkened soul that had descended upon the land in vengeance. Creatures came out of their hiding spots. Birds chirped in the light of the sun, and butterflies floated through the fields of flowers, grazing each one and happily starting for the next. Oz was alive once more with thriving life. The wastelands were gone.

Everyone gasped when they looked at Nick. They

watched as his body transformed right before their eyes. He was no longer made of tin. His body had been returned as it was so many years ago, before the Wicked Witch of the East played the cruel game on him. He looked at his hands and touched them to his chest. He could feel a real heartbeat beating within in breast. For the first time in many, many years, he cried without having to fear he was going to rust again.

Maryjane descended from the sky, still holding Charlie in her bright white light. Once they touched the ground, the white light slowly faded, and you could see the two clearly as day. Maryjane was still bent over Charlie, crying. He still didn't move. She slumped on his body, burying her face in his chest, and sobbed.

"The kid did everything in her power. She restored the land and even returned Nick back into his flesh. Why won't they give her what she wants the most?" Lion asked, looking to the ground in grief.

"It should have worked," Ozma breathed. "I don't understand. You are a Magus Mortem now, the most powerful of all beings. It should have worked!" she exclaimed in disbelief.

Maryjane sat up and stroked his face one last time. "Your one fear has become my pain. Goodbye, my love. We will be together again one day," she cried while gasping at each word.

She kissed his forehead one last time and laid his head down on the ground. She put her head in her hands and cried. Dorothy had turned away from the sight. It was many years ago, but she knew exactly what she felt at that moment. The loss of the one person you imagined growing old with eats away at your heart.

After everything she has done, you're going to take the one thing away from her that she needs the most? She will have no one else left for her once I am gone, and so you take the only people she could have turned to and ripped them from her heart. Why? When she

222

has given up so much for your land, why do you do this to her? she asked silently.

Nick stepped away and turned away from the two. Lion backed up and did the same. They stood beside Dorothy and looked out at the new Oz.

"It will never be the same again," Nick said, peering out at the land.

"What do you mean?" Dorothy asked, holding back the tears behind her eyes.

"Everything has changed. We can't go back to the way life used to be. We've been through too much. The land has been through too much. It's a new land, and we owe it all to that child," he said, turning to look at her. "And it definitely wouldn't be the same without you."

Dorothy understood what he meant and leaned over and kissed his cheek. "Don't cry, you'll rust yourself," she said, choking back tears and hugging him. She was prepared to die. She no longer feared it. "I think I'll stay here, though, until it's time," she said, smiling at him. He returned her smile and placed his arm around her shoulder.

Ozma was still in shock at the whole situation. *How could we not have seen this coming? How can he be gone after everything we've done to save this land...? Why? It doesn't make any sense. She used every ounce of power to return everything back to life, but he did not revive.*

She walked over to a tree, slumped against it, and down to the ground. She bowed her head in defeat, and for the first time in years, she wept.

Chapter Twenty-One

"Charlie, Charlie, wake up, Charlie," the voice floated around his head. *"It's not your time, son. This is not your ending. You need to open your eyes and go back to Oz."*

"What if I don't want to go back?" he asked. *"Why can't I stay here? It's so peaceful here. It reminds me of how Oz used to be, not the shambles it is in now."*

"Oz has been restored, my son. You two accomplished your destiny together. It's time for you to go back now."

"I don't have any reason to go back. Everything will be different. No one needs me there," he said, walking further into the bright sunlight.

"They need you in Oz, son. Maryjane needs you most of all," the voice replied.

"Maryjane will go back to her world. It will all be ok. I want to stay here with you," he replied.

"Maryjane isn't going home. She is staying right here in Oz with you, I can assure you that, and as much as I'd like you to stay, you can't stay here with me, even if I were to will you to stay, the Elders have plans for you. It was my time to go. The end of my rule comes with my death and the beginning of your rule. Your time is just beginning. Now awaken, my son. Join your queen, rule this land as I have foretold."

Scarecrow stood watching Maryjane. She was distraught. He looked from Maryjane to Charlie. He bowed his head in shame as he thought of the words he had said to him earlier that day. He never got to apologize for his temper. The kid wasn't as bad as he thought he was. He wished he could take back the words that the kid would wake up, something to get rid of the feeling within him. Poor Maryjane had been through a lifetime worth of heartache, heartbreak, and fighting for survival. She deserved more than this outcome. He looked back up at the poor kid lying on the ground. He gasped.

Charlie moved

When he awoke to find everyone crying, he didn't understand what had happened. Maryjane wrapped her arms around him and refused to let him go. He hadn't even known he had died, but thought he had been asleep. Apparently, the love that Maryjane had for him was enough to return his soul to his body. Of course, it took a nudge from a guardian angel who was now watching over Oz. He looked to the sky, and he could see the face of his mother in the sky smiling down on them all. She waved her wand, and a bright rainbow popped across the sky. Charlie smiled at her while still holding onto Maryjane. She nodded in approval, and her apparition disappeared from the sky.

Ozma sighed in relief. "You are my brave warrior," she said, kissing his forehead. "Your troubles have come and passed. You no longer need to live in fear or in the shadow of doubt. You don't have to live in the fast lane anymore," she said, holding his hands.

"Yeah, a little birdie convinced me it was ok for me to come back," Charlie said, winking at Ozma. She looked off to the sky and nodded as if answering someone's call to her.

Scarecrow walked up to him, "Kid, look, I'm sorry for what I said earlier," he started.

Charlie held his hand up to quiet him. "It's exactly what I needed to hear," he said, smiling. "Don't worry about it."

Everybody strolled up to give him hugs and smiles. He was a little surprised when a man he had never seen before walked up and gave him a hug, crying. "Nick, is that you?" he asked, staring harder into his face. Nick shook his head yes, unable to answer from the flush of emotions running through him.

Dorothy walked up to Charlie last and gave him a hug. "Welcome to the family, son. It's wonderful to add you to it, even if we don't have that much time together."

Charlie kissed her hand, and she felt something shock her when he did so. "Maybe it will be longer than what you think," Charlie said, grinning. Dorothy was confused by his statement as she walked off with the others.

Maryjane stood at the back of everyone. Everyone cheered and hollered in celebration of the defeat of the Red Sorceress. From the gates, they could hear the entire city buzzing with adrenaline and celebration. He ran over to the body of the dragon while Maryjane watched in confusion. He walked back over to her while everyone else walked off to the gates of the city. In his hands, he held her staff. He handed it back to her.

"I think this belongs to you," he said as she took the staff from his hands.

She looked the staff over and tossed it to the side. "I don't think I need it anymore," she said, stepping closer to him.

"So, you brought me back. Are you going to leave me to return to the human world, or are you going to stay with me forever?" he asked, stroking her cheek.

She looked up at him. "You already know that answer," she said, leaning in close and kissing him.

They were suspended in the air. Charlie's clothes changed into a suit of white with purple trimming fit for a king. Maryjane's clothes changed into a beautiful, flowing, Victorian ball gown that was purple with white trimming. Her hair was danced up into beautiful hanging curls. They looked down at their clothes while descending, and then looked over to see Ozma smiling at them, standing at the gates of the city.

"My King and Queen," she said, bowing, "your public awaits you. The people of Oz wish to thank the heroines for saving their land and meet their new king and queen. Please, join us."

She began to walk through the gates and into the city when she turned around, "Oh, and Maryjane, your mother's health has been restored. Neither you nor she has to worry about her dying anytime soon," she said, smiling. She winked at Charlie, who nodded back at her as she walked through the gates.

"Your kiss on her hand healed her, didn't it? Of course, you would be the one to heal her sickness, you do, after all, give life as opposed to taking it," Maryjane said, wrapping her arms tight around his shoulders.

"Well, it was either heal her or move to the mortal world with you two. I just don't think they would have been ready for all of this handsome, powerful, gorgeous-bodied man to be in their world. It would simply be too much for them to handle," he laughed as she gently swatted his arm, laughing.

He brushed her cheek with his thumb, staring into her eyes. "Are you ready?" Charlie asked, grabbing Maryjane's hand.

She smiled. "I've been ready since I was born."

The two locked fingers and strode to the gates. They breathed a deep breath and walked through the threshold to everyone in Oz. Everyone cheered as they saw them make their way down the carpeted halls of Emerald City. The throne room Scarlet had fashioned for herself had been moved to the entrance of Oz. Ozma stood at the steps that led up to two separate thrones. This wasn't any usual coronation celebration. Everyone wasn't simply waiting for them to be crowned king and queen. They were waiting for the final consummation of Charlie and Maryjane's power. Their marriage.

Kasey Hill has lived in Franklin County, VA, for most of her adult life and is a versatile writer known for her work in several genres, including urban fantasy, horror, thriller, paranormal romance, and metaphysical/New Age topics. She has authored both fiction and non-fiction, with a particular interest in Wicca, specializing in Trinitarian Wicca as the historical archivist with an upcoming historical account of the shift from polytheism to monotheism in Abrahamic religions, where she has published non-fiction works exploring the subject.

Her fiction often dives into the supernatural and the macabre, blending mythological elements with modern storytelling. She has published multiple novels, poetry collections, and short stories. Notable works include her *Guardians of Light* series in the mythology fantasy genre, and her poetry that has received recognition for its depth and emotional resonance. As she grows in the horror genre, she has a particular penchant for Southern Gothic storytelling, such as her Adult Horror novel *Devil's Claw* and her Young Adult horror series, *The Whispering Spirits* featuring *The Haunting at Foxwood Village* and *Dark Coven*. She has several Horror short stories circulating for anthologies and Ezines featuring her unique style of worldbuilding.

In addition to her writing, Kasey Hill has also contributed to the Wiccan and occult community through her non-fiction work, making her a multi-faceted author with a broad range of interests and expertise.